DRILL ME SERGEANT

Edited By

ERIC SUMMERS

Herndon, VA

Published in the United States by STARbooks Press

PO Box 711612, Herndon, VA 20171

Many thanks to graphic artist John Nail for the cover design. Mr. Nail may be reached at: tojonail@bellsouth.net.

STARbooks Press Titles
by Eric Summers

Muscle Worshipers

Love in a Lock-Up

Unmasked – Erotic Tales of Gay Superheroes

Don't Ask, Don't Tie Me Up

Ride Me Cowboy

Service with a Smile

*Never Enough – The Lost Writings
of John Patrick*

*Unmasked II: More Erotic Tales of Gay
Superheroes*

*Can't Get Enough – More Erotica Written
by John Patrick*

Unwrapped: Erotic Holiday Tales

Teammates

Big Holiday Packages

Rock & Roll Over

Who's Your Daddy?

Mob Men on the Make

Unmasked & Undressed

Drill Me Sergeant

CONTENTS

PRISONER OF WAR
By Garland

Garland is the penname of a full-time actor and writer, living in Hollywood, whose has written three novels and been published in more than forty anthologies. www.garlandserotictales.webs.com

They came to our village in the night. My mother had told us she suspected they would invade us soon. She had always been a strong, brave woman; nothing ever shook her. Not even my father's death from the fever last year. But last night when she was saying goodnight to me and my little brothers and sisters, I saw something in her face that scared me, something I had never seen before. She kept glancing out the window of our hut, staring into night's inky blackness. Even though I was a man and supposed to be brave I couldn't help but shudder as ominous goose bumps sprouted up on my arms. I had no idea what caused them.

The screams jolted me awake. I looked around, disoriented. The heavy smell of smoke suffocated me, choked me. My eyes welled up with tears as my lungs burned.

Springing out of bed, I looked out the window and couldn't believe what I saw. The screams and cries grew louder as the villagers ran for their lives. The thatched huts crackled as the soldiers burned them to the ground.

Shots rang in the air as the soldiers took over my village. I couldn't believe it. I just stood there, frozen with fear. Not even in my worst nightmares could I ever have imagined something like this.

It wasn't long before the soldier caught my eye. The dancing flames illuminated his face, giving him an eerie orange glint. His camouflaged uniform blended into the jungle like a chameleon. Smiling, he raised his rifle and shot. The loud bang whipped me back to reality as I felt the hot bullet whiz past my ear.

Turning from the window I ran out of the hut as the roof gave in under the weight of the flames. I wondered where my family was. It was impossible to see them in the thick smoke and calling their names did no good; my cries were just swallowed up by the chaos. I prayed they were still alive.

What did the soldiers want with us? I wondered looking around in utter confusion. What were my people going to do?

Another shot made me jump. Turning, I saw the same soldier walking towards me, rifle raised, finger itching to pull the trigger. The soldier smiled, and I finally got a good look at him. He was from the north, our sworn enemies. Suddenly this all made sense. The northern people had wanted to wipe us out and make us their slaves for a long time.

My instincts took over, and I ran into the jungle. The only thing that was going through my mind was survival.

I heard a whoop behind me. Turning I gasped. The soldier was in hot pursuit. Digging deep, I ran faster, ignoring the branches that scraped my arms and legs. My breath was loud in my ears. My heart was pounding against my chest, and I couldn't help but gasp in pain from the stitch in my side. I could hear the soldier crashing through the brush. It sounded as if he was right behind me, but I was too scared to look back.

Don't let him get me, I silently begged. *Please don't let him get me*.

"Little monkey! Little monkey!" He mockingly called out after me. "Come here monkey!" He kept yelling the nickname the people from the north had given us. My people had long been tree people, able to climb and swing through the jungle with ease. That had always given us the upper hand against the northerners; until now.

"Monkey," he continued. "Don't run away from me monkey!"

I ran faster. I felt as if I was about to pass out. My head was dizzy, and I saw spots before my eyes.

Suddenly, I felt my feet leave the ground as the soldier tackled me. His strong arms encircled me tightly as his rifle landed on the forest floor with a careless thud. Seconds later, I, too, landed on the hard ground with a loud oof.

Laughing, the soldier roughly turned me over and straddled my chest. Picking up his rifle, he pointed it straight at my head. I didn't dare move. I was scared to breathe.

"Caught you, monkey," he said breathing heavily.

Even though the sun was beginning to rise, the stars were still twinkling proudly in the blue-black sky.

The soldier smirked, and his deep chocolate colored eyes sparkled with mischief. I had never been this close to a northerner before. He really didn't look that different than us. His hair was blacker, and his skin was a little darker shade of chestnut, but aside from that and the slight difference in dialect, we could have been brothers.

I don't know why, but as I stared at him, I felt a strange sensation begin to stir in my body. I couldn't tear my eyes from him. The back of my neck burned crimson as I felt my cock begin to stir. I had never been this close to a man before, though I had longed to be for some time. Plus the fact that he was an enemy soldier who could easily kill me made it that much more exciting.

"Such a pretty little monkey," he whispered leaning down and gently caressing my cheek. His palm was silky smooth, and as his hot breath brushed against my earlobe, I couldn't help but shudder.

Leaning down, he kissed me. Long and deep. My eyes bugged out, and I gasped before relaxing into the kiss. His lips were moist and full against mine. His tongue slipped into my mouth, flicking against mine. My dick was rock hard, straining against my pants, begging to be freed.

When he parted, he sucked on my chin before making his way lower down my body. A small little squeak spilled out of my lips as the soldier kissed and licked my throat, sucking on my Adam's apple.

My breathing grew rapid as his mouth traveled lower and lower, lips brushing over my bare chest. Because of the heat, I hadn't been wearing a shirt to bed. I was glad I had made that decision.

His mouth greedily sucked my erect nipples, biting and pulling on the tip, making me moan out into the night. My hands grasped at the underbrush as the soldier sucked on my stomach causing my body to writhe blissfully on the jungle's hard floor.

I couldn't help but gasp in surprise as he tore off my pants, finally freeing my hard dick. He clutched my dick tightly in his fist almost making me come.

"Do I excite you, little monkey?" The soldier asked squeezing the head of my dick and slowly running his thumb over the tip. All I could do was bite my bottom lip and nod vigorously.

A little scream fell out of my throat when the soldier lowered his mouth onto my dick and slowly bobbed his head up and down. My eyes rolled back into my head, and I screamed with passion. I had never experienced anything like this before. I never wanted it to end.

My stomach tightened. My hands clenched and unclenched. My cries rose as I felt my balls tighten. The soldier increased his sucking. His fingers traveled over my chest, pinching and pulling my sensitive flesh.

"Oh," I cried out, rising up on my elbows as I exploded into the soldier's mouth. He greedily swallowed every last drop.

"You taste good, monkey," he complimented as I fell back into the dirt, exhausted. "Now it's your turn to taste me," he said once again straddling my chest and beginning to remove his fatigues.

4

"I've never been with a man," I confessed scared. What if I wasn't any good at it? What if I couldn't please him as he had pleased me?

"Well, now you are," he stated firmly.

Gripping the back of my head, he pulled my face up to his stomach. Lifting his shirt, he pulled down his pants. His dick sprang to life, hitting my chin. I loved the feel of it against my skin. This was the most exciting thing I had ever experienced; doing something like this with an enemy soldier. The ultimate taboo.

"Kiss me. Taste me," he ordered gripping my hair harder.

Timidly, I kissed his stomach, trying to imitate the way he had kissed me.

"Be a man about it," he commanded tightening his grip. "This will make a man out of you," he promised pushing me back onto the ground and positioning himself over my mouth.

Roughly he rubbed his dick over my lips. It was so big; I must admit I was a little scared of it. It was thick and pulsated with lustful blood. His balls were full, and his dick was already leaking pre-cum.

"Open your mouth, monkey," he demanded.

I did what I was told. His dick entered my mouth. I was surprised I could accommodate his whole length.

Not giving me a chance to get used to him, he fucked my mouth with great speed, grunting and groaning like a wild dog in heat. The sounds he made while he used my mouth turned me on even more. The tip of his dick tickled my tonsils, and his salty-sweet pre-cum trickled down my throat. His heavy balls hit my chin, and he kept his eyes locked on me; they were burning with lust. Sweat glistened his brow as he picked up speed. It wasn't long before I felt his dick throb as he shot an impressive load down my throat. Closing my eyes in bliss, I enjoyed his thick load, amazed at how much there was.

"Good little monkey boy," he complimented breathlessly, giving the top of my head a little pat.

Slowly, he pulled his dick out of my mouth and stuffed himself back inside his fatigues before getting off me.

Grabbing my arm roughly, he pulled me to my feet. Picking up his rifle, he pointed it at me. I froze and felt my blood turn to ice.

Oh God! He's going to kill me, I thought panicked. *He got what he wanted and now the jungle is going to be my grave.*

I gulped.

"Walk monkey," he ordered turning me around and giving me a hard nudge with his rifle. I didn't ask where we were going. I didn't even ask to get dressed.

We walked for what felt like miles. My legs were heavy as lead, and I prayed that every step we took would be our last. Everything that had happened that night seemed so surreal, like a dream. If only it was.

The sun had fully rose by the time we entered a clearing buried deep in the middle of the jungle. I was taken aback by what I saw. A homemade army base had been built using bamboo and the fallen palm fronds. I wondered how long it had taken them to construct it. They had everything they needed: barracks, a watch tower, and a row of cages, obviously meant for the trophies they collected during their invasion. The only other sign of life were two other soldiers who chuckled when they saw me.

They walked toward us, whistling with approval when they got closer. Their eyes ran over my body, and they smiled.

"Look at the pretty monkey," one of them said licking his lips with desire.

"He's a stranger to men," the one who had brought me explained as he ran his hand over the curve of my ass, giving it a hard squeeze. Rising on my toes, I felt my cock start to stir.

"We'll have to make him familiar with men," the second soldier continued.

Wasting no time, the three soldiers stripped out of their uniforms and circled me like sharks as they stroked themselves to hardness. I gulped, scared and excited at the same time. My own cock grew as I looked at their perfect bodies: tall, muscular, smooth. I wanted all of them, and that made me blush.

The soldiers continued to circle me, moving closer and closer. They never took their eyes off me as they smiled knowingly.

I gasped at the first feel of their hands on my body. It wasn't long before they were kissing me. Moaning, I closed my eyes, enjoying the feel of their lips all over my body. I wondered if they did this with every prisoner or if I was just one of the lucky ones.

"Look at how much the little monkey likes it," one of them snickered.

"Get on your knees," the one who brought me said, pushing me down, though it was unnecessary. At that moment, I was overflowing with lustful euphoria I would have done anything they wanted.

My captors looked down at me, stroking their hard dicks and grinning. My heart raced with anticipation as I imagined all the things they would do to me. The three soldiers ran their cocks over my face. I knew what they wanted, and I wanted to give it to them.

Opening my mouth, I slowly swallowed the soldier's hard dick. Holding my head in place, he bucked his hips back and forth. My hands were wrapped around the other two cocks, blindly jerking them off as the soldier fucked my mouth.

It wasn't long before they were passing me around like I was a glass of fine wine. I loved it. My heart skipped a few beats knowing they were using me just for their pleasure.

"Should we make the little monkey a real man?" One of the soldiers asked beating his dick against my face.

The other two nodded. I gulped. This was it. I was going to give my body over to them completely.

They bent me over, exposing my ass. I sighed at the first feel of the cool liquid one of them drizzled on my hole making it pucker. Clutching at the dirt I held my breath when one of them started to enter me, not letting it out until he was completely inside me.

The soldier only gave me a second to adjust to him before moving in and out of me. He started out slow, gradually picking up speed as he found his rhythm and got used to my tightness. The other two soldiers stood over me, slowly stroking their dicks as they awaited their turns.

The soldier fucked me faster than I thought possible. His balls slapped against my ass. Gripping my hips tightly, he ground into my ass, making me scream with orgasmic abandon as every one of my g-spots were awakened.

"How is he?" One of the soldiers asked.

"Not bad. Want a turn?" His friend responded pulling out of me.

The second soldier quickly kneeled behind me and shoved his dick inside my eager hole. Wrapping his arms around me, we fell back together.

"Ride me," the soldier ordered slapping my chest.

Repositioning myself I rose up and down on the soldier's stiff dick. The other two stood on either side of me, allowing me easy access to their cocks. This all felt too good to be true. I prayed it never ended.

Holding onto my hips the soldier pounded my hole like a jackhammer. Screaming in bliss, my cock erupted like a volcano, spewing virginal white cum all over my chest. The soldiers whistled, obviously pleased by the sight.

The soldier pushed deeper into me, filling me with his cum. Instinctively, my hole tightened around his dick, milking him dry. My chest rose and fell with heavy satisfaction.

"Open your mouth monkey. We're not done yet."

I obeyed. The two remaining soldiers positioned their dicks in my mouth. They were stroking their lengths so quickly their hands were nothing but a blur. Within seconds my mouth was filled with hot cum. I greedily swallowed every last drop.

"What should we do with this little monkey?" The soldier underneath me asked, dick still hard and buried deep in my ass. "Should we kill him like we did the others?"

The other two soldiers glanced down at me and smirked.

"Nah," the one who brought me answered. "Let's keep him. I think he'll be a very valuable prisoner of war."

I couldn't help but smile. Even though I was a captive, I had a feeling I was going to like it there.

A PRIVATE PARTY
By R. W. Clinger

R. W. Clinger has numerous books and stories published through STARBooks Press. He can be reached by e-mail: kenitorico@verizon.net.

1. PRIVATE MAXIM COLE

The doorbell on my Cape Cod rings, as expected. My personal accountant and best pal of forever, Luke Cinders (blond hair, five-ten frame, 165 pounds of muscle, forest green eyes, no facial hair, no piercings, and a knob the size of the Eiffel tower), answers the door. Luke is nice to look at, but taken. He's at boyfriend status with a chemistry professor of Condore College; the two have been hooked for the last six months. It doesn't stop me from looking at him in the naughtiest manner, though. What single guy like me wouldn't?

Luke lets Private Maxim Cole inside the Cape Cod. We all shake hands. Luke and I stand a few feet away from the man and do synchronized once-overs of the Army dude's hot bod. Maxim is about the most handsome military man on God's planet: six-two frame, scruff on his chin and cheeks, sandy-brown hair that is cut in a mandatory-short military fashion, wishing well blue eyes, Walt Disney prince-sloped nose, dimple in the middle of his rugged chin, bulky shoulders like a Hummer, and thighs of American steel. He has a firm grip that only Superman can aspire to, and his eyes never leave ours. The man carries his sunglasses in his left hand, which he places on top of his pretty head, storing them away for the time being.

I check out his uniform: Fossil watch on his left wrist, tight olive-green tee that clings to his hulking chest, military green slacks, matching belt with a gold slide-through buckle, black shoes that are freshly polished and shiny. I close the foyer's door behind him and politely ask, "Should we have a seat and discuss our business arrangement?"

I have notes to review with the soon-to-be-hired military man as a stripper: the birthday boy's name is Carter Dixon; he's turning twenty-four this Saturday; a lap dance is necessary during Maxim's striptease; I will gladly pay the ex-Army guy/stripper extra to let Carter touch his chest; the striptease can be as long as Maxim wants; the birthday party begins at eight o'clock in the evening at The Robin Hood Inn on Route 7; I expect Maxim to show up at nine, and not to be a minute late.

Private Maxim takes me in, Ben Enger, and absorbs my twenty-nine-year-old office monkey looks: five-eleven frame, muscular build, amber/brown-colored eyes, ripped tummy, ink-black hair that is curly, broad shoulders, nipples hard under my Rufskin tee. He shakes his head in a direct manner, decides to remove his sunglasses and place them on a nearby Tiffany glass table to his left, and instructs, "Let's cut the bullshit, guys. I'll show you what I've got. You cut half of your check today. The other half is due right after my performance."

Luke looks at me. I look at him. We both turn to the stripper and say, "Bring it on, man."

Maxim doesn't waste any time at all. He steps into my Architectural Digest-decorated living room, stands in the center of the room, demands that we have a seat as his prized two-person audience, and he peels his shirt off with utter zest. In doing so, he admits, "Of course I'll be dancing to music while the striptease occurs. You can give me a list of the birthday boy's favorite artists, and I'll choose the best song for my performance."

Honestly, Luke and I don't hear the stripper's last few words, although they are shared. Instead, our mouths hang open and our interests become intense and engrossed in his now-bare chest. Side-by-side in the foyer, like high school boys who have never been kissed before, we huddle together. What we admire is nothing less than chiseled perfection. Maxim sports a rock-hard torso with deep lines designed by numerous workouts, spirals of sandy-brown hair between his bulging pecs, pointed nipples of Army steel, and a line of treasure hair that falls into his military slacks, positioned beneath his dented navel. Our tongues literally hang out of our mouths. And, the packages between our legs begin to swell with excitement.

"Obviously you both approve of my torso. The show isn't over as of yet, just so you know." Now, he kicks off his freshly polished and shiny shoes on the Berber carpet, swings his tight and bulbous ass to and fro in our faces, undoes his gold belt buckle, pulls his nylon belt through its loops, and drops it to the floor. Within seconds, the stripper unbuttons his government mandatory slacks, teases us with his bulging crotch, which he cups, rubs, and grinds both of his palms over.

"Bring on the sausage party," Luke whispers at my side. He literally has saliva at the right corner of his mouth; evident proof that he is totally turned on by Maxim's performance.

Supportive of his relationship with his professor, I lean into him and whisper in his right ear, "Think of Robert. This way you will feel less sinful."

He chuckles.

I chuckle.

And Private Maxim decides to finally remove his slacks from his ripped body, continuing his gig.

2. THE SHOW MUST GO ON

P-E2 Maxim Cole's history proves intriguing, of course. He served two years in Afghanistan as a grunt in combat with the 23rd Ground Davison. He was honorably discharged because of hearing loss due to military action in the field. He's from Dallas, Texas, new to Trenton, and lives with his younger brother in a two-bedroom apartment on Shetner Street. Stripping is a part-time job that he enjoys on the weekends, which makes extra money for the man and lands him numerous dates with guys and some heavy-duty naked action in the bedroom, among other areas for male-with-male companionship. His full-time job entails paper pushing at an insurance agency in Ewing, a suburb of the city. He drives a Jeep Wrangler and …

None of these details seem to matter when Luke and I are seated next to each other on the English sofa in my living room, and when the military dude's slacks come off. What is exposed beneath his fabric, minus underwear, is nothing less than a queer gift from God. Seven soft inches of veined and cut tool swing between Maxim's legs. The limp shaft is accessorized with a V-shaped patch of curly, sandy-brown hair that is freshly trimmed, and two clean-shaven balls in a drooping sack.

"Sausage time all the way," Luke exclaims at my side. "Look at this fucker's dick, Benjamin."

I am blown away by the sight of the naked stripper in front of me. Maxim is proof that God is queer and enjoys the company of a military man. Not only is the ex-Army brat drop dead gorgeous, but he knows it.

What follows during this pre-show that will surely land Maxim the job on Saturday evening at The Robin Hood Inn on Route 7 is rather enlightening for Luke and me. The stripper decides to step in front of me and positions his droopy cock a mere few inches away from my mouth. In doing so, he begins to swing his hips left and right. Balls and cock flap against my chin in a rather forward manner, driving me to self-pleasure by dropping my jeans to the floor and jerking off. This beef-handling to my fully hard, eight-inch cock only occurs in my head, though. Instead, I keep my composure together and allow him to continue with his stripper pre-show.

Seconds pass, and Maxim now shifts his upright body in front of Luke. He begins to tease my sidekick on the sofa. Luke is falling in love with his boyfriend, though, and sits back in the sofa, distancing himself from the stripper's goods. "Dude, you're swinging those in the wrong face … I'm almost married."

The stripper doesn't take offense to Luke's confession and decides to continue his dick-shaking in front of me. Again, he stands directly in front of my mouth, positions his tool next to my lips, and asks down at me, "Do you want to make it hard, man?"

When was the last time I was intimate with a fag? Six weeks ago? Seven? I really can't remember. If I hold out any longer regarding sex with a guy, I will explode.

Just as I'm about to open my mouth and slip the tip of Maxim's still-soft shaft between my lips, the bad boy says, "Some guys will want to suck me off at the party, which I don't mind. The birthday boy will get a facial if he wants one; it's up to him. I can even fuck a guy, or get fucked, for an extra two hundred dollars. It all depends on how the gig unfolds."

Luke is rather ballsy and chants up to the stripper, "Shut the fuck up and let my friend suck you off, man. What do you say?"

"Only if Ben wants to," Maxim admits. "I don't like to force anything on anyone. I'm not that kind of guy."

As if this is my cue, I take the military tool into my mouth, cup Maxima's balls in my right palm, and bring his thumper to life. Seven soft inches turn into eight … nine … ten veined and throbbing inches of protein. The stripper bashes his beef down the back of my throat, slightly pulls away, bashes it inside again, tickles the top of my lungs, and continues this process for the next few minutes.

"Damn, Ben … I wished that thing was in my mouth," Luke utters with a gasp, perhaps wanting to be single for the first time in his life, unemotionally attached to his boyfriend, Robert.

My palms discover the stripper's hips, and I assist him in bashing my throat with his meat-plunger. Quick and steady forward and backward lunges with my lips and throat ensue on the man's pick. He grunts and groans above me, bucks his weight forward, pulls away, and swiftly bolts forward again. His balls slap against my chin. Saliva drips out of the corners of my mouth and falls to the Berber as I lean forward, into his mid-section, positioned between his legs. More grunts and groans echo within my living room, this time from both of us. Together, we continue this blowjob action for the next four … seven … ten minutes, until he finally pulls away from me. "Damn, Ben, you're pretty good at that. If I don't stop you … you'll be wearing my load."

"That's too bad, because I'm sure I wanted it," Luke says at my side, lounging with his head back on the expensive sofa. One of his palms cups the denim-covered erection between his legs, which is probably leaking sticky spew into his cotton, CIN-2 briefs.

Honestly, I don't know what comes over me. Maybe I'm just needy of a man's naked company and desire nothing less than a Tuesday evening fuck with a stranger by the name of Private Maxim Cole. As the stripper backs away from me, snapping his massive cock off his rippled stomach, I unbutton my jeans, raise my hips, push the denim down to my ankles, and expose an uncut, eight-inch flag between my legs.

"Nice," P-E2 chants above me, glowing from ear to ear with a hungry smile. He licks his lips, toys with the tip of his cock with two fingertips, and demands from me, "What do you have in mind next, guy?"

Luke prattles at my side, "Yeah, Ben … what the fuck are you doing?"

"I'm testing out the goods, Luke. We're not hiring him for Carter until we know how great he really is at his job." I begin to stroke my pole up and down with two fists, let out a huff, give my palms a little thrust with my hips, and feel a bubble of pre-ooze leak out of my cock's head.

Luke feels a little uncomfortable next to me and ends up in a plush chair to my far right, hard as a rock between his legs, ready for whatever is about to unfold next between Private Maxim and me.

"Find a condom," I tell the stripper in a rather demanding nature. "You're going to ride my cock."

Maxim's cock bobs up and down on its own. He now grins from ear to ear, nods his head with satisfaction, and salutes me in his military manner. "The Army taught me to take instruction well. Let me get some plastic from my slacks, and you can ride my ass for as long as you want."

3. BENJAMIN BOUND

I tell the stripper to roll the condom down and over my prick, which he does and adds a generous amount of lube, too. Now, he strokes the bolt up and down with his right palm, stares at me, grins wildly at me, and says, "I have to make it super stiff if I'm going to take all of it at one time."

"Suit yourself," I reply.

On his chair, Luke has his palms between his denim-covered middle, and rattles off, "Where is Robert when I need him? I can't believe this is happening."

What is about to happen is quite simple: Private Maxim Cole is going to back into my stick, lower himself onto the pole, and find pleasure in pouncing up and down. Basic gay stuff. Elementary queer events between one man and another man. The icing on the cake regarding his pony show this evening, some four days away from the birthday party at hand.

"Do it," Luke coaches from his chair, into our play. He adds, "Fuck yourself with his cock, Private. Don't be shy."

P-E2 is hardly shy about anything. In truth, he's horny as hell and ready for the ride of his life with my swollen bar. The man backs into me with skill, spreads his ass cheeks with two palms, and quickly lowers himself onto my staff with utter bliss. A roar of pain mixed with sudden enjoyment echoes within my living room. His voice ricochets off the walls, filling my ears.

The site at hand, a steady and impulsive rocking on my firm piece of steel by the private, is nothing less than a turn-on for my friendly sidekick, Luke. Now, the man has his denim open and his nine-inch flag out for fun, watching the stripper and me at work. Luke says to us in the most homoerotic manner, "Show daddy what you've both got. Make me spew."

"Can't let him down," Maxim replies above me, jostling his weight in a north and south motion, riding my inflated wand with pure delight.

Of course, I hold onto his hips with all my might, jack myself upward, into him, and breathe against the man's back. My ride inside his man-cavern is just as pleasant as his ride on my branch. Together, we work like professional XXX stars on my English sofa, humping wildly, sweating, moaning, and groaning.

To my left, the accountant is busy working his own tool. Luke has his legs spread wide open and his stiff wanker protrudes from his jeans. The guy still has his shirt on, but some of his hairy stomach is exposed, accented with sculpted abs and a concave navel that looks absolutely delicious. Both palms work steadily on his nine-inch shaft, willfully cruising up and down on its excess skin. The man lets out a growl of infatuation, pouring sweat from his brow. Gurgles of pleasure escape his partially open lips as he continues to view our random act of cock-in-ass.

Man-action continues among the three of us in synchronized lust: Luke bobs his fists up and down at his middle, huffs and puffs, growls and grunts; Private Maxim bounces up and down on my masculine limb, obeying his rump-hunger, pleasuring the both of us; I jostle my eight-inch toy inside the stripper, buck his bottom with consistent bangs, arch my neck back with pure elation, and feel an orgasm just about surface.

A video of our sexual feat can be a prize for the three of us to enjoy at a future time: a twenty-eight-minute mix of desirous and filthy men at play inside my living room. To no avail, a video camera is not in possession and rolling, a film crew is not on hand, and our spew-spraying extravaganza that is about to occur will unfortunately not be visually and audibly recorded. Not that this deters the three of us from shooting our loads, of course. Why should it?

My best friend comes first. Luke throttles the mass between his legs, pumps his fists with speed, lets out unrecognizable mumbles, and grits his teeth. Now, obviously windblown and in a state of orgasmic pleasure that is irreversible, the accountant explains through his clenched teeth that he is about to empty his creamy cargo. Just as this warning exits his mouth, white spirals of Luke-ooze bedazzles his navy T-shirt. The sticky sap spins out of his cock's mushroom-shaped head and twirls against the cotton that tightly conceals his chiseled and boyfriended chest.

The stripper comes next. Continuous bottom-thrusts are carried out on my solid flag. Five self-strokes with his right palm to his ten-inch post explodes his seed on the Berber carpet. Resolutely, he fires his pent freight against the floor and accumulates three puddles of his man-liquid. A melodious groan of euphoria erupts from the man's mouth, which is now followed by a string of short grunts as he finishes emptying his system. Two final strokes to the fleshy lever between his legs follow. Seconds later, P-E2 climbs off my spear, spins around, and grins wildly down at me. "It's time to get you off, dude."

"Trust me," I reply, "this is going to take all but a minute."

Truth is it takes less than a minute for my hose to blow. With Private Maxim's help, standing over me ever so slightly, locking his lips to my lips, the condom is rolled off my gear and tossed to the floor. His right palm shifts sporadically up and down with speed on my tube of meat. The man's tongue darts into my mouth, down the back of my throat, pulls away, and darts inside again. His kissing is mind-blowing, dick-hardening, and just about Hot House perfect. The moment becomes intense for me, an unlimited apex of enjoyment that I will surely not forget anytime soon.

While these acts are being carried out between Maxim and me, Luke decides to clean the mess off his T-shirt. Fingertips gather up goop from his cotton and enter his mouth, one at a time. My sidekick begins to moan with robust pleasure, delighted with his Tuesday evening snack, savoring the seed with every finger-dip into his mouth.

As expected, I come with just a few dick-jolts. Ooze leaks out of the spigot between my legs, flies against his plated chest, over the dude's fingers, and even nails the man in the chin. Once this transpires, he politely pulls away from me. "Lick it off me, pal … You know you want to."

And so it is done: I slip my tongue out of my mouth, lap up the goop from his narrow chin and consume my chow, drop by drop. The moment is festive and delightful at the same time. I become hungry for my seed, devouring it from his skin, and cover every inch of his rigid chest with my mouth, cleaning its surface until it gleams.

"Nicely done," he coaches me.

"I'll get it all," I reply, consuming every drop of my sap from his flesh.

"Of course you will."

Our evening together ends rather abruptly, I admit. The stripper dresses, asks for half of his full payment, and exits with a blistering smile and a check in his right hand. On his way out of the Cape Cod, he politely whispers into my ear, "You really know how to fuck a man, Ben."

I pat him on the back with my right palm in a butch manner, heartily laugh, and provide, "Come back for round two anytime you want."

P-E2 winks at me, waves his goodbye, and leaves me alone for the evening with my cohort, Luke.

My best friend is already half-asleep in his chair, post-sexed and exhausted from his self-play. I give him a little shake and tell him to go home, that his boyfriend awaits his company … and maybe even something more. Luke agrees, vanishes from my side like the stripper. In due time, not that I'm aware of it at this very second on this Tuesday evening, both men will come into my life again: one as a friend, and the other on a mission to be my boyfriend.

4. PUTTING OUT

Two nights later, and two nights before Carter's birthday/sausage party, Private Maxim shows up at my house a second time. He carries a tiny video camera at his side that he intends to use, a condom in one of his pockets, and a ten-inch throbbing erection between his legs. Of course, I welcome him into the Cape Cod, serve him a longneck beer, sit with him in the living room, study his tight and T-shirt covered ripped body yet again, and inquire, "What are you here for?"

"Seconds ... or maybe longer."

"What's the maybe longer entail?"

"A date. Alone time with you. Something real maybe."

"Do I have to pay you this time?"

He laughs, almost spitting out a swallow of his beer, shakes his head, gathers his composure, and admits, "Not this time."

"What if I want to get lucky with you, though? Will I have to pay then?"

He snuggles next to me on my English sofa, rubs fingers over my chin, seduces me with his handsome eyes, and confesses, "This isn't about the gig on Saturday. This is about you and me."

"Private Maxim and me."

"Yes ... us. I rather like the sound of that."

I want to laugh at him, but keep my composure together. "You're a romantic at heart, aren't you?"

"Guilty," he admits. "But I can still be naughty."

"I would hope so."

He leans into me, rubs his nose to my nose, and dots the center of my lips with his outstretched tongue. "How do you want me to be naughty, Mr. Enger?"

I pull away from him, attempting to play hard to get. "First, you can dance for me."

"Then what?"

"You can strip, and I can have my own sausage party."

He laughs, and adds, "Then what?"

"I think you know what will surely happen next between us, Private Maxim."

He rises from the sofa, finds some music to put on the stereo in the corner and begins to dance. "I don't put out on the first date."

I like the guy. Maybe more than I should since he's a promiscuous stripper. His military qualities blow me away, though, which I find totally irresistible. "Something tells me you're going to put out tonight."

He dances a little, strips off his shirt and drops it to the floor, shows off his perfectly cut chest for me, and continues our intimate evening together with: "Once again … you're right."

DRESS REHEARSAL
By Logan Zachary

Logan Zachary (LoganZachary2002@yahoo.com) lives in Minneapolis. His new book Calendar Boys *is out, and his stories can be found in dozens of anthologies.*

"If you want the production to be accurate, you need to hire a real live Naval officer for me to meet with and go over their uniforms, conduct, motions and such." I closed my laptop and pushed it away from me on my desk.

"Can't you just watch the DVD?" Mike Sabers, the director, dropped a copy on top of my computer.

"No. I knew you'd say that. If you want me to do this right, you'll do it my way. Place an ad, call a friend, whatever it takes, but I need this expert if you want this production of *South Pacific* to be perfect."

There was a sharp rap on my office door.

"I am the best in the business, and I do things right."

Another rap hit the wood.

"Now what?" I pushed up from my desk and ripped open the door. "What?"

A startled Naval officer stood with his hand ready to knock again.

Mike pushed past me. "If you need anything else, just ask. You can thank me later." He nodded at the man in uniform and kept walking.

"Did I come at a bad time?" the man in uniform asked.

I took a deep breath and forced a smile. "Mike and I have worked together for many years, and at times he tries to cut corners, and I wasn't going to do that this time."

"I'm Captain Gary Rogers. I understand you have some questions about our uniforms and mannerisms that would help you in your play's production."

He was the most handsome man I had ever seen. Short dark wavy hair, freshly cut, clean shaven face, erect posture, which caused me to get an erection, and a finely pressed uniform. His shoulders held epaulettes with four gold stripes and a star. He stood at attention and looked at me. His deep blue eyes were like the sea, and I wanted to dive in.

"I … I don't know where to begin." I felt my face flush.

"Let's start at the beginning, that's the very best place to start." He smiled and curled his lips into a pucker as the lyrics came out.

Was he toying with me? Did he realize what he said? Or was I reading too much into it?

"The more stars and bars a service man has the more respect he demands and deserves. We have our dress uniforms and then our regular uniforms, each man is issued these." Captain Gary pointed to his rank.

"I want them to be authentic, but I also want them to look good on stage and on the actors."

"I see," he said. "Soldiers are in the army, and we have sailors in the Navy." He put his hands behind his back and thrust out his pelvis, which stained against the fabric of his pants.

"We have a winter blue uniform and a white summer uniform, since the play takes place in a warm climate, so the white one would be worn."

I grabbed my notebook and flipped it open. I searched for my pen and couldn't find one.

Captain Gary stepped closer and reached for me.

I held still as his hairy arm moved closer, and I felt him pluck the pen from behind my ear and handed it to me. One of his fingertips brushed along side of my face, and my cheek burned.

"Is this what you are looking for?"

"In more ways than one," escaped out of me before I realized what I said.

He smiled and stepped back. "Since the play is set in the tropics, many men would modify their uniforms, cut the pants into shorts, cut sleeves off shirts, or go shirtless, since much of the action is on the beach."

I wrote something down in the notebook. Not a clue what it said, but who cares.

"The higher the official the more likely, he'll wear his full uniform and metals to show his rank and status. The enlisted men would shed their uniform easier since they haven't worked as hard or invested as much of themselves yet." He started to unbutton his shirt.

"If a superior officer enters the barracks, all the soldiers, sailors, whoever must stand at attention for inspection or whatever information is being passed. If they're changing or in the shower, everyone must hurry to their post and stand at attention."

"Even dripping wet with a towel on?" I asked.

"Yes." Two more buttons opened.

"That must be embarrassing." My eyes darted down to follow his fingers down his shirt.

"It's all part of the military life. The service owns these men for the tour of their duty. They feed, clothe and offer shelter until they are discharged." He pulled his shirt tails out of his pants and let them hang. He stood straight and tall.

I had to ask another question, what did I want to know? "Do many guys have tattoos?"

I watched as his hairy chest came into view. He undid his cuffs and slipped his shirt off. He carefully folded and set it on my desk. His arms were muscled and toned. His skin was bronzed under his thick pelt of fur that covers his pecs and over his sculpted abs.

"Most guys have a tattoo on their upper arm..." He flexed his biceps and made his arm bulge, just as my pants were. "... but some guys choose to have one on their inner forearm." He flipped his palm up and showed a popular place.

Nothing marred his beautiful skin as I looked over his body and memorized every inch.

"You don't have any tattoos?"

He smiled. "I thought you wanted to know about uniforms, not me."

"I guess getting to know a real Naval officer helps me understand the works of the man and his conduct." Good save.

"Mind if I sit?"

I motioned to the chair opposite my desk. "Sure, have a seat."

He pulled off one shoe and then the other. He set one on my desk and handed me the other one. "See how polished and shiny it is. There are no scratches or scuffmarks, ever."

I turned the big black shoe in my hand to see all sides. You know what they say about a man with a big foot. I set his shoe on my desk.

He took off his black socks and handed them to me. "These are government issue socks. We can't wear white tube socks."

I looked at his bare feet, beautiful long toes with hair sprouting from each one of them. They were bronze just like his chest. I inhaled deeply and smelled all male and all man. He had a musky sweat, but clean soap and water scent, too. I doubt he wore any after shave, even with his five o'clock stubble starting to show.

He reached to his waist and unbuckled his shiny gold belt buckle. It had the bar that slid and held the webbed belt in place around his hips. He pulled it free from his belt loops and handed that to me.

I set his socks on top of his shoes and examined his belt. The belt was khaki, and the golden buckle held a silver eagle hanging onto a shield, behind it were crossed golden anchors. The tension bar rattled loose in the buckle.

Were my hands shaking that much?

Captain Gary didn't seem to notice, or if he did, he ignored it. "Any questions so far?"

My mind was racing in so many directions that I couldn't think of what to ask next.

"Should I keep going?" He looked into my eyes and stood up. He unhooked his pants and unzipped them. He pushed them down his hairy legs and stepped out of them. He flattened them and gave them to me.

They were soft and warm to the touch. They smelled of him, a scent my body was responding too on so many levels. My nipples pressed against my shirt and seemed to be rubbed raw after all the moves I made. My cock strained in my pants and hurt from the angle it was twisted. I needed to adjust myself.

Then I looked at him.

Captain Gary stood clad only in a pair of white boxer shorts with the fly peeking open. Dark hair escaped and a bump was easily seen from the cotton. He nodded to the pants and sat down. "Check them out; get all the details you need."

I reached inside the pants and felt the dampness of his sweat and heat of his body. My hand ran down the inside, imagined cupping his balls, rolling them between my fingers and combing through the hair all over his body, and then caressing his ...

"We are supposed to wear only white briefs. Most choose boxers to allow for more freedom. Ball room if you wanted to know."

"We all need that." My gaze darted down to his crouch and noted his fly was wide open and something hairy and pink peeked out one of his leg holes. There was a big bulge that stretched the fabric.

"We don't have any talcum powder for those guys who are sweaty down there, and the barracks can become pretty ripe in the summer. And jock itch can become a problem." He touched himself down there.

I doubted he had crotch rot, but the word alone inspired a scratch even on the driest balls. I adjusted myself behind the shield of his pants and had a flood of relief in my pants. I smiled and let out a deep breath.

Captain Gary dug a finger into his fly, and the snap of crackly hair echoed through the office.

The sexual tension in my mind was making me dizzy. His scent, his handsome hairy look, and such a sexy, confident presence radiated from every pore in his body.

I wiped the sweat from my forehead with the back of my hand and his pants. "Whoops."

"I'm hot and sweaty, too, so a little more won't hurt." He stood up and stepped forward.

I figured he was coming to get his pants back, but he surprised me.

He hooked his fingers into his elastic waistband and pulled them away from his torso. His eyebrows rose, questioning me. "Ready?'

Ready? Ready for what? Did he mean?

He pushed his boxers down his long legs, the electric sparking sounded all the way down as the hair rubbed against the fabric. He handed them to me and 220 volts shot through me as his skin touched mine.

I went blind. I couldn't see. I couldn't breathe. I was going to throw up.

I brought his boxers to my nose and breathed in deeply, and I savored ever second they were there. My tongue stuck out of my mouth, hoping to catch a drop of sweat from his balls.

Then I realized he was standing right there. Naked. Staring at me.

"I'm so sorry," I said lowering his boxers, and my eyes looked lower and lower.

WOW!

"This is what a Naval Officer looks and acts like." He stepped closer and took the boxers from my hand and threw them on the desk. He sat his bare ass on the corner and spread his legs. "I don't manscape, I don't shave." He pulled up his low hanging balls and rolled them for me to see. His massive cock dangled from his thick pubic bush, and he stroked it.

I licked my lips and tasted his salty sweat on them. I wanted more.

"Maybe you need to look closer." He motioned for me to come to him.

I walked into his arms and almost kissed him on the lips.

Captain Gary grabbed my head and guided it down to his chest. He brought my head to his pec, and he rubbed over his nipple as it rose to a sharp point.

He smelled so fine, and my tongue licked through the hair and circled the point. My teeth rolled it, and the flavor was pure beef with salt.

"See how the hair spreads out over my chest and funnels down to my abs."

His hands held my head and had me kneel as I licked lower and lower. His hairy belly button needed extra attention.

My tongue, tickled by the hair, enjoyed his navel. My hands couldn't resist any longer. They grabbed his torso and slipped over his hips and massaged his ass, buns of steel. His furry ass was warm and so tight. My fingers pulled his cheeks apart and slipped into his crease.

His hair funneled into his crack, and my fingers happily followed. Warm and moist made my exploration easy.

Something brushed under my chin.

Old Glory rose to full mast, and it was all mine. His thick pubic bush glistened like morning dew, and his cock stood straight out, demanding my full attention.

I licked the tip and tasted a pearl of sweetness. Licking down his shaft to his balls, I felt Captain Gary's whole body tense. I licked along the crease between his testicle and his leg, driving him nuts.

"I'm here to help you," he said, trying to rise up to a sitting position.

"Oh, you are, and you taste so good, too. I enjoy watching you and pleasuring you." I guided my hand between his cheeks and explored the hairy crease.

His butt pressed down on my finger, encouraging me to slip it in deeper. He brought his feet up on top of my desk and widened them for easier access.

I've had many fantasies about a hot naked man lying across my desk, but I never believed it would happen.

Was my office door locked? My whole body stiffened. Slowly, I withdrew my finger from his tight ass and stepped back.

He looked up at me worried.

"I need to lock the door." I motioned to it.

"Great idea. Take off your clothes when you come back, and that's an order." He rolled into a side-lying position to watch me. His balls rolled over to dangle as his cock pointed directly at me.

I locked the door and pulled my shirt off over my head without unbuttoning. My finger fumbled with my belt as I kicked off my shoes. My pants exploded open and sank to the floor. I dove on top of the desk and landed on him.

His hands pulled my briefs down and squeezed my ass as they lowered to half mast. "Ahoy matey, anchors away." He pulled the underwear down in the front and freed my cock.

My balls swung free like pendulums, as my cock stood straight up.

Captain Gary guided my cock to his mouth, and he swallowed me whole, deep throating all eight inches. He grabbed my hips, pushed and pulled me deep into him. His tongue pulsated along my shaft.

Pre-cum oozed out of me and added to his saliva to slip in and out easier and easier. The sensation grew as I quickened my pace.

His fingers pulled my cheeks apart and dug in deeper and deeper. A tip brushed against my pucker and sought entry like a heat seeking missile. He pressed the spot and entered a little deeper.

I pushed forward into his mouth, and then backed up on his hand. I wanted so much more. Rocking my hips back and forth, the pleasure rose.

Drool poured out of the corners of his mouth as he worked my rod. He pulled his finger out of my hole and grabbed my balls. He pulled them down and stretched them as far as they would go. He pulled his head back and sucked my cock to the fat head and kissed it.

Pre-cum wet his lips, and he smiled. "Do you have lube and a rubber?"

I rolled off of him and pulled the bottom drawer open on my desk. I rifled through the files and pulled out a small bottle and a foil square packet. "Is this what you want?"

He sat up and slapped my ass. "That is what I want." He took the condom and tore it open with his teeth and handed it to me. "Wrap it up."

I stretched the rubber over his dick's end and rolled it down the thick girth to his thick pubic bush. I squeezed his balls and felt how full they were.

"Lie on the desk," he slipped off the edge and stood, motioning for me to climb on top.

The cool surface made Goosebumps rise on my ass, and I tried to slip back, but my skin stuck due to the dampness.

Captain Gary helped me lie back and stepped between my legs. He flipped the top open on the bottle and poured some into his palm. He slathered his condom coated cock and ran up and down my crease. His lube covered finger pressed into me.

I moaned and felt my ass swallow his finger.

He pulled his finger out and slapped my ass with his dick. Lube splattered as his meat made contact.

The hair on my balls absorbed the lube. I took a deep breath as he guided his cock into my hole. He set his bare feet on the floor and pushed into me.

My pucker resisted as he tried to sail into me.

He felt the tension and grabbed my dick and started to stroke me. He pumped me as he humped me. Slowly, he entered me.

My butt relaxed and stretched to allow him inside; inch-by-inch his rudder steered his course toward my prostate. His tip pressed against my gland, and pre-cum flowed out of me.

My hand brushed against the pile of his clothes. His uniform threatened to topple off the desk, but we stopped and adjusted it, respecting them enough to keep them safe.

Captain Gary resumed and rammed into me full speed ahead. He anchored my cock in his hands, and he stroked me as he poked me, faster and deeper.

Even without his clothes on, I wanted to salute him, and part of my body was. I moaned with each thrust and felt my balls rise. The sensation grew through my body and each nerve ending tingled, ready for the big release.

"I'm …" was all I got out of my mouth.

"Me, too." Captain Gary doubled his speed and thrust into me. He anchored his dick in me and shot his load.

I felt wave after wave of spunk hit my prostate, and it drove my orgasm out of my cock. The eruption spewed between his fingers and sprayed over my torso. Another spasm emptied my balls, but a few more wracked my body. Every muscle tensed as each nerve ending intensified.

Captain Gary's hand slid down my hip, and my body rose off the desk. I shuddered as pleasure washed over me. I gasped as my heart raced in my chest.

Captain Gary collapsed on top of me and spread my seed over our bodies. Wet warmth squished between us, as we held each other.

I shifted my body, and his cock slipped out of me. I laughed from the pure joy and emotional release. I rolled off the desk and found a towel for myself and him. Without a word, we cleaned up our fun.

"Will you be here opening night?" I asked, as I stooped to gather my clothes.

"I'll be here any night you want me. And I hope to see you outside of this place, too." Captain Gary pushed up from the desk and looked for his clothes.

"What is the next step for you? I mean, in your career path."

"I'll be a Rear Admiral on my next promotion." He bent over and picked up his underwear. His beautiful ass rippled as he moved.

"I know you'll be perfect for that position. I'll even give you a glowing recommendation."

He looked over his shoulder at me and smiled. "It's part of my oath to protect and serve."

"Well, I'll take the service."

And I did, many times.

THE MAN BENEATH
By Mark Apoapsis

Mark Apoapsis doesn't currently have a website but may be reached at mapoapsis@excite.com.

"My God," Rodrigo muttered, crouching beside me on the tree branch. "It looks like a giant preacher."

"¿Un predicador gigantesco?" I echoed, confused. After almost a year, I was very fluent in Spanish, but my misunderstandings and misstatements were a continuing source of amusement to my comrades.

"A mother snake," he offered.

"He means a Saint Teresa, Josh," Guillermo whispered beside me. Despite the dire situation we faced, he grinned at me and punched my arm. "¡No es un pastor!"

Mateo leaned past Guillermo to whisper, "Una mantis religiosa."

"Mantis!" I said. "Got it. Yes, more or less." With the bug eyes and roughly triangular head, the thing striding toward us did look vaguely like a giant silver praying mantis three times the height of a man, but it walked on two legs, and the two arms looked more human than mantid and ended in hands with five long fingers, three equipped with wicked claws. Its barrel chest was shaped like that of a burly man, scaled up: anything but stick-like.

It crashed through the jungle, effortlessly sweeping away vines like cobwebs with no need for anything so primitive as a machete, thrusting aside small trees, and trampling the undergrowth. It was making straight toward our encampment, as precisely as if it had a GPS in its head – which it almost certainly did – and knew the exact coordinates, which was more surprising.

Scary as hell, whatever you compared it to. Every instinct screamed at me to run away. Every instinct but one, apparently, because I found myself trying to rise and head straight toward it, to try to stop if before it reached my buddies, my comrades.

"Josh!" Rodrigo put his hands on my shoulders and hauled me back down. "Maintain your position, man," he whispered in my ear. I couldn't even claim a convenient lapse in my language skills; *Mantén tu posición* would have been unmistakable enough even on the day I'd first arrived to offer my services to the rebels.

"If that thing is armored with the material I think it is, the guns will be useless," I whispered back. I was fluent enough now that I could manage complex sentences without thinking, which was a good thing because all I could think about now was that my buddies were about to be slaughtered, and I was holding our two best hopes of defense.

"We can't afford to lose you, man," Rodrigo said, squeezing my shoulder. "Are you sure no one else can operate those things?"

I glanced down at the cobbled-together box in one hand and the wire-wrapped cylinder in the other. "I didn't exactly have time to make them point-and-click," I said.

"It's too late anyway. It's almost at Raul and Jorge's position."

Raul and Jorge, two of our best marksmen, were very nice guys. Like most of my comrades, they were young: no older than I, and I was just out of school. Raul had shyly offered to teach me to shoot, if only for my own protection, but seemed to accept my decision to not carry a gun. Jorge had talked me into grappling lessons. Those had actually been fun, and I'd learned a lot, even if they usually ended with me pinned down helplessly, with my nose buried in Jorge's armpit. To tell the truth, that was a good incentive for me to keep at it; that and the opportunity to admire Jorge's sinuously muscular brown arms, normally hidden by his outer uniform shirt. He did leave his undershirt on. He was one of the few guys to wear one; between the tropical heat and the limited funds, most guys contented themselves with one layer of shirt.

A moment later, semi-automatic weapons fire erupted from the bushes – aimed at the monster's torso, as I'd recommended. But they bounced harmlessly off the advanced-materials armor plating, not even leaving a mark. The stream of bullets played briefly up and down the metallic body in hopes of finding a chink in the armor.

The monster could have ignored the minor annoyance, but it bent down and fished Raul out of his hiding place. It held him up, struggling in terror, at bug-eye level to inspect him or to savor the moment. Then it flung him away. He hit a tree trunk two stories up with a meaty thwack, and slid down to land like a discarded rag doll.

Jorge had broken cover when the thing had grabbed his buddy. He'd held his fire, presumably because the ricochet might hit the dangling Raul. When it hurled Raul into the tree trunk, he ran between its legs and tried shooting into its crotch from below, then in the back, with no more success than before.

Moving impressively quickly for its size, it turned around, bent down, knocked away his gun and grabbed his wrists between thumb and forefinger, dangling him at eye level. He screamed in terror as the claws of the other hand raked his chest, tearing his heavy outer shirt open and leaving his undershirt in ribbons, giving me my first and last look at his muscular chest, which was smoother than I'd pictured it. Then the claws ripped through the skin and into the muscle. Jorge screamed in agony. Both of Rodrigo's hands were on my shoulders, physically holding me down; apparently I was trying to go to him. I hadn't realized I was that suicidal. I could feel Rodrigo's hands shaking as we listened to the dying screams of our comrade. They seemed to go on forever, but it was probably only a few seconds before another swipe clawed open his lungs or his heart. I remembered listening, countless times, to that heart hammering, with my head pinned against his chest, as he struggled to keep me from breaking free. Now it would never beat again. I was so absorbed in my own grief that I didn't notice Guillermo's stunned reaction to his buddy's death until I saw him being comforted by Mateo. Mateo was one of the most empathetic guys I'd ever met; naturally, he'd picked up on our buddy's grief right away.

The metallic monster tossed away the bloody remains of its plaything and resumed its progress toward our camp, where dozens of men who had become my only friends and family were waiting, effectively defenseless and utterly vulnerable. We'd been forced to abandon our only cannon in our last retreat.

I activated one of the two jury-rigged devices I held: the boxy one. It had limited battery power, but the thing would soon be close enough, and at this rate we were all likely to die long before the battery did. But it failed to immediately stop the monster in its tracks.

A stream of bullets hit it from above as it ducked under a stout tree branch. They bounced off its head and shoulders, and it reached up into the tree and pulled out the gunman, who turned out to be José. Everybody liked José; he was always cheerful, and he told a lot of jokes that were apparently hilarious if you knew the subtleties of the language and culture better than I did. I liked him anyway. Had liked. A short time later, he, too, was thoroughly dead. Not nearly short enough.

Three more men broke cover, carrying our last rocket-launcher between them. It was Bernardo, Leandro, and Enrique. Enrique was my closest friend, not counting the ones I'd abandoned in the United States and Canada. He was the only one fluent in English, and when I'd first arrived, I'd know enough Spanish for utilitarian purposes, but not enough to joke around with anyone, or to have a meaningful conversation about my hopes and fears and torn loyalties. I'd known Bernardo and Leandro for just as long, and with them, I had a bond that didn't depend much on language. When I first arrived, we'd been even shorter on tents than we were now, and they'd let me crowd into their two-man tent with them, one of those tiny pup tents you have to enter by crawling. I've always thought they didn't deserve to be called even "two-man" tents because the two men would have to be real friendly. I'd learned soon after getting here that it was necessary to be real friendly. Fortunately for me, Bernardo and Leandro were very likable, open, easygoing guys – much like Mateo, whose tent I was now sharing, ever since his previous bunkmate was shot in the leg and had to return to the dubious safety of his village. I didn't have much in common with Bernardo or Leandro, but we'd forged a bond, lying side by side with our bare shoulders unavoidably touching, talking softly before we drifted off to sleep. I'd spent countless hot summer nights watching their bare sweaty chests rising and falling in the moonlight. We'd often done things together, though not with each other, if you know what I mean.

As fast as they could, the three men set up the rocket launcher and began trying to aim it. They weren't fast enough. The monster had drawn within arm's reach and was bending down to pick up the nearest man, which happened to be Bernardo. It grabbed him by the ankles and used him as a flail to knock his buddies from its path. Then it brought him down several times on the rocket launcher until it was ruined, possibly beyond my ability to repair it and finally flung what was left of him to the ground. We had a high enough vantage point to see that it had deliberately dropped him on top of the unmoving body of Leandro.

"He's dead, isn't he?" Guillermo whispered numbly.

"Oh, God, I hope so," Mateo breathed.

"Leandro might still be alive," I said. "Maybe we can get to him before ..."

"Before he wakes up and sees what that thing did to his best friend," Mateo finished for me. I'd been thinking more along the lines of, before he bleeds to death, but the blood soaking into his shirt looked like it was all from Bernardo's body.

"I wish the thing really was a giant insect," I whispered miserably.

"If it were a mindless insect doing this, it wouldn't be quite so horrible, you mean?" Rodrigo asked.

"Exactly. Even a giant killer robot."

"Are you sure it's not?" Guillermo whispered.

"Robots don't torture their targets," I said. Of course, that was partly because they weren't smart enough, but more importantly, because the software would be officially reviewed by several people.

Official, systematic torture was something the dictator we were fighting might engage in, but his allies – my own country – would not stoop quite that low, I hoped. I patted the box. "Someone is operating it. Let's hope he's doing it by remote control. If so, this jammer should stop it as soon as it gets in range."

"Quiet," Rodrigo hissed. "We don't know how good its hearing is."

As the thing continued its relentless advance, drawing closer to my position, Hernando and Arturo broke cover and ran toward the monster, carrying a heavy chain stretched between them, hoping to trip it up. The giant's mirrored bug-like eyes looked down expressionlessly at its small attackers. Bending at the waist, it deftly grabbed the chain in the middle, causing the two men to be slammed against each other, ten feet up. Arturo hit the ground running, but when he saw that his stunned comrade was being scooped up in the monster's claws, he valiantly doubled back. He grabbed one end of the chain, darting between the monster's legs to wrap it around its ankle. It started walking, yanking Arturo off his feet and dragging him along the ground. He held on. He loved Hernando. We all did; his nightly singing by the campfire was one of the few forms of entertainment we had. But, I knew Arturo would have done the same for any of us.

Desperately, I pointed my other homemade gadget, the wire-wrapped cylinder, at the monster and pressed the button. I could tell from the sound and vibration that it had gone off, but the only thing that happened was that the power light in my jammer winked off. No loss; that one should have worked by now if it was going to.

"Out of range?" Rodrigo whispered.

"Probably. Of course, it could be shielded."

"Wait for it to get closer. Don't expose yourself."

The thing, still carrying Hernando's struggling form, stopped and looked down at the annoying little creature on its ankle. Deliberately, it held Hernando where Arturo could see him, and began pulling at his arm with its free hand. Hernando screamed. I looked away, unable to watch. When the screaming stopped, I looked at Guillermo instead. He had his face buried in Mateo's shoulder, and was mumbling something. I caught the word for "body" and for "pieces."

"In English, we have an expression, tore him limb from limb." I translated it literally. "Did it ..."

"Yes."

I looked back. I couldn't see Hernando's body in the undergrowth, mercifully, but now it had Arturo. It was holding him aloft by his ankles with one hand. I could see his navel; his shirt had slid toward his head, baring just a little of his belly, about the width of one of the clawed fingertips. I thought I saw something I'd never thought I'd see on Arturo's handsome face: fear. Instead of immediately ripping into flesh or shirt, it poked him in the chest with the pad of a fingertip to set him swinging.

I jumped out of the tree, defensive weapon in hand, taking everyone by surprise, including myself. The cylinder only had enough power for a few tries, so I got as close as I could, not stopping until the monster was looming above me. It turned its bug-eyed gaze on me and raised Arturo above its head, as though winding up to break my ribs with my comrade's skull, or possibly just to give me a better view of what it was about to do to him. Now or never! I pressed the button and held my breath. Nothing happened.

After a few seconds, I realized that was a good sign. The monster stood there frozen, with Arturo still dangling by his ankles.

"Arturo! Are you okay, sir?"

"Never mind me, man! See if Enrique or Leandro is alive." He bent at the waist and athletically grabbed the claw that held his ankles and swung up onto it. I wondered what his abs must look like, to be able to do that so easily, and wished his shirt had slid just a little further.

I turned around and was relieved to see Enrique on his feet, dragging a woozy Leandro out from under his dead buddy. As I watched, Enrique tore off his dazed comrade's shirt, which was soaked with the blood of his best friend, and threw it over the dead man's battered face, then put his shoulder under Leandro's armpit and helped him hobble away from Bernardo's body. From the way they were limping, I guessed that they had only two or three uninjured legs between them. I started toward them, intending to put my shoulder under Leandro's other armpit and wrap a supporting hand around their backs, but then I heard the crashing noises. Something very big was headed our way very quickly. They heard it, too, and hurried as best they could into the shelter between two sturdy tree trunks.

Not sturdy enough. Another shiny giant, the twin of the one I'd just defeated, came up behind them and uprooted the trees they were cowering between. They tried desperately to crawl away, but it picked Enrique by the back of his shirt and made him watch while it stomped on Leandro's legs, then his naked torso. Then it crushed Enrique's ribcage like a beer can and tossed him aside.

I could never have reached them in time, I told myself, but the fact was that I'd been close enough to hear the ribs cracking; I'd been paralyzed by terror and horror and hadn't even tried to move toward them. I'd been called a coward many times since fleeing to Canada, and maybe they'd been right.

The cylinder was probably good for one more electromagnetic pulse. As the new monster approached, I stood my ground, which sounds a lot better than "stood frozen in terror."

I had to make this count. I waited until it was actually reaching down to grab me before I pressed the button.

This one didn't freeze. Instead, it sank to its knees before me. I realized later that was a safing mechanism; the pulse must have burned out some of the electronics and motors but left it working well enough to reflexively minimize damage. As the knees hit the ground, a ruler-straight crack appeared down the center of its torso, from mid-chest to waist.

I looked around. My half dozen surviving comrades had not moved from their hiding places in the trees and undergrowth.

"Guys, help Arturo get down," I directed. "And cover me while I get this thing open."

I slid my fingers into the thing's belly and found a latch. The panels swung apart when I pulled, revealing a man's naked torso, pale and not particularly well-muscled for a soldier, breathing hard, with electrodes pasted to various points on the chest and belly. The only thing he was wearing that was visible to me was a chain lying against his chest, on which were strung dog tags and a tiny electronic device that looked like it might contain a few megabytes of data.

"I surrender!" he said in Spanish, with an accent worse than mine. His voice was muffled; his head and shoulders were buried somewhere around where the heart of the giant would be, where he'd presumably been viewing the world through screens that were now dark. It covered him down to just above his nipples, which were at a height just out of my reach. I noticed the electrodes were pasted onto his skin over each major muscle group, and more wires trailed down his body toward his hidden legs. "Please, don't kill me. I surrender!"

I'd never punched a man in my life, let alone a trapped and helpless one, but right now I badly wanted to use that exposed belly as a punching bag. It was positioned conveniently right around my shoulder level, with the suit kneeling like that.

"So it's really just a man inside?" Mateo said, approaching warily.

"Just a man, like you and me," I agreed. Actually, I was ashamed to realize he was more like me than like him, judging by guy's accent and his skin color. I'd been hoping for light brown, which might mean he was a local, acting under the orders of a dictator already known to be a sadistic scumbag. Any other color meant he was from the country I'd once called home. This guy was pale – as pale as I, and I'm blond.

Rodrigo was trailing behind. He got a look at our vanquished foe and called to the surviving rebels, "You see? The enemy is not an invincible monster. He's just a man. A man who can be defeated. A man who has been defeated." He added quietly to us, "Get him out of there. Be careful."

"I like him the way he is," I growled and drew back to get in at least one good punch before he was released.

Mateo grabbed my wrist. "What are you doing, man?" he whispered. "If all of us start doing what we feel like doing to him, he's not going to survive the day."

Guillermo walked up and stuck the barrel of his rifle into the prisoner's exposed belly, practically grinding it into his navel. "Come out of there, pal. Slowly," he ordered.

"To need ... I need ... help. The suit no does to function," he said in bad Spanish, and added in English, "Even when it's working right, I need a hand climbing out."

I translated the English, then watched my buddies pull out a lanky, frightened man no older than I, clad only in olive drab boxer shorts. His bare feet must have fit in stirrups inside the knees of the suit. Once I was sure he was in no position to pull any technical surprises, I went to see to Arturo. Our remaining comrades had lowered the suit onto the ground on its back and pried the fingers off his ankles. Or maybe Arturo had done it all on his own, knowing him. We had to use a crowbar to open the chest compartment on this one. Muffled English words were coming from inside – actually, just two particular Anglo-Saxon words, over and over.

When they got the chest open, the first thing I saw was a concave navel with some wisps of black hair above it. They got it open further, exposing a muscular chest, with dog tags and an identical electronic thing lying between his pecs, half buried in thick curly chest hair. His torso was rising and falling rapidly with suppressed fear, or maybe rage.

# # # # #

44

By the time the suits were empty husks and their operators were being led away with their hands bound behind their backs, barefoot through the undergrowth in their underpants, most of the survivors had gotten over the shock and were giddy with victory, with the fact that we were unexpectedly still alive even if seven of our buddies were not. I was slapped on the back by more hands than I could count and hoisted onto the shoulders of two sturdy comrades, Ernesto and Pedro, where I could look down on the slumped bare shoulders of the limping prisoners. Others dragged the suits behind us, forming an impromptu victory parade back to the camp and the waiting comrades we'd just successfully defended.

Once they'd set me down, I spent most of the next half hour with Pedro's brawny arm around my shoulders, Ernesto watching shyly, as everyone related the story to the guys back at camp. It felt good.

"Uh-oh," Pedro said, looking toward Rodrigo, who was stalking toward us now that the crowd of admirers had thinned out. "I know that look. He's going to bawl somebody out."

"Can I talk to you for a minute, Josh?" Rodrigo said quietly, and took me aside. "First of all, I know you probably saved all our lives today, man. Don't think I'm not grateful. I know you haven't sworn an oath like the others; I don't have as much authority over you as if you were willing to wear our uniform."

"Yeah," I agreed cheerfully, still exhilarated by triumph, "if I'd let my own side draft me, I'd probably have been shot for insubordination by now."

"I wouldn't have you shot for that. But if you were wearing our uniform, you wouldn't be wearing it much longer if you continued to disobey my direct orders."

"I don't need to be here, you know. I was safe in Canada." That country had gotten fed up enough with its southern neighbor's increasingly aggressive actions to officially grant asylum to draft resisters. I understood that it had also been a de facto haven the last time there was a draft. The war and the reinstatement of the draft were unpopular enough with the international community, but what really alienated the Canadians was the President's decision to conscript only males, after Congress refused to update the law to give her the authority to extend the draft to both sexes.

"I know," Rodrigo said. "I respect your altruism and bravery; you gave up a safe life to help us, whereas the rest of us are fighting out of desperation to save our families and villages and because our only alternative is to cooperate with a corrupt government. And I'm well aware that you can walk away if I ever push you too far. And we need you now more than ever. Nevertheless, you have to obey my orders next time."

"Or what? You said yourself I don't have a uniform for you to take away."

He looked me up and down. "Don't think you have nothing I can take away. I think you really care about what you're doing here, so it should be possible to devise a punishment that won't be so harsh as to ..."

The awkward confrontation was interrupted by Mateo, who hurried up and said "Sir, what would you like us to do with the prisoners?"

By giving me a chance to step back from the argument and think about it a minute, he instantly became my new best friend. Come to think of it, he literally had instantly become my new best friend a short while ago. We were already very close. Not quite as close as Bernardo, Leandro, or Enrique, but they had just been abruptly and horribly eliminated from the competition.

Rodrigo looked as relieved at the interruption as I felt. "Rig up a temporary platform and put them up on it where everyone can see. It'll be good for morale, to remind the men that the attackers weren't unbeatable monsters, just men like themselves with better technology. Um, I suppose we'll need to put up mosquito netting or give them some clothes."

"No you won't," I said. "The Army gave ... will give ... um, will have given them the same shots I got from my doctor in Canada before I came here. Not only are they immune to the most common diseases, the mosquitos won't go anywhere near them."

"I've noticed they never seem to bother you, man," Rodrigo said. "But then, you still never take off your shirt. Are you sure they won't be eaten alive?"

"It's true," Mateo said. "They won't even come into our tent. We leave the flap open when it's hot, and never bother with mosquito netting." He tugged at the neckline of the green T-shirt under his uniform, miming being overheated. He was just about the only guy besides poor Jorge who wore two layers in this tropical heat; I wondered if anyone had noticed. He started to add, "And when I borrow ..."

"Don't you have a platform to construct?" I interrupted, embarrassed.

"Right. I'd better round up a few guys. Hey, carpentry is sort of like engineering, isn't it? How are you with a hammer?"

"No," Rodrigo said. "I want him to see if he can salvage the suits."

"I'll get right on that, sir," I said. I generally avoided calling Rodrigo by his first name, and like everyone here he kept his surname a secret to protect his family. What we didn't know, we couldn't reveal to the government if we were captured. And, he didn't have an official rank.

"Let's go round up some guys to carry the suits," Mateo suggested. When we were out of earshot, he whispered to me, "It looked as if you needed rescuing."

"Thanks. I owe you one."

"Owe me one? Are you kidding?" He squeezed my shoulder warmly. "We'd all be dead if you hadn't been so incredibly brave out there, buddy."

"Just doing my part for the cause," I said, trying to sound modest. It felt good, though, especially after so many people back home had implied I'd dodged the draft out of cowardice and not on principle.

"You are so full of shit! Do you really believe you risked your life because the Resistance couldn't afford to lose some cannon fodder?" He drew me into a long, warm embrace. Men were allowed to do that to their buddies, here.

# # # # #

I was excused from backbreaking grave-digging duty – and heartbreaking body bagging duty – so that I could try to get the captured suits working again. One of them had a fried CPU, and the other had some burned-out motors, but I was able to cannibalize them and make one working suit. I figured out how to run the diagnostic self-check, and the current levels looked good, but it refused to move a single joint. The screen buried inside the upper chest compartment kept flashing "No User Detected" in yellow when I stuck a mirror in for a peek. By nightfall, I had worked up the courage to get in. I took off my shoes and awkwardly wriggled into the supine suit, which seemed to be designed to be entered when it was in a kneeling posture and not horizontal. It still said "No User Detected." Finally, after glancing around, I tried taking off my T-shirt. The message remained yellow, but changed to "Not Authenticated." There was a keypad that I guessed was for a passcode. I began pressing digits at random. It took six digits before the message changed to "Access Denied" in red. One down, nine hundred ninety-nine thousand-nine-hundred-ninety-nine guesses to go. Feeling very vulnerable, I didn't want to find out what it did to an unauthorized user after a handful of incorrect entries.

I heard someone approaching and hurriedly pulled my T-shirt on and clambered out of the suit. It was Pablo, a guy almost as big as Ernesto or Pedro. He offered me a hand – he almost could have lifted me out all by himself – but I managed on my own. He'd been sent to tell me the graves were ready, and they were about to start the funeral.

At the graveside, Rodrigo said a few words. Someone must have taught him to open speeches with a joke, since he began, "As I'm sure José would have said, the only predicators within ten kilometers are six meters tall with metal claws, so I guess I'll have to do." Men groaned at the pun, and wept at the bittersweet reminder of our fallen comrade.

After the short ceremony, Rodrigo took me aside. I thought he was going to continue the argument we'd started, but he said, "I'm going to allow a large bonfire tonight. The enemy obviously knows where we are." Usually we kept it small, just enough to cook by, and trusted the dozens of solar-powered heaters our scouts had strewn around to be enough fool the satellites' thermal sensors. I'd designed those myself online and had them mass produced and airdropped along with the shipments of fresh uniforms that I hoped had been produced by machines and not underpaid kids in Asian sweatshops. The devices hadn't been cheap, considering how many we needed, but Rodrigo had deemed them higher priority than things like additional tents.

"Yes," I told him. "I'm sorry, I was sure the visible-light satellites couldn't detect us through the canopy. But then, who knows what military satellites can do? It's not like I ever had a security clearance."

"There are other ways they could have found out. Diego knew our current position."

"So you think he was captured?"

"I'm afraid so. He should have gotten back by now. Diego's tough, but they may have had him for several days, and of course, the government has expert torturers."

That was, of course, one of the reasons I was here. That is, why I'd turned traitor and was giving aid and comfort to the rebels fighting my own country's ally.

"Poor guy," I said.

"I wonder how Arturo will take it. He must already fear the worst."

I joined in the fireside wake, where we all got at least a little drunk on our remaining supply of booze. Many of my comrades were standing with their arms around a grieving buddy's shoulders. Men could do that here. There was a lot they couldn't do, but in some ways they could show affection more openly than were I'd come from.

Arturo, whom I'd always been secretly in awe of and had been too shy to get to know well, came up to me and clasped my shoulder. I felt a warm flush that wasn't just the booze. "You saved my life today, man. Thank you."

"Think nothing of it," I said.

"I thought for sure it was going to rip me to pieces when I went back for Hernando."

"That was very brave of you, sir," I said.

He looked at me strangely.

"That was very brave of you, man," I amended.

He clapped me on the shoulder and went back to his friends.

It was hard to address a man I admired so much with such familiarity. Damn the language for forcing me to make the awkward choice between the polite and familiar "you" every time I talked to someone.

"You really did save his life, you know, man," Pablo said, stepping closer. "He's always taking big risks, and somehow, something always saves him. He's like one of your American action heroes."

I grinned up at the big man. "I noticed that about him."

"Well, this time, you were the something. How does it feel?" He clapped me on the back, almost hard enough to send me sprawling into the bonfire.

Just about everyone came up to me that night with a word of gratitude or a word of congratulations. I was so physically exhausted and emotionally drained as the night wore on that the single most welcome word was the one Mateo finally said softly to me: namely, "Let's go to bed."

OK, I guess that would be four words if you translated it to my native tongue, but I'd gotten past translating things in my head and was thinking in Spanish by now. Now if only the verb conjugation meant a conjugal bedtime. Mateo was a really hot guy, with a face as attractive in its own way as the ruggedly handsome Arturo's, and a lean and nicely proportioned body. After I'd somehow been lucky or unlucky enough to wind up sharing a tent with him, I'd had a few sleepless nights before I'd gotten inured to the knowledge that he was sleeping within easy reach, almost naked. At least with only two of us we weren't physically pressed against each other. We did have to share a blanket.

"Didn't you just get to the party ten minutes ago?" I asked him.

"Yeah, but I'm exhausted, and you look as tired as I feel."

That was another thing I loved about Mateo. He was always in tune with how those close to him were feeling.

We undressed outside the tent as usual, since the so-called two-man tent could comfortably hold two men lying down, but trying to sit up and undress in it was just asking for an elbow to the skull. I always chose a spot at the edge of camp to pitch our tent, and the opening was facing away from camp, so we had more privacy than most of the camp did.

As we took our shirts off, I said, "Haven't seen you all night, man. Were you at the burial?"

"I'd have liked to be, but someone had to guard the prisoners. I guess we haven't had any prisoners since you joined us, but it's sort of one of my jobs." He stepped out of his pants. "They're tied up securely, so I'm not worried about them escaping, but if no one had been watching them, I think they'd have been beaten to death by our comrades."

"I know everyone's pretty upset, especially those of us who saw what they did. But would any of our brothers really attack an unarmed, bound and helpless man?" I bundled up my pants and socks and stuffed them into a corner of our tent.

Sliding past me to do the same, Mateo said, "You were the first one I had to stop, remember?"

"One punch, that was all I asked, and it was the heat of the moment. I wasn't going to beat him to death."

"Believe me, I had to talk several guys out of it. That kept me so busy I didn't even get a chance to talk much to the prisoners." He crawled into the tent.

I tossed my T-shirt loosely on top of my bundle and crawled in after him. "It may be callous to say this so soon, but with the men we lost tonight, I wonder if more of us will be able to have our own tents."

"I don't know about you, man, but right now I wouldn't want to sleep alone even if I had the choice."

"Maybe a blanket for each man, then, so we don't have to share."

"It's too hot tonight for blankets anyway. Although I commandeered two for the prisoners, since they're out in the open."

We soon started drifting off to sleep. The tent never had much room, and we were in the habit of having to sleep with our shoulders almost touching, due to the need to share a blanket. Tonight I could feel the heat radiating from him.

I woke from a light sleep to find Guillermo crawling into the tent with us. That didn't surprise me; he joined us sometimes when his own bunkmate needed privacy, even though it left him crammed between Mateo and the tent fabric and Mateo even closer to me than he was now. But he always found it even more embarrassing to be in his own tent when his bunkmate was jerking off. I could understand that, although with Bernardo and Leandro, we'd all just pretended not to notice what the others were doing. Mateo and I, when we were alone, did it even more openly. As Mateo said, we were young men, full of life, out here in the jungle with just other guys, and we didn't have the luxury of privacy. I don't know what the rest of the camp did, since no one talked about it, but I knew that Rodrigo kept ordering much larger quantities of socks than we could possibly be wearing out even when we were on the march.

I was about to say, sleepily, "Is Jorge at it again?" Then I realized my mistake. Jorge was dead. Guillermo had been sleeping alone, after watching his friend tortured to death before his eyes. I imagined what it would be like to sleep alone without Mateo's familiar warmth and soft breathing beside me, and really felt for the guy.

Departing from our usual custom, we slept that night with Guillermo sandwiched between us. He fell asleep weeping quietly on Mateo's bare shoulder, and my chest snuggled tightly against his back, skin to skin. I reached around him and put my hand on Mateo's other shoulder, holding them both in my arms as we grieved for our fallen comrades.

# # # # #

Guillermo was gone when I woke up the next morning. I vaguely remembered him slipping out of the tent at the first hint of light. Was he ashamed for the other guys to find out that he'd sought comfort? I was sure they'd have understood.

Mateo had rolled over to close the gap, probably in his sleep, and had his head pillowed on my bare chest. He'd never done that before. I wasn't sure what to do, but it felt warm and good. I resisted the temptation to stroke his thick black hair.

I drifted off again and later woke up fully when Mateo stirred. He opened his dark eyes without lifting his head from my chest, and said, "Please tell me it was just a nightmare, and they're still alive."

"Sorry, bro," I said. "The nightmare was real. We lost seven of our comrades in one battle."

"I'm glad you're still alive, anyway," he mumbled into my chest.

"Death makes us appreciate the friends we still have, doesn't it?" I said, squeezing his brown shoulder. We lay there a long time, holding each other tightly, as if we believed we could physically keep each other on this Earth. Finally Mateo laughed and said, "After this, I won't even need to borrow your T-shirt from yesterday to keep the mosquitos away." He patted me on the chest and sat up.

# # # # #

"I may need your help today, man," he said as he got dressed outside the tent. I noticed he put on my T-shirt despite his earlier words, maybe out of habit. I'd never believed it did him all that much good after a night of drying out, but he'd come to treat it like a good luck charm.

"Sure. I was going to spend today trying to salvage the extra radio from the suits and make it work standalone, but what do you need?"

"One of the prisoners, the one with the hairy chest, claims not to know any Spanish, and my English sucks. Anyway, I wouldn't be able to ask technical questions even in Spanish."

"Do you think they'll be willing to answer?"

"Oh, I'm sure they will. They were pretty arrogant last night, especially the hairy one, but the situation must be sinking in by now."

# # # # #

"We took them to the latrine and gave them a little water, like you said, sir," one of the men who'd drawn overnight guard duty told Mateo. "And we gave them a quick shower at dawn. We've got them tied up separately, so you can question them one at a time."

"Perfect."

We walked over to the first prisoner, who was sitting against a tree, draped in a blanket. He pressed his lips together when Mateo approached and said in Spanish much worse than mine, "All I have to tell you, sir, is the name, the rank, and my number of the serial. I already told you these things last night."

Wordlessly, Mateo jerked away the blanket. The prisoner was naked underneath, tall and lean and smooth and blond. He flinched, and his arms jerked as though he was reflexively trying to cover his crotch, but his arms were tied behind his back, around the tree. He recovered quickly, though. For a bound and naked man, he radiated self-confidence, as though he thought he still wore the suit that had allowed him to kill my friends with one casual swipe of his claws. He turned his icy blue gaze on me and said, "You look like you speak English. I can't say this properly in Spanish, but tell your friend that he can do with me what he will, but other suit operators will come after us and squash him like a bug."

"What, you think he's going to torture you?" I asked.

"Of course he's going to torture me. What kind of idiot are you?"

"The dictator you're supporting is the one who believes in torture."

"What are you guys saying?" Mateo asked me. I suddenly realized that for all he knew I was striking a deal to betray him and free the prisoners. Yet, I could tell from the utter lack of suspicion in his voice that it didn't even occur to him not to trust me. It warmed my heart. And of course, he was right. Beside the fact I'd decided my allegiance before I came here, he and I were bros; I'd never betray his trust.

"He's making cocky threats about what his buddies will do to us," I said. "Also, he assumes you're going to torture him."

"Ah, I thought I heard a word that sounded like *torturar*." He laid a gentle hand on the prisoner's pale shoulder and spoke slowly, in a reassuring tone. "My friend is going to ask you some questions about the suit, pal. Just answer as best you can, and you don't need to worry about anything. Afterward, we'll get you a meal and see what we can do about some clothes."

"See?" I said in English.

"Ask him whatever you need to know. Don't bother to translate if it's something technical, but anything else, make sure the details get repeated to me or to whoever can use the information, okay?"

"How do you log in to the suit?" I asked in English. "It says "Not Authenticated" when I stick my head into the helmet. The thing you were wearing on the chain with your dog tags seems to turn it on, but there's something else we need. I tried the other guy's, too. What else do we need to work it?"

The prisoner clamped his lips together and looked away. Mateo patted him on the thigh in a friendly manner, about an inch from his balls. "You really should pay attention when my friend is talking," he said cheerfully.

I tried again. "I'm guessing there's a passcode you need to type on the keypad. Look, you can at least shake your head yes or no to that."

"You can go fuck yourself, turncoat," he snarled at me. "You're an American, right?"

"Is he cooperating at all?" Mateo asked.

"No. Wait, why are you taking off your belt, man?"

"Why do you think, dumb-ass?"

"Wait, buddy, let's talk about this."

"Back off and let me do my job, buddy." He folded the belt and rubbed the edge of the leather against the prisoner's pink nipple in an insultingly familiar way. "This is your last chance," he told him, speaking slowly and clearly. The man spit in his face, and he calmly wiped it away and took a step back, holding the buckle of the belt in his hand.

Tough as he'd seemed, the prisoner cried out readily enough by the tenth time my friend's belt slapped against his chest, intersecting the pink welts already crisscrossing it. When Mateo was finally finished with him, he slumped in his bounds, his pale, compactly-muscled chest heaving in silent sobs. After a moment, he looked up with watery eyes and said bravely in Spanish, "Is that all you've got, pal?"

"We're just getting started, my friend." He signaled to one of his assistants whom he'd sent away on an errand earlier. The man handed Mateo a small object.

"What's that?" I asked.

"You know those really hot peppers you used to complain made it feel like the lining of your mouth was burning away?" he asked me, and held it out for me to see. It was a pepper, cut in half.

The prisoner's eyes widened as Mateo bent over him with the chili pepper. "Wait!" he said in English. He started to say in Spanish, "Only one man is able ..." then looked pleadingly at me and said in English, "No one else but me can work it. Please tell him. For one thing, I had months of training."

Mateo had taken his hand away and straightened up, but after I translated, he began rubbing the chili on the helpless man's chest, right against the reddest of the welts. I hadn't heard a man scream so loud since ... well, unfortunately, since less than twenty-four hours before, and that time the scream had been coming from a man whose arm had just been ripped off.

# # # # #

The screaming in the distance turned to whimpering, and a few moments later I felt a hand on my shoulder. "I need you to come back, man. He's almost ready to talk."

"I came here to help you fight against a government that was torturing its own citizens," I said tightly.

"That's different."

"How?" I whirled around to face the man I'd been sharing a tent with for months, whom I had thought I'd known better than I knew my own brother.

"He may feel humiliated, he may be in pain, but he'll still be whole when I'm done with him. He'll recover quickly."

"It's still torture," I said.

"I never told you why I joined the cause. My brother-in-law was taken, just for selling supplies to the rebels. They eventually let him go when they'd wrung everything out of him, not that he had any real information. He used to be a big strong fellow. He'll never be able to work with his hands again. My sister has to spoon-feed him. When we go to a place with public restrooms, I have to unzip his pants for him and hold it at the urinal. Thank God it's only the urinal; we have modern toilets in the city, or I'd have to ..."

"I get the idea." Going back to using toilet paper was one of the hardships I'd had to endure at camp. And it chilled me to realize that with their third-world medical care here, injuries that would have meant nothing worse than long-term and big hospital bills in the United States, or an annoying recovery period in Canada, would become lifelong disabilities. Even something as simple as a severed finger probably couldn't be grown back here, or pulverized bones, or any of the other painful horrors I was imagining. Medical practice here mostly consisted of surgically removing anything that didn't belong, stitching up wounds, and relying on the human body's all-too-limited natural regenerative ability.

"Look, man," he continued when he saw his point had hit home, "I know all you see is a pathetic, helpless, naked prisoner now. But don't forget, this is the same guy who killed one of your best friends yesterday and deliberately threw his bleeding body onto another of your best friends. The same guy who calmly ripped poor Jorge's chest open, and tore Hernando apart. He butchered five of our brothers. And that suit is just what we need to protect ourselves against more of them. Maybe even rescue Diego if he's still alive. Let's hope he's in one piece, and Arturo doesn't have to feed him for the rest of their lives."

"I want to get Diego back as much as you do, but not by stooping to their level."

Mateo's face darkened, and he stalked off to take his frustration with me out on my helpless countryman. Although it was true that if anyone deserved to be tortured ...

It seemed like an eternity, even to me, before he came back. "I think I may have broken him. He keeps repeating these same six numbers over and over in English and Spanish, and they're not part of the serial number he gave me last night." He handed me a slip of paper.

"These must be the code. I can try it with his key," I said without enthusiasm. Then I brightened and added hopefully, "So I guess you can stop torturing him now."

"Sure. For now. Maybe for good, if you verify that it works. But if it doesn't, he's going to be really sorry he lied."

"I'll try it and let you know."

"One thing, though. He seemed to object when I walked away with the paper."

"Well, of course he did. He just gave a powerful weapon to his enemies to save his own skin, and he feels guilty."

59

"No, I sensed he was afraid of more torture to come, even though I was walking away. He said something in English, but the only words I understood were 'won't work' – doesn't that mean '*no trabajará*'"?

"Oh," I said with a sinking feeling. "It can also mean '*no funcionará.*'"

"I told you my English sucks. If you want to spare the guy some unnecessary pain and humiliation, you really need to come and translate, so there's no misunderstanding."

I reluctantly followed him back to the prisoner. His naked body was covered with pink welts and had been rubbed down with oil, darkening and slicking down his sparse golden body hair and making the sunlight gleam off his stringy muscles.

"Oil?" I asked Mateo. "Is that part of the torture?"

"Just the opposite. Quicker relief than water."

Gently, I said in English, "How are you doing, buddy?"

I fully expected a sarcastic reply along the lines of "How does it look like I'm doing" or "I'm not your buddy, the torturer's your buddy," but instead he turned his blue eyes pleadingly on me and sobbed, "Please, don't let him hurt me anymore. I've told him everything I know."

"So this is your passcode?" I read it back to him.

"Yes, but it won't work for anyone else, even with the key. They explained it in training. The key is keyed to me."

"Ah. Some kind of biometric information encrypted on the key along with the passcode?"

"I guess. I really don't understand that stuff."

I translated, and commented, "I think he's telling the truth."

"You must have some technical questions for him."

I thought for a moment. "Do you enter the passcode before or after you insert the key?"

"After. I insert and remove the key, and then I have one minute to enter the passcode."

"Is that before or after you hook the electrodes up?"

"Before they hook them up."

Mateo's was watching closely, his body language suggesting that he thought he could wring more information out of the poor guy with a little more torture.

"And you have no idea how the biometrics work? Is there a fingerprint scanner, like smart-guns have? Retinal?"

"No, it just happens. Watching other guys, sometimes I think I see a green laser flicks over their chest just before it grants them access."

"Hmm." One last question occurred to me. "Have you ever tried entering your passcode before you ... took your shirt off?" I hesitated in reminding the naked man that he used to own clothing.

"Once. It said 'Not Authenticated.'"

I squeezed his pale shoulder, feeling wiry muscle and thin bones beneath my hand, and said, "Thanks, man. That's very helpful."

I persuaded Mateo to come with me and help verify his story. We took turns sticking our head into the helmet and entering the passcode we'd been given, and a random six-digit number, with and without the key, with and without our shirts. We verified part of the captive's claim: it took the combination of the key, a six-digit number, and a bare chest to get the screen to say "Access Denied," as opposed to "Not Authenticated," "No User Detected," or nothing at all. For the prisoner's sake, I wished with all my heart the designers had chosen a specific error message like "Incorrect Passcode" or "Unrecognized Biometrics" to show we were on the right track.

"It's a pretty standard security precaution to not give specific feedback like 'Invalid username' and 'Invalid password' separately," I assured Mateo. "He probably gave us the right passcode, but we have no way of knowing."

"I'm inclined to believe him," Mateo said. "I can usually tell when a man is holding something back, and when I've broken him. And I've broken that guy. Let's leave him alone for now and question the other prisoner to see if their stories match."

# # # # #

The second prisoner was even more of a tough-guy than his compatriot. Or maybe it was just the contrast of going from the weeping, pleading, meekly cooperative wretch we had just left to a fresh, unbroken captive.

"Tell him I don't fucking speak his fucking third-world language," he said, ignoring Mateo. Why did they both assume I spoke English? Must be the fair skin, blond hair, and blue eyes, but for all they knew, I have could been from Scandinavia.

This one was physically a stark contrast to the other, except for both being white. He was stocky and barrel-chested, with lots of curly black hair between his well-defined pecs, although the pecs themselves were hairless, either naturally or because he'd shaved them for the electrodes. His belly was flat and hairless except for a trail of fine black hairs in the center, and even that ended at his navel, leaving the pale white skin above his pubes completely smooth.

"I thought you guys were officially 'military advisors' – we never declared war. How do you advise these people without being able to talk to them?"

"So you are American. I'm not going to argue politics with you, traitor."

"Did he just call you a traitor?" Mateo asked mildly, unbuckling his belt.

"Well, technically, I am," I said.

The Constitution defines treason as "aid and comfort" to the enemies, and although a defense lawyer might try to argue the rebels weren't legally enemies, I was unquestionably aiding them, and I'd certainly done my best to provide comfort to two of them last night.

"Never mind the insult. Just let me ask him the questions." I turned to the prisoner and switched back to English. "Your buddy told us that the suits have a three-factor security system: a passcode, the electronic keys we took from you, and a biometric scan. Is that true?"

"I'm not telling you nothing." His square, heavily stubbled jaw was set in firm determination.

"That's what the other guy told us, but by the time my friend was through with him, he was very eager to tell us everything. To tell the truth, it was really hard for me to watch, and I don't want to go through it again. Can we just skip the macho posturing and all the torture, and cut straight to the part where you tell us everything you know?"

"You claim you already know everything. Why do you need to hear it again?"

"Because each individual's passcode and the biometrics have to hash to the same code that's encrypted on his key," I said. That was my working hypothesis, anyway.

"I thought you spoke English," he said tauntingly. "Not Geek."

"Your buddy gave us his passcode," I explained patiently, "but there's only a slim chance we've got someone who happens to match whatever physical traits are supposed to identify him. How slim depends on the fuzzy – um, on how picky the machine is. If you give us your passcode, it'll double our chances. But most likely, we either won't need it or won't be able to use either of them. That's why I tried to persuade my friend that it wasn't worth torturing you today. But he wouldn't listen. So now I'm telling you. Is it really worth getting tortured over six numbers that probably won't help us?"

The prisoner's response was scathing and filthy. "What did he say?" Mateo asked.

"'Tell that worthless scumbag what he can do with his belt,'" I translated loosely. Actually that was bowdlerized; what he'd actually said had included several racist epithets and had been very explicit about what my buddy could do with his belt, buckle first.

"Help me get him up onto his knees," Mateo requested.

The guy was as tough as he looked. Each lash was rewarded only by a sharp intake of breath, not a scream, even though half of them unerringly crossed one or the other of his dark nipples. Not until the pepper juice began soaking into his abused skin did he begin groaning, then screaming and struggling uselessly. Even then, he didn't talk. I could see that Mateo, even as he repeatedly attacked the prisoner's twisting torso, was already eyeing the ball sac swinging loosely between his powerful hairy legs.

Much later, after writing down the passcode the wretched prisoner was eager to repeat for us as often as we liked, we left the burly man whimpering softly into his chest hair, as thoroughly broken as his buddy.

# # # # #

"That was a good day's work," Mateo said as we stripped for bed.

"I can't believe you would do that to a fellow human being. You must think of them as things, not as men. You almost seemed to enjoy it. I'll bet you pulled legs off of insects when you were a kid."

"I do enjoy it, sort of. But no, I never forget that the prisoner is a man. That's what makes it fun. You're wrong; I was never one of those kids who dismembered insects or hurt animals; I think that's just gross.

It has to be another man, another young man. I enjoy taking a strong, self-confident man and stripping away his machismo, his training, his very self-respect, layer by layer, and revealing the man beneath."

I crawled into the tent after him, having nowhere else to go but never had I been so reluctant to sleep side by side with this man.

No sooner were we settled down than I heard the familiar soft rustle of Mateo pulling his boxers down. I turned and saw he had his dick in his fist, and it was already hard.

"You can do that now, after the day we just had?"

"Well, it's been, what, days? And I sure wasn't in the mood last night."

"I'm even less in the mood tonight. I feel sick to my stomach after what I had to help you do today."

"Well, I feel horny. You don't mind, do you, bro?" Asking was just a pro-forma courtesy; we had an understanding about such things. Usually, I didn't mind at all, and would usually watch, and often join in.

To my discomfiture, he continued talking as he stroked himself. "Those guys seemed so cocky at first, didn't they? They didn't look so tough once I was done with them." He was breathing hard. "That guy with the muscular, hairy chest, crying and begging for mercy ..."

I propped myself up on my elbow and said accusingly, "You're picturing them while you jerk off, aren't you?"

"I thought we agreed never to tell each other what we were picturing."

That was because his descriptions of the women he usually pictured instantly turned me off – and because my own favorite inspiration was no visualization at all, but just watching the handsome, nicely built Latino beside me jerking off before my eyes. I'd never told him that, of course. So I had no answer.

65

"Man, I thought that guy would never break," he said, breathing hard and arching his back, which made his chest muscles flex. "I'm glad I finally came up with the idea of taking the little seeds from the pepper and forcing them one by one into ..."

"That's it!" I shouted. I wriggled quickly out of the tent and stalked off into the night.

By the time I realized I'd left my clothes in the tent, it would have been awkward to go back for them. I sat down on a log in my boxers, shivering and feeling sorry for myself. When I heard someone come up to me in the dark, I assumed it was Mateo and pointedly ignored him.

"Aren't you afraid of mosquitos, man?" It wasn't Mateo's voice, but one a little less familiar.

I turned and peered at the face beside me in the dark. "Arturo?" I asked tentatively. It was easy to see him nod, a shadowy head against the moonlit jungle canopy. "Mosquitos won't come anywhere near me. The benefits of modern medicine. I wish my country would spend more money on medical aid to you guys and less on propping up tyrants." Ironically, half our modern medicines came from a drug discovery program that sifted through botanicals found in this very rainforest. The U.S. biotech industry was very interested in maintaining access to those supplies, which was widely believed to be the reason the U.S. Government wanted a stable government here, even if it was an autocracy that hoarded the wealth, made the people live in squalor, and brutally punished opposition.

"Aren't you cold, though?"

"A little. So what are you doing up?" I remembered this time to use the informal "you."

"I haven't really slept in two days, between seeing Hernando ripped apart right in front of me and thinking about what they must be doing to Diego."

"I'm sorry," I said. "You shared a tent with Diego, didn't you?"

"Um, yes, and he and I ... are very close. What are you doing up, man?"

We didn't know each other that well, but Arturo had always seemed like a noble guy, exactly the sort who wouldn't approve of torture, and after all, who else could I talk to? Of the close friends I usually confided in, all but one was dead, and the surviving one was himself the torturer. So I told Arturo all about my day, leaving out the more intimate details in the tent.

"Oh. That's a better reason than the usual one. Usually when a guy is out of his tent for awhile, I figure it means his bunkmate needs some privacy, if you know what I mean. I think most guys pretend they don't notice, or are even open about it between each other, even though they don't talk about it."

"Yeah, I know what you mean. I don't know why anyone is embarrassed. We all do it, right?"

"All these healthy young men, away from women for so long? Of course we do."

"Actually, that's exactly what Mateo is doing right now."

"Is that why you're out here freezing your ass off in your boxers?"

"It's not just that. Usually it doesn't bother me." Now I really was embarrassed. Naturally I didn't add that I usually copied him, or that I watched. "But tonight he was bragging about how good it felt to break the prisoners, even while he ... I think he was thinking about them."

"Oh. True, that is a little sick."

A chilly breeze came up, and I shivered and wrapped my arms around myself.

"Come on, man. You look like you're freezing. And I've got a Diego-shaped empty space in my tent, and a nice warm blanket." He shifted slightly. Somehow I got the idea from his body language that he was making a heroic effort to hold himself back from gathering me into his arms to keep me warm.

I felt myself blushing and was glad it was dark. I couldn't imagine imposing on someone like him. "That's really nice of you, man, but Mateo should be done by now, and he always falls asleep right afterward. So at least I won't need to listen to him bragging about how he made helpless men scream and beg for mercy."

Arturo sighed. I belated wondered if the guy could actually be lonely. "Then, see you in the morning, bro," he said.

# # # # #

"This feels like the end of Cinderella," Rodrigo said as yet another man ducked in through the mosquito netting. They were worse here than they'd been in the old, compromised location we'd just spent the previous day moving the camp away from. But the netting was not to protect me or Rodrigo, nor the empty, kneeling suit that served as its tall tent pole.

"OK, man, take off your shoes, socks, shirt and pants," I said for about the twentieth time today. "Everything except your undershorts." It should have gotten boring by now – I'm sure the staff at the induction center I'd avoided back home must feel that way – and I tried my best to sound bored and professional, but the truth was I never got tired of saying those words. To Rodrigo, I said, "I prefer to compare it to the sword and the stone. Um, do you know the Arthurian legends here, sir? Those are from England, so it's part of English-speaking culture."

Rodrigo smiled. "I know about them from the same source as everyone knows Cinderella."

"Of course," I said distractedly, watching the latest man, Dario I think his name was, obediently strip off his uniform until he stood before us in his ragged boxer shorts. Under my feigned disinterest I was thoroughly enjoying this. Until today, Mateo, my late bunkmates, and

Guillermo were the only ones whose bodies I'd gotten to admire close up, and even touch.

"Now step into the suit," I told him. "I'll give you a boost. Put your hand on my shoulder." I had this down to a science now. The twentieth bare foot of the day planted itself in my waiting interlaced hands, and the twentieth pleasantly musky bare chest brushed past my face as my comrade climbed into the inert suit. "Your feet should fit into the stirrups inside the knees, so you can stand up. Great. Here's the first key; insert it into this slot here and remove it. Good. Now duck your head under there and straighten up. See the screen? Now, look down at the keypad and enter these six numbers." I recited them from memory. There was a barely perceptible flicker of green light, and I knew that a laser had scanned up and down every inch of the muscular brown torso before me, faster than my eye could follow. "Good. Look back up at the screen. Is it displaying two words in red letters?"

"Access Denied," he read, mispronouncing the English words only slightly. Half the guys were illiterate even in Spanish due to the almost nonexistent education system here, but a few like Dario could read English.

By now, we'd experimented with stuffing the gagged and bound prisoners into the suit. I'd squeezed my shoulders into the chest compartment with them to insert the key and enter the passcode for them, so we now knew they were telling the truth. It worked for them, as long as we used each man's own passcode and key. At least, I could catch a foreshortened glimpse of green lettering if I pressed my ear against the guy's chest and looked up past his chin at the screen. Unfortunately, it had shut down automatically as soon as we pulled him out.

Next in line was young, tall, broad-shouldered Ernesto. He grinned shyly when I directed him to take off his shirt. Almost every man before him had nonchalantly begun unbuttoning his shirt immediately when asked, but Ernesto hesitated for a few seconds before finally unbuttoning it, revealing a smooth brown chest with rounded muscles, and then well-muscled arms as he shrugged out of the sleeves. He hesitated again before he finished undressing. He seemed to be blushing slightly, but it was harder to tell with him than with me. I don't know what he was ashamed of; he had the most impressive body I'd seen so far. Finally, he placed a huge bare foot in my interlaced hands, and clamped his big hand on my shoulder. I grunted as I supported his considerable weight long enough for him to step into the suit.

Ernesto struck out, too. His equally beefy and slightly older friend Pedro was next in line. Pedro proved to have a lot of hair on his chest, just where some of the electrodes for sensing the motions of his pectoral muscles would go. We'd have to shave him, I decided, if he was the one. But the suit didn't grant him access either. Nor the man after him, or the next. Finally, much later, Mateo entered.

"Are you the last?" I asked him, peering over his shoulder through the layers of netting.

"Of course. Like you asked, buddy."

I'd asked him to bring up the rear because if we happened to have two men who matched the biometrics, I wanted someone, anyone but Mateo to be the first match. Of all my comrades, Mateo was the only one I could imagine using a suit in the vicious and sadistic way we'd seen them used. If I could have prevented him from trying it at all, I would have. I was apprehensive as he stripped, as he placed his bare foot in my hand, as he brushed past me, his familiar scent lingering in my nose. I was enormously relieved when he reported a red error message.

As Mateo put his pants on, Rodrigo poked his head out of the mosquito netting. "Is that it? No one else?" he called.

He withdrew his head and turned around.

"It was worth a try," I said. "Is that everyone?"

"All but a few of the wounded and the most badly traumatized. In a day or so I'll have them try. But every day we wait ..." To my surprise, he began unbuttoning his shirt.

"You're going to try it, sir?"

"Of course." He was only a few years older than most of us, and a little thicker around the middle, but still extremely fit. He stripped to his briefs and waited expectantly for me to give him a boost.

After that ended with the usual disappointment, he dressed in silence, eyeing me speculatively. Finally he said exactly what I feared: "Now you."

"I told you, sir, if I was willing to use weapons ..."

"I know, if you were willing to use weapons you wouldn't have resisted your own country's draft. But this isn't a gun. It's a powerful, flexible tool that could turn the war to our advantage."

"I won't even use a stunner, and I'm sure as hell not using this. This is exactly what I resisted the draft to avoid doing," I said hotly. "I wouldn't even be here to help you ..."

"You're here because you know we're defending our liberty from a tyrant. You avoided the draft because you didn't want to lend military support to that tyrant."

"There's very little chance it will work for me when it didn't work for anyone else. The biometric parameters must be very tight."

"Maybe one of the things it looks at is skin color."

"They wouldn't use skin color. There are too many people with the same skin color, and each guy's skin can change from day to day if he's out in the sun with his shirt off. Did you notice how tan the bigger hairier guy is, and how white his crotch is?"

"What if it's eye or hair color? The other prisoner ..."

"I'm sorry, the answer is no."

"You realize I could order you stripped and stuffed into it unwillingly, just like your two countrymen? The men like you a lot, but they'll obey orders."

"You can force me into it, but you can't force me to use it."

"One step at a time." He shouted an order, and three beefy guys, Ernesto, Pedro, and Pablo, ducked back into the netting to crowd around me. None of them looked exactly happy to be threatening me. Pedro and Pablo wouldn't meet my eyes, while Ernesto, in particular, looked down at me apologetically, his big brown eyes begging my forgiveness.

Rodrigo said quietly, "Please, Josh, don't make me do this. Take off your shirt, man."

"No," I said, wondering if I should make a break for it, or go limp like they taught in nonviolence training just to make it slightly more difficult for them.

Rodrigo sighed. "Strip him."

They got my T-shirt off after a brief struggle, and Pedro wrapped his arms around my torso, pinning my arms to my side and lifting me off my feet, to allow Ernesto and Pablo to remove my shoes and socks. They were trying to get past my thrashing legs to undo my pants when someone entered the netting.

"Is it too late for me to try?" he said. It was Arturo. To Rodrigo he said, "Sorry, I overslept. Sir, you might have had someone wake me."

"I know how upset you were, man – the news about Diego, on top of seeing your friends killed before your eyes and narrowly escaping death yourself. I wanted you to rest for a day or two."

I wondered if Rodrigo knew that Arturo had been walking around sleeplessly at least one of the three nights since the massacre.

"No, I want to see if the suit works for me."

"Fine. Let Josh go, guys," Rodrigo said. "No, leave your shirt off, man," he added sharply as I bent down to retrieve it. "You're next after Arturo. Unless he's as lucky with this as he is with everything else."

I'd been mentally scoring my comrades all day, and Arturo had the most impressive body in the company. Not as husky as Ernesto or Pedro, but trim and muscular, with the best abs I'd seen all day. He must have been genetically gifted to have muscles like that without especially good nutrition or access to a modern gym. I felt very self-conscious, standing next to him with my own shirt off and four guys looking at us, three of them big and brawny. As Arturo put his hand on my bare shoulder and vaulted effortlessly into the suit compartment, I decided he even smelled the best: a clean, musky, nutty male aroma.

The first key and passcode failed, like it had for everyone before, and I dreaded the confrontation that was about to resume. Then we tried the second one. I held my breath as the laser played over his muscles.

"Green letters this time," Arturo reported. "It says, um, Eseestem Actee ..."

All of us drowned him out with our whoops. "I knew it!" Rodrigo crowed.

Ernesto, Pedro, and Pablo were taking turns giving me bone-crushing hugs that probably left handprints in my bare back, obviously relieved that they wouldn't have to force me into the suit against my will. After I helped Arturo out, he excitedly gathered me into a skin-to-skin embrace as the bigger men pounded him on the back.

"Must be that square jaw," Rodrigo said teasingly, reaching past my shoulder to cup said jaw affectionately in his hand.

Arturo finally released me, only to throw his arm around my shoulder and slap me affectionately on the chest. "I guess we'll be working closely, Josh. You'll be training me, right?"

# # # # #

"Careful, man", Arturo said. "I'm *cosquilloso.*"

I paused in attaching electrodes to each of Arturo's well-developed muscle groups. "What?"

"I've got *cosquillas.*" He paused to think of a definition. "I'm ultra-sensitive to being touched in certain ways in certain places, like the ribs and belly. It makes me laugh uncontrollably."

"You're kidding!"

He grinned down at me. "Why is that so surprising?"

"To tell the truth, I've always thought of you as being practically superhuman."

"And with the suit, I will be. But every superhero has his secret weakness, right? Now you know mine."

"I'll try to resist using that knowledge to get you under my power."

"Just remember I can squash you like a bug, buddy. If we get this working."

"Just two more connections. Are the lights along the bottom of the screen still turning green?"

"Yes, and there are exactly two red ones left, so I think you're doing it perfectly."

"Good." I'd worried that the last one I'd attached, against his abs, might not work because it was off-center. I didn't want to center it because then at the end of the day we'd need to rip it off the delicate-looking, wispy-feeling black hairs that began at Arturo's navel and trailed upward for a few centimeters. Then again, the prisoner whose key and passcode we were using had an almost identical trail. It belated occurred to me that this could well be one of the biometric parameters the suit was looking at, in which case there'd been three or four other guys who might have matched if I'd shaved off the part of the trail that continued past their navels.

I attached the penultimate wire to his bulging left biceps and the final one to his tree-like right thigh.

"All green," he reported. "And you know one of the words on the screen looks just like '*menú*' without the accent. Does that mean the same thing in English?"

"Yes. Is the cursor still following your eye movements?"

"Yes. Should I blink?"

A deliberate blink was like clicking a mouse, we'd been told. I didn't like to think about what it had taken to extract that tip from the prisoners.

"Yes, go ahead and blink."

"It worked. The text changed to a list, and ... hey! What's the word for '*lenguas*'?"

"'Languages.'" I spelled it for him: "*Elle, ah, enne, hey, oo, ah, hey, ay, esse.*"

"Thought so. Hey, we're in luck! The choices are English and Spanish."

"Convenient for us, but you realize what this probably means?"

"Oh. That your government is planning to give it to mine."

"Or at least that someone thought about it. Well, maybe it doesn't matter. They couldn't use it any more cruelly than the American operators did."

Arturo loved his new toy, and either he was a fast learner or the suit interface was very intuitive. He was walking almost immediately, although for our first session I had to be fast on my feet to keep from getting stepped on accidentally as he stumbled around. At least the suit kept its balance well enough that it didn't fall flat on its face, with me under it. It would be just my luck, having survived being ripped to shreds by the suit, to wind up being killed by friendly pratfall.

Once he got the hang of walking, he started practicing moving his arms, which at first involved a lot of flailing around on his part and ducking on my part to keep him from accidentally braining me. Finally, my T-shirt soaked through, I called a halt. Arturo complained he was just getting started, but I was exhausted. It was a strange experience, arguing with someone three times my size who could literally tear me apart if he wanted to, but in the end, he got down on his knees and let me open his chest up, exposing brown flesh that was sweating less than mine was. I reached up and began the long process of removing wires without getting them tangled and without tickling my trapped comrade.

"You might be more comfortable taking your shirt off next time, man," Arturo suggested, when he was standing on his own feet. He emphasized his words by actually lifting up the hem of my T-shirt. The air did feel cool on my exposed belly. "Especially since you don't have to worry about mosquitos. What is it that keeps them away?"

"Some kind of generic engineering. I think it has to do with the way it makes my sweat smell." I pushed his hand away and yanked my shirt down.

"I don't know what their problem is," he said with a grin. "You smell fine. If I were a mosquito, I'd think you smelled delicious and would sink my teeth into you every chance I got."

My face felt hot. "Only if you were a female mosquito."

"Oh. I had the impression ..."

"No, only the females bite. The males eat plants."

"If I rubbed myself down with your sweaty T-shirt, would the little bitches leave both of us alone?"

"Probably. But I'm not taking it off."

"Who said you had a choice? Do you think you can stop me if I want to take it off you?"

"What's gotten into you, man? You're never like this."

"Oh. Sorry." He took a step backward and said sheepishly, "I think it's something about being six meters tall for the last few hours, and strong enough to do whatever I wanted. It goes to the head."

"That's all right," I said, and stuck out my hand. "We're still friends."

Ignoring my hand, he grabbed me in a bear hug. I laughed and hugged him back, my sweaty arms against his bare back.

While I made secure the suit was safely shut down, he put on his pants and shoes and swaggered shirtless over to the two men who were digging a drainage ditch from a swampy area that had been identified as a mosquito breeding ground. I'd noticed the poor guys in the distance, swatting at their arms every few minutes. From his body language, Arturo was bragging about how he was invincible to mosquitos. It hurt to realize that his embrace had had an ulterior motive. After a minute, he took one of the two shovels – fairly aggressively, it looked like – and began digging. As soon as I was done stowing the suit, I went over to help, taking the other shovel so that both men could get out of the infested area. I did it because it made sense, and because I'm a staunch egalitarian. If it gave me a close-up view of Arturo's chest and arm muscles flexing as he worked, that was just a fringe benefit. I kept my own shirt on, not caring to flaunt my own mosquito-resistant powers.

# # # # #

"I wish we could let the prisoners go," I griped to Arturo on the second day of training. I was feeling comfortable around him; he felt like someone I could vent my frustrations to, even when he towered

77

over me in his suit. "We got the information we needed out of them, clearly."

"Yeah, but they know our current position, our numbers, and the how well we're armed," Arturo said, his voice coming from the external speakers. "Which is not very well, except for this suit." Even if we'd had better funding, guns were one of the few supplies even the Chinese merchants wouldn't sell us over the Internet to be airdropped by XUPEx, our usual delivery service, whose planes neither the United States nor the locals dared to shoot down. "We don't kill prisoners, so until we can arrange to have them locked up in a village we control, we have to keep them. At least Mateo has stopped torturing them."

"Unless you count the forced push-ups and sit-ups. And making them wrestle each other."

"That's for a good cause. He's harvesting their sweat. It smells better than our usual bug repellant, and it's free."

"He enjoys it way too much. I can tell ... at night."

"I've already offered to let you share my tent, buddy."

Somehow that still seemed like being allowed to bunk with Superman, especially now that Arturo had real superpowers. To cover my diffidence, I tried to make a joke of it. "How do I know you won't dream you're still in your suit and try to squash me like a bug in your sleep?"

"Don't worry about that." It sounded like he was grinning. "What you should be worried about is that I'll dream you're Diego."

I didn't know what to make of that, but the more I worked with Arturo, the more he seemed like there was regular guy behind that handsome face and impressive physique, one I could actually be buddies with and not just worship from afar. And I did need to get away from Mateo. So eventually I agreed.

"Great!" he said. "And as a bonus, I get my own personal bug repellant. Mateo says that all of you guys smell better than bug spray, but he likes your scent the best. Fancies himself something of a connoisseur."

# # # # #

When Arturo got to the point where he could pick up a red cacao pod between thumb and forefinger without crashing it, I knew he was ready. I told him as much and called a halt for the day.

"One final test," he insisted. "You're sure I'm good enough to operate this thing without hurting anyone unless I want to, right?"

"Of course, or I wouldn't say you were ready. If it were up to me, you'll never kill anyone with – what the fuck are you doing?" I realized I had yelled the last part in English. He had wrapped his long metal fingers around my chest. Not bone-crushingly hard – we both remembered very well what those fingers had done to Enrique – but very gently, not even as crushing as the hug he'd given me with his own strong arms at the end of our first session.

"What are you doing?" I repeated in Spanish, surprised that I could still breathe, as he lifted me to eye level.

"My final exam," he said. "You know I would never hurt you, man. So this shows how confident I am in my control." He moved the other hand behind my head, and I felt it pluck at the neckline of my T-shirt. He opened the hand that was wrapped around my ribcage, and I found myself suspended by the fabric of my T-shirt bunched up under my arms.

He proudly carried me through the camp that way, with my belly ignominiously exposed, as men scurried out of his path like lizards. He stopped in front of Rodrigo's tent, where our leader was studying a map. "Look, sir!" he said, sounding for all the world like a five-year-old who'd captured a bug. "My teacher's so confident in my dexterity that he was willing to bet his life on it."

Rodrigo looked up with a twinkle in his eye. "I think you're ready for your first mission, man."

A bunch of guys I was casually friendly with had gathered below, laughing and pointing. "Raise your arms and slide out, man!" they called. "We'll catch you."

"I don't trust these guys, Arturo," I said over my shoulder. One of them was enough of a prankster that I could imagine him letting me land on my ass, and another had once held me down and tickled me in retaliation for an unintended insult. "Please put me down."

To my relief, he did, and very gently at that.

# # # # #

I couldn't help but notice, helping Arturo out of the suit later, that his boxers were tented. I didn't say anything, but that night, as we stripped for bed in the moonlight, he had an even more obvious boner.

He caught me looking and said, sheepishly, "Sorry. It's been like this all day. It's been so many days since I've had the tent to myself, and I wasn't sure if you were comfortable with me doing anything about it right in front of you, even though we agreed it was nothing to be embarrassed about."

"Don't let me stop you, bro. Mateo and I used to do it right in front of each other, sometimes at the same time. Didn't you and Diego ...?"

"We don't talk about that," he said sharply. "But, well, I didn't want to say anything, but I noticed you've had a few boners, too. I'd be less embarrassed if you did it at the same time."

"Really? OK. Do you want to turn away from each other?"

"I always do it on my back. You can do whatever you like. You can watch, for all I care."

Arturo had a nicely shaped cock, of fittingly heroic proportions. I came within minutes, that first night. We both did.

# # # # #

The next day, Arturo set out to do battle, completely alone. No surprise that he was brave enough to do that; after all, he'd confronted a suited soldier singlehandedly, and this time he was on the right side of the armor. I wished I were one-tenth as brave as he was. I'd been called a coward often enough when I'd fled the draft, and sometimes I wondered if the real reason I was here was to prove to myself that I'd fled out of conviction and not cowardice. What I hadn't counted on was that I spent more time worrying about my comrades' lives than my own. Like Arturo, out there alone, even with the suit.

Arturo made it back safely, flushed with excitement as I helped him out of his suit after his first mission. "You should have seen them scatter in panic!" he gloated. "And the way their Jeep felt between my hands when I destroyed it, it felt just like crushing a beer can." He put a hand on my shoulder and vaulted out of the kneeling suit, nimble as always, landing barefoot on the well-trodden jungle undergrowth.

"Please tell me you didn't have to kill anyone."

"Don't worry, I didn't, they were so outmatched. I have to admit, though, that I felt some temptation, feeling so all-powerful. I never thought I'd say this, but I can almost understand how the prisoners could rip our friends to shreds. It was like playing a video game, and I could almost imagine having something squishier than a Jeep in my hands, the crunchiness of a ribcage giving way ..."

"You're scaring me, man."

"I don't blame you. I'm scaring myself." He was silent for a moment, looking thoughtful. "Would you do something for me, buddy?"

"Of course. Anything."

"I need to wrestle someone."

"What?"

"I need to feel myself pitting my own natural strength against the strength of another man, to remind myself I'm only human. I need a reality check."

"You'd totally beat me, I'm sure."

"That doesn't matter. You'll put up a good fight, and that's all I need. You just have to make me work for it, work up a sweat."

I thought about it as I watched him get dressed. "You didn't humiliate me enough in front of our comrades the other day, when you carried me through camp slung from my own shirt?"

He grinned sheepishly. "Sorry about that. I told you the suit goes to one's head. We can go somewhere private."

"Maybe where the mosquitos are swarming?" I suggested seriously.

"Sure. I'll be safe from them as long as I'm wrestling you, right?"

"Probably."

"If I manage to get your T-shirt off, can I keep it?"

"Only if I can have your undershirt." It was a little cooler today, and he was putting one on under his uniform. "I'm not coming back to camp bare-chested."

"Deal." We headed off into the jungle.

# # # # #

Over the next few days, Arturo did a lot of damage to the enemy forces, and even more to their "advisors" from my county, who seemed to vastly outnumber the allies they were advising. He disrupted supply lines, knocked over communications towers, and tore through one small U.S. camp like an anthill. He was able to avoid picking on anyone his own size; he could literally spot them a mile away because they hadn't yet thought to disable the transceivers in their suits as I had done to the one I'd found in Arturo's. There didn't seem to be too many of the suits in the country.

His second time out, he came back with an armful of captured supplies: badly needed rations, and ammo that was compatible with some of my comrades' weapons. I had mixed feelings about the latter, but my contribution to acquiring the bullets had been several levels of indirection away from the men whose bodies they might eventually find their way into, so I could live with it. I rationalized that I was no worse than a medic who saved the lives of soldiers who then returned to "duty" to kill again.

But his third time out, he captured a giant handful of smart-guns. The lethal kind: not stunners, but the kind that shot streams of bullets. They'd been dropped by the fleeing American soldiers who'd been ineffectively trying to find a chink in his armor. This wound up putting me in an extremely difficult position. It was my own fault; I should have kept my mouth shut when Rodrigo said in my hearing, "It's too bad these are useless to us. I know this kind only fires for its owner – for exactly this situation, so the other side can't use them if they capture them."

My engineer's habit of truthful assessment betrayed me. Before I thought better of it, I blurted, "Not exactly this situation. It's more to prevent someone picking it up on the battlefield and immediately turning it on its owner." Oh, for the days when I wasn't yet fluent and had to actually think before speaking!

Rodrigo looked at me speculatively. "You mean they can be rekeyed?"

"It would be a stupid design to make it impossible to change owners at all," I admitted. Thinking hard, I added honestly enough, "It might require a special gadget to reprogram them, though."

"Could you take a look at them, please?"

"Ah ... I really don't think I'd be comfortable with that."

"That was an order," Rodrigo said mildly.

"Here we go again. Sir, you know how I feel about weapons."

"I'm not asking you to shoot one yourself. In fact, you don't have to key one to yourself, so you won't be even able to use them. These are the perfect weapons for you to have around: one you can't ever be asked to shoot."

"Arming my brothers to do the shooting for me is no different than if I pulled the trigger myself."

"You don't have a choice. We may be pretty informal around here compared to a regular army, but this is one of those times I'm going to have to insist you follow orders, or ..."

"What are you going to do? Turn me over to Mateo to be tortured until I obey?"

Rodrigo looked shocked. "How can you say that? Even if I were that ruthless, I couldn't do that. Mateo is your friend. He'd die rather than hurt you. Don't you know that?"

"I don't understand him at all anymore."

"But I will find a suitable punishment if you refuse."

# # # # #

They came for me the next day, right after I'd gotten Arturo into his suit and seen him off: Ernesto, looking like he'd rather be anywhere else on the planet, and several other big guys, any one of whom could have easily overpowered me. They had prudently waited until my super-powered friend was out of sight, then politely but very firmly escorted me to the center of camp, flanking me and gripping me firmly by the biceps to ensure I didn't bolt.

With everyone hanging around looking on, they bound my hands over my head. When Mateo walked up to me with a knife, I was sure he was going to torture me after all.

"Don't look so scared, buddy," he said earnestly. "I'm not going to cut you up. I can't believe you thought I'd torture you if Rodrigo ordered me to. But humiliation, that's another matter." With that he began slicing my T-shirt to ribbons. He made no attempt to rip the shreds away, but when he was done, he turned to the crowd and said, "Many of you have been asking me for rags soaked in the sweat of the prisoners. By now you know it really works as a mosquito repellant. Our comrade here had the same treatment. Help yourselves."

Laughing, the men surrounded me. Over my protests, greedy hands ripped the shredded T-shirt from my body. In seconds I was bare-chested, still being attacked from all sides as they grabbed the last scraps clinging to my sweaty skin. My chest looked pathetically pale in contrast to all the brown hands groping it. A few guys, I didn't see who, started playfully tickling me, until Mateo said sharply, "Back off, you guys! No one but me makes him *cosquillas* until I say so."

They all withdrew to a respectful distance. Mateo grinned at me and said, "You don't know how many times I've thought of doing this. Do you have any idea how tempting it was to have you lying there beside me in easy reach every night, wondering how *cosquilloso* you are?"

If I hadn't already learned the words *cosquilloso* and *cosquillas* from the other end from Arturo, I'd have found out now what they meant, the hard way. Mateo ran his fingers lightly along the bottom of my ribcage. He was better at it than the guys who'd touched me a minute ago; this time I couldn't choke back my laughter.

"All this creamy, vulnerable looking-skin right beside me all that time," he taunted. "And at dawn when you would throw your arm over your eyes, with all these fine wispy hairs sticking out of your armpit, completely exposed, like they are now ..."

He must have taken an hour, easily, to deftly work over every inch of exposed skin from my armpits down to below my navel. It felt like longer. I was gasping for breath by the time he paused to ask for volunteers from the audience. He soon had four guys on me at once: one on each armpit, one attacking my belly, and one standing behind me to reach around to my ribs.

Suddenly, an inhumanly loud voice bellowed, "Hey!" Everyone instantly stopped and looked up. It was a suit – and fortunately for us, the voice was Arturo's. He was using the external speakers and had "accidentally" turned them up to full volume. "What are you guys doing with my *escudero*? I need him to get me out of this suit."

"Fine, he's had enough," Rodrigo said, eyeing Arturo nervously. "Let him go, Mateo. For now."

# # # # #

Arturo, who of course I'd told all about my argument with Rodrigo when we'd bedded down for the night, had not only come back earlier than usual and rescued his "squire," as he'd dubbed me, he had come bearing more captured smart-guns: a dozen handguns and a few rifles. But these were all stunners. Without even being asked, I immediately set to work figuring out how to configure one of the small stunners for a new owner. A red LED winked on through the solid-looking gunmetal of the handgrip as soon as I touched it, presumably its own way of saying "Access Denied." It winked out when I let go.

The first thing I did was to remove the clip, so it couldn't go off in my face. Once I looked closely, it was obvious that behind the clip there was a tiny recessed button, the kind you need a bent paperclip or a pen to press. I found a tiny twig on the ground and poked it. The red light immediately turned yellow. Unwilling to key it to myself, I let go. The yellow light began blinking. I looked around, saw Guillermo watching from a short distance away, and recruited him to grip it. The yellow light stopped blinking and stayed on, but nothing else happened at first. Then another yellow LED lit up beside it.

"A progress bar, maybe," I muttered in English.

A third light came on opposite the second one, and I explained my theory to Guillermo.

"Either that or a self-destruct warning," he joked, but bravely kept a tight grip on the gun, and a fourth light came on.

I told him my theory: "It may be designed to take a minute to register a new owner, so an enemy soldier can't just pick it up in the middle of a battle and use it."

Sure enough, a fifth light came on ten seconds later, and ten seconds after that, the yellow lights were replaced by a steady green light. It went out when Guillermo put down the gun and turned green again as soon as he picked it up. It turned red when I took it from him, green when I passed it back.

"Let's put the clip back and go test it on one of the prisoners," I said.

As we approached, we saw Mateo standing next to the skinny blond prisoner, who he was forcing to do sit-ups to work up enough of a sweat to harvest as mosquito repellant.

"Perfect. Get him while he's lying down, so he doesn't get hurt. But we have to get much closer. The handguns aren't very accurate, I've heard; that's what the rifles are for."

"I've heard it doesn't actually cause unconsciousness."

"That's right. Just ... how do you say 'paralysis'?"

"Pretty much like that. So the guy remains completely aware of what's happening to him, and he can still feel everything?"

"Right. There's no numbness."

"Are you sure you don't want me try it from here and accidentally hit Mateo?"

"It's tempting," I admitted, laughing. It was all too easy to imagine carrying his limp body off into the jungle, stripping him to the waist, stretching him out, and relentlessly digging my fingers into the thick black hair I knew he had in his armpits.

# # # # #

The rifles were a little more secure against theft. They had a second LED near the butt that only lit up when it was held against a man's shoulder, and remained red even when the one near the trigger had been made to turn green. I eventually realized the extra LED was for a sniffer unit. Even civilian technology was superior to the human nose these days, and for all I knew, military technology could rival a bloodhound. Certainly it would have no problem telling one man from another by his unique personal scent. Even I could probably do that, if they blindfolded me and made me smell the armpit of each of my comrades. Now that was a punishment I wouldn't have minded suffering through for my principles.

The sniffer had its own tiny switch, hidden under a sliding cover and impossible to press by accident, and it showed a yellow linking LED when I pressed it against Guillermo's shoulder. I hoped the smart-gun wasn't smart enough to notice that it was pressed against the wrong color of uniform.

"Why's it blinking?"

"Let's try something. Could you unbutton your shirt a little?" He complied without hesitation. I stuck the butt of the rifle into his shirt, and as soon as it touched his skin, the light on the side turned a steady yellow. But no other light came on after ten seconds. We waited patiently, and were rewarded with a second light after a full minute.

"How long do I have to stand here?"

"I've heard stories about soldiers sleeping with their new weapons. I always thought it was a joke implying some kind of sick fetish. But that would make it really secure against it getting picked up in battle, wouldn't it? Where's your tent?"

I checked on him an hour later, by crawling into his tiny tent on my hands and knees and straddling him. He still had the rifle cradled against his bare chest as I'd instructed. He asked, "Any sign it's working?"

"Seven LED's are yellow. Can't tell how many there are."

"Shit. Well, I don't want to let go now and have to start over."

"I'd stay and keep you company, but I have to help the others reconfigure their own guns. Think of it as a good excuse to take a nap in the line of duty." I patted him on the chest and crawled backward out of the tent.

# # # # #

Rodrigo started sending a team out with Arturo, armed with stunners. I felt good about that. Normally they'd be carrying conventional weapons that would wound or kill, but thanks to me they were carrying nonlethal weapons instead. Rodrigo had agreed with my point that the stun guns were better for guerilla warfare, being utterly silent. They were also more accurate and didn't need frequent reloading like the old-fashioned weapons, although admittedly the same was true for the lethal modern weapons I still refused to touch. I wondered how many lives I'd saved by arming my comrades with stunners.

The next day, Arturo came back pushing a Jeep ahead of him. Except for how far he had to bent over, he looked much like a man wheeling a grocery cart from the meat counter to the checkout stand, right down to the beefy cargo piled in the passenger compartment and even draped over the hood. The foot soldiers ran ahead, bragging about how many men they'd captured. The enemy had predictably fled in terror when Arturo stomped up, and he'd flushed them right into the waiting arms of the men armed with my stunners. The captives wore

American uniforms. All men, of course; with the dwindling volunteer forces already deployed half a world away, the Western Hemisphere was the province of draftees.

"We need all the help we can get unloading them," one of the food soldiers said. Two of his buddies hurried by carrying a limp body under the knees and armpits. I noted absently that he had a thick trail of hair starting at his navel and running up under his shirt, a dark brown contrasting with his pale belly, though his slack face was tan. Two more guys walked by carrying a slim young Asian. Then a relatively light-skinned African American, then a redhead with broad shoulders and impressive abs.

"What are you going to do with them?" I asked nervously.

"What do you think? If we'd wanted them dead, we would have slit their throats where they lay."

I should have known. Within half an hour, they were all strung up by the wrists, stripped down to their military-issue boxers. Even before they were able to move, Mateo was pacing up and down the line, taunting them, running his forefinger possessively down one prisoner's sternum, pinching the next man's nipples cruelly. When they began to stir, the interrogation began. The screaming and moaning lasted well after dark.

"Next time we'll have to really try to find some loyalist troops," Arturo told me that night in our tent. "These Americans don't seem to know anything about where Diego would have been taken. That's only one of the questions Mateo has been asking them, of course."

"Arturo, doesn't it seem wrong to you that we're doing the same thing to our prisoners as they're doing to Diego?"

Arturo looked distraught. When he answered, it was so softly I had to roll closer to hear him over the distant screams, even though we were lying side by side. "I wish there were a better way. But more than that, I wish I could believe what they're doing to Diego is as mild as what Mateo is doing to his prisoners."

# # # # #

Neither of us felt like jerking off over the sounds of torture, not being Mateo, but I woke up in the blessed quiet of predawn with a raging hard-on. It was just light enough for me to see that Arturo was awake, watching me. He said softly, "You, too, huh?"

I looked down and saw that he was as hard as I was. "Maybe we should both take care of this."

"Both of us, or each of us?" he asked teasingly.

"Both, I mean, each," I stammered, my language skills suddenly failing me. "What's the difference?"

"Let me show you," he said, and pulled my boxers over my cock and down out of the way.

I gasped, and then gasped again as he took my cock in his fist. "This has to be a dream," I whispered.

"If you were dreaming, we'd be in a bigger tent and I'd have room to do more than this. Do you think anyone would notice if my legs were sticking out of the tent? It's almost light, but sometimes on moonless nights ... well ..." and he mumbled something that might have been "It doesn't matter," "It's none of your business," or even "Do you mind?" – I didn't stop to ask. He was still squeezing my cock rhythmically. I moaned and arched my back, and he took this as permission to roll against me, his arm skin against mine, his unshaven cheek and soft lips against my chest. Having wrestled with him before, I knew I wasn't quite so outmatched that he could pin me and still have a hand free to do whatever he wanted to me. But for the moment, I was happy to surrender myself to that fantasy.

# # # # #

"How quickly do you think you could train Felipe to take over as squire for Arturo?" Rodrigo asked me the day after I'd sent Arturo off with his team, both of us acting like nothing had happened the previous night.

"What? Why? I thought I was doing fine. Look, is this about what happened before dawn? I don't know what anyone thought they heard or saw, but it wasn't what they thought. We were just ... wrestling, you know. Just a little ..." my Spanish was failing me in my panic, "you know, playful clowning around."

Rodrigo actually looked flustered, and gestured for me shut up. "I don't know what you mean! That's none of my business ... would be none of my business, whatever you might have been doing. We don't talk about stuff like that here! God! No, it's not that I want to keep you away from Arturo. You're doing a great job, and so is he, and anything else, I don't want to know about. It's just that I figure anyone can be his squire, and I have a better use for you."

"Oh."

"I want to send you on a mission of your own. One only you can do. It'll be dangerous, so I won't insist, but it would really help us."

"More danger than we face here every day?"

"Well, no. Maybe 'dangerous' isn't the best word. More like stressful. Here you're surrounded by supportive brothers facing danger together. On this mission you'll be alone with the enemy, undercover. If you get caught, you'll be imprisoned, of course. Possibly executed, but I doubt it."

"Does it involve my engineering skills?"

"No. It's just that you're the only guy we've got who can pass as a North American, because you are. Even our most fluent English speakers could never pass themselves off as a Latino-American without raising suspicion; very few of your immigrants come from this region, and we certainly don't look Mexican or Puerto Rican. And our local accents would be hard to disguise."

"I think you're giving my countrymen too much credit for making those distinctions, but I'm sure you're right that a blond-haired blue-eyed guy with an authentic American accent would be less likely to raise suspicions. But aren't there records? ID cards?"

"It's not like the suit security. The regular soldiers do carry IDs, but the technology is decades behind the times, even by our standards. Would you believe they still seem to think that adding a hologram over the picture makes it unalterable? We have some guys who are very good at forging documents."

"I would think they would run them through a reader and display the real pictures from central records."

"You might think so, but the prisoners all say they've never encountered more than a cursory manual inspection."

Mention of the prisoners and the helpful information they'd given us made me uncomfortable, as always. I knew Mateo was spending all his time interrogating the ones Arturo was bringing in before sending them to a POW camp the insurgency had built a day's march away. At least he was making do with other interpreters now that the information he was extracting wasn't technical.

"You see," Rodrigo continued, "Arturo and others would like to find out where Diego's being held – if he's still alive – so he can try to rescue him. Or, well, at least put him out of his misery. Maybe they can even free others being held at the same facility as well. The prisoners from both armies have been very informative about where their own units are camped, but Mateo says he's convinced they know nothing about the location of the detention camps. But we did find out that your military is routinely getting intelligence from our government's torture chambers. It turns out that one of the men Arturo and his team captured in the raid last week had been working as a translator. You can't take his place; they must know he's missing and would be suspicious if someone showed up using his name. But yesterday on the road, we intercepted his replacement on his way to report for duty at one of the surviving American camps. Come with me. I'll show you."

I reluctantly followed him to an area of the camp I'd been avoiding, where my old buddy Mateo interrogated the prisoners. He led me over to a man of medium build, about my age, with light brown hair, a moderately hairy chest, and wispy tufts of armpit hair. He was on his knees with his hands bound to a branch overhead and a gag in his mouth. He looked up apprehensively at our approach.

Rodrigo picked up the dog tags that were resting on the prisoner's chest and made a show of reading them. "This is Lt. John Davis." He pulled the chain with the dog tags over the helpless man's head and handed them to me. "The uniform we took from him might even fit you. If not, we have plenty of others in various sizes, and of course the name and insignia are just attached with Velcro."

Now that I was confronted with it, the idea of wearing the uniform of my own country for deceptive purposes was no more appealing than the idea of wearing it to "serve" my country. And being introduced to the poor guy whose identity I'd be stealing wasn't helping either. But I cared about Diego. I cared even more about Arturo, who had never gotten over the loss of his friend and would never really be happy again until he got some closure. It was the toughest decision I'd made since deciding to risk my life coming here to fight against my own country.

I stared at the dog tags in my hand. "I'll do it," I finally said. I pulled the chain over my head and stuck the dog tags into my shirt. They felt cold against my skin.

"We captured his Jeep and his driver, that guy right over there." He pointed to a man with black hair, a muscular, hairless light-brown chest, and black bushy armpit hair. "Another piece of luck: The driver has a Spanish surname, so we can even fake an ID for the guy who drives you through the gate, and they'll never know we made a substitution. With luck he won't have to say one word to the guards at the gate, but just in case we'll pick the most fluent guy we can spare. He'll be the last friendly face you see for awhile. You'll be on your own after he drops you off."

I'd never have guessed that the little bit of acting experience I'd gotten in college and community theater would ever be a survival skill, but I was able to hide my nervousness and fake a military bearing well enough that no one seemed to suspect I was a traitor in their midst. The sentries glanced at my fake ID and directed me to a trailer where I reported for duty. This involved a certain amount of bureaucracy that would have been boring if I hadn't been busy trying to hide the fact that I was afraid they would check my fingerprints or pull up the real Davis's picture from their computer records. Apparently they didn't because the private who they assigned to escort me (I knew what one stripe meant because Mateo had given me a quick refresher on U.S. Army insignia, using his growing collection of captured uniforms as illustrations) led me not to a firing squad but to one of the officers' barracks to drop off my pack next to a vacant cot, then to the mess hall for a quick snack and cup of terrible coffee, and finally to the communications shack, where I'd be working. He left me there with a young lieutenant. I was doing a pretty good job of remembering to salute at the right times.

The lieutenant, a handsome dark-haired guy about my age if not even younger, had a friendly smile. "Hi, I'm Danny. Can I call you John?"

"Of course," I said, and resisted the temptation to add nervously, Because that's my name, you know. "Nice to meet you, Danny."

"Want some coffee? I just made a pot."

"I just had some, thanks."

"What, that commercial stuff from the mess hall? The stuff that's shipped from this part of the world to the U.S., stored for a year, roasted, ground, stored again, and then sent back here months later to sit around for hours over a burner? Let me give you some of the good stuff. I buy it with my own money. It's locally grown."

Back home, I'd always associated "locally grown" with environmentally and socially responsible purchases. Here, I realized, that meant it was grown by farmers who were practically slave labor. It smelled delicious, though, and I accepted some to be friendly. It tasted as good as he'd promised. This guy could easily seduce me into forgetting why I was here, if I didn't watch out.

"Let's get you set up with a computer account. You'll be working on this one." He booted up the second workstation. He'd been working on the other one when I came in, flipping between spreadsheets and maps. Danny was some kind of logistics officer, I eventually gathered. But when he'd risen from his chair to greet me, he'd carefully locked his screen. It was now displaying his screensaver, a picture of himself wearing unbuttoned fatigues over a while T-shirt, with his arms around the shoulders of two other guys our age, both shirtless. One was a muscular, slightly overweight African-American, the other a broad-shouldered white guy with a tattoo on his chest. All of them were grinning, looking happy and relaxed.

"I'm really glad you're here. We have about a fifty-hour backlog of interrogation sessions since the other camp was attacked."

"I heard about that, of course."

"The whole world heard about that, even though it's supposed to be classified that that we have those suits at all, let alone that the terrorists stole one, or that one of them is running around loose with it. I just hope we're safe here. We used to have two suited guys guarding our perimeter, but now they've been redeployed."

"Damn. Is that permanent?"

"Rumor has it that they're assigned to hunt down the enemy suit. So we'll probably get our protectors back just as soon as we don't need protection so badly anymore. Anyway, our allies send us more interrogation footage every day. I can get by with written Spanish, but I could never translate recordings. Some of our guys do speak Spanish fairly well, but we have trouble getting anyone to stick with it."

"That boring?"

"That disturbing. Are you sure you're up to it? Have you ever witnessed extreme interrogation methods before?"

"Oh, yeah," I said truthfully and ruefully.

But I wasn't prepared for what I saw in the first video. Mateo had been right: as torturers go, he didn't look all that bad compared to the government he was fighting. He never maimed or mutilated anyone, and rarely spilled even a drop of blood. After awhile I couldn't take it anymore and fled outside, feeling like I was going to barf. I fell to my hands and knees. The fresh air helped, and I managed to hold down my lunch. For some reason, I was reacting worse to this than I had to the even more gruesome sight of my own friends being torn apart. Maybe this seemed worse because it wasn't a battle, or maybe it was because I wasn't in a position to race to the rescue of the guy in the recording. Hell, I was pretending to be on the torturer's side.

I felt a gentle hand on my shoulder. "Hey, buddy," Danny said softly. "You okay?"

"I didn't expect ... I've never seen ... I can't believe anyone could do that to another human being."

"I understand. If it helps, keep in mind that these guys had it coming. After all, they're traitors to their country."

I shuddered in his arms. I resembled that remark.

"I know, I know," he said softly, massaging my neck, "even traitors deserve better than that."

I looked up at his sympathetic gray eyes. "This job is going to take some getting used to," I admitted.

"You know what? You can work up to it slowly. The session you were watching is worst than most of it. They don't really start doing anything nearly that bad until a prisoner's been in custody for months, and they're trying to wring the last bit of intelligence out of him before they either release him or execute him. You don't have to translate the

97

rest of that one today or anytime soon. Like I said, we have like fifty hours of the stuff, with more coming in, and it's not prioritized. You can do it in any order you want. So when you're ready to go back in, we'll have a beer, and then I'll help you set up a filter, so you only see the first few weeks of each prisoner's questioning."

Inside, he produced two ice-cold bottles of beer from a stash in a small fridge and placed one in my shaking hand. While he was helping me set up the search filter, I noticed that the other search parameters included age and gender. "Please tell me they don't torture woman and children," I said hollowly.

"They don't seem to have any limits, but we can filter those out, too, if you like."

"Definitely. Please. And old men, too." I had an ulterior motive, of course: this would make it more likely I'd come across Diego's recordings and find out which facility he was in.

"Well, the good news is that all these criteria only narrow down the backlog to thirty hours. Work slowly enough and you may be able to avoid ever having to watch the worst of it. But look, it's getting late. Why don't you turn in, get a fresh start tomorrow, when you feel better, dude?"

# # # # #

Being a spy was hard enough, but if wearing my own country's uniform dishonestly was hard, taking the uniform off in front of the other guys was another challenge. I hadn't thought about it, but I was being plunged into military life suddenly and had to hide the fact that I was adjusting to it for the first time. The guy I was impersonating would have long since gotten used to casually stripping to his shorts in a whole barracks full of other male officers, or stripping naked and stepping into the shower next to other guys, their equally naked bodies already soaped up and ranging from shiny pink to polished mahogany. Showering in our one-man camp shower was something I'd finally gotten comfortable with, but while it exposed me to the whole camp, I was visible only from the knees down and from the clavicle up. I'd never gotten completely used to being crammed into a tent with Leandro and Bernardo, and after that it had taken me months to get used to sleeping next to one guy I'd known well – or thought I'd known well. Now I was surrounded by a dozen softly snoring enemies, completely vulnerable to them. And them to me: if I hadn't been a pacifist, I could have easily slit their throats or at least stunned them all in their sleep. I didn't know a single one of them; there were two other barracks for officers, and Danny slept in one of the others.

# # # # #

The next morning, starting my first full day of work, I found that the first torture session matching the new criteria was something I could deal with: a shirtless, muscular man around thirty strapped spread-eagle to a table, bare chest rising and falling with ragged breaths as two thugs clamped wires to his nipples. I could almost pretend it was a porn video. Hours of footage later for me, eight days of leisurely torture later for the poor guy on the table, he was naked and the wires were clamped to his balls. He was a plumber who'd been taken into custody after one of his customers was arrested for conspiring with the rebels. They were grilling him for any bit of revealing information he might have overheard while fixing the sink.

I worked right through dinner, which gave me an hour alone to skip around in the videos trying to find Diego, and also to use my phone to send a secure text message reporting my status and what I'd learned: if they were following their usual pattern, Diego was very likely still alive and in one piece. I also advised them to warn Arturo that he was probably being stalked by two or more suited enemies, and that the silver lining was that this camp might be more vulnerable than usual to attack, if need be.

When I heard Danny returning, I flipped back to a video I'd paused in the middle, this one of a guy in his early twenties who still had pants on at this stage and continued typing my translation: "Please, I told you, I don't know anything. I'm just a – why are you taking off my shoes? What's – no, please, don't – (expletive deleted) that hurts!"

"How's it going, buddy?" Danny said. "I know you said you didn't have much of an appetite right now, but I brought you back some food anyway."

"Thanks, Danny. That was nice of you."

"I'll make us some more coffee. I'm going to get some more work done myself. You make me feel like a slacker." He sat down at his locked workstation.

"Who are those guys in the picture?" I asked, mostly to be friendly, but also because it gave me an excuse to come over and shoulder-surf, trying to see the password he typed to unlock it. He'd let slip by now that he dealt with exchanging goods with the local government forces, including the detention centers where the videos I was translating were being made. I was pretty sure his workspace had maps showing those detention centers, maybe even hints about their security systems.

"This one is Vance," he said, pointing to the African American. He was killed in action two months ago."

"I'm sorry."

"The other one," he said, pointing at the well-muscled shirtless guy, who had a small tattoo on his chest, "is Bryce." I could hear the fondness in his voice. They were good buddies. "I just had dinner with him, in fact. Funny how losing one friend makes you really appreciate the ones you have left."

"I know exactly what you mean," I said. "I've lost some good friends in battle."

# # # # #

The metadata on the videos included the location of each interrogation – the name of the location, anyway. The sobbing man on my screen at the moment, a twenty-eight-year-old with the word "TRAIDOR" branded across his broad chest in big block letters, was being held in Detention Center 2. I could see Danny studying a map on his own screen, with color-coded dots representing his own army bases and the facilities used by his allies. I was too far away to read the labels.

# # # # #

"Have you seen the latest news?" Danny asked grimly when I showed up the next morning. I was about to log in when he added, his eyes still fixed to his screen, "I can't believe how much one guy in a stolen suit is damaging the war effort."

That got my attention. I hurried over and looked over his shoulder. He was watching streaming video of a column of half-naked men, most of them white, black, Asian, or mixtures thereof – Americans, in other words – dejectedly marching toward the camera, most of them carrying comrades on their generally bare backs. The men being carried had splints on their legs and were otherwise as half-naked as their buddies carrying them, none of whom wore more than military-issue boxers or briefs and the occasional white T-shirt or tank top.

"He obviously attacked them while they were asleep in the barracks, the coward, and snapped the legs on half of them like they were twigs."

I resisted the urge to point out he could have slaughtered them with less trouble, and that an outnumbered rebel force had little choice but to resort to guerrilla tactics. Our American history books lauded our own revolutionaries for being clever enough to hide in the forests and shoot at the British troops who stupidly wore bright red uniforms and marched in the open. Personally, I was proud of my friend for his bravery and restraint.

Danny didn't seem to notice my silence, didn't even turn around, so my efforts to hide my satisfied grin were wasted. He added, "I can't believe our government lets the media air this humiliating stuff. They should crack down."

It would have been wise to agree with him, but I couldn't resist at least saying, "I thought our Constitution guarantees freedom of the press."

"Not for embedded reporters. If they want access to our troops or even to this country, they'd better start playing ball."

# # # # #

On Friday, as I paused a video of a young guy being stripped of last scrap of clothing, next to a barrel on its side and a table full of suggestively-shaped objects arranged in increasing order of discomfort, Danny said, "Hey, by the way, me and my buddy Bryce are driving to the capital tomorrow. Want to come along? I'm sure I could talk the CO into giving you a weekend pass, too. You haven't been here long, but you've been working your ass off."

I still hadn't met Bryce, but I remembered he was the guy in the screen saver, the white one with the tattoo. "Uh, let's see how much of this backlog I get through today," I said. I needed time to think about it. There was a Canadian embassy in the city, I knew. Ever since I'd seen what Mateo was doing, I'd been questioning my whole reason for being here. This would make it easy, if I wanted out, to say "a pox on both your houses" and return to the safety of my adopted country.

And leave Diego to rot. I couldn't do it. I remembered him, smiling and happy, roughhousing with Arturo. I had to try to help him, for his own sake and for Arturo's. And the truth was, although I might feel torture in any form was wrong, Mateo had had a point about there being a difference. I'd just watched a terrified young guy, who would have been a college student in a better time and place, being threatened for an half hour with a knife held against his toes, and finally stopped it when I became convinced they were really about to carry through with their threat. And that was nothing compared to what I'd watched on my first day.

In the end, I turned down Danny's well-meant offer. And so I had the tent to myself all weekend, and I put the time to good use. First I changed the search parameters to include only sessions that already had translations, instead of excluding those; also to show only the first session, and to narrow the age range. Diego had looked to be in his mid to late twenties, so anyone guessing his age would have put in a number between twenty-four and twenty-eight, I estimated. Then I began watching ten seconds of each result. It didn't take me long to find Diego. It was nice to see his face again, even if we'd never become close. He was still unharmed in this old video, and they hadn't even taken off his shirt yet. I wished it had been my job to translate Diego's cocky taunting of his captors. The guy showed more bravado than any of the last ten men I'd seen. Of course, it was his first session, and they hadn't done anything to him yet except show him a few of the instruments of torture. He struggled when two of his interrogators propped his foot up in the lap of a third, but they had all the leverage, and he was unable to kick them as his shoe, then his sock, were slowly removed. I paused it and turned away. I didn't know exactly what the man had planned for the bare foot he held in his hand, but I didn't imagine he would settle for tickling. Usually for the first session, bamboo shoots were involved.

There was plenty of other footage of him listed when I adjusted the criteria. Some of it was recent. He was still alive, then, which was a mixed blessing. I couldn't bring myself to watch the latest footage just yet, even though it might be useful to know what he had told them. It would have been reassuring to verify that they hadn't done any permanent damage yet. Not only was I was afraid to find out, but also I couldn't bear to see Arturo's closest friend strapped naked to a table pleading for his life, which was about the best I could hope to see.

He was being held in Detention Facility 5. That would have been my second guess; over a third of the prisoners who had been combatants and not innocent civilians seemed to be sent there. The only problem was I had no idea where Detention Facility 5 was physically located. Danny surely knew; he routinely sent weapons and guards to that and the other facilities, and it was presumably marked on the a map I'd seen him consulting.

I spent the rest of the weekend searching his desk drawers in hopes of finding a Post-it note with his password hidden away somewhere. No such luck.

# # # # #

"Dude, you gotta see this," Danny said excitedly the next Wednesday afternoon. I had just paused a video to puzzle over the translation of an unknown word; the interrogator had told his assistant, "clip the other end onto his *prepucio*."

"What's up, buddy?" I was almost beginning to believe myself when I called Danny that, and for some reason I'd always liked the sound of the word in my native language better than *amigo* or *compinche*.

"They finally captured the guy in the stolen suit. Here, I'll rewind it for you. This is awesome!"

I plastered a fake smile on my face and watched in growing horror as one suit was surrounded and grappled by three others, its arms eventually pinned behind its back, and its chest pried forcibly open, exposing a familiar naked brown chest. The clip ended with a close-up of a defeated and terrified Arturo, in his boxer shorts, hanging helplessly by the arms from an outstretched enemy claw. I knew how demeaning that felt, even at the hands of a friend. Now it was his turn to be utterly humiliated, not just in front of his comrades but in front of a worldwide audience. The views for this video were already in the tens of thousands on this site alone, I noticed, and it would presumably be broadcast on the evening news. Unfortunately, humiliation was the least important problem he faced right now.

The scene switched to an anchorman. "Sources say the terrorist has been turned over to his own government."

"They'll torture him, won't they?" I said hollowly.

"I hope they do, after all the men he's wounded. When you get the recording of his first session, can I watch?"

I pulled myself together. "Sure, buddy," I said, no longer meaning it.

"Yeah, I'm sure they'll torture him. They'll want to know how he broke through the suit's security."

"I'll be watching for it," I said. I sat down and pretended to work. Resuming the video made the meaning of *prepucio* all too obvious when the assistant rolled it down, stretched it out cruelly, and clamped the teeth of an alligator clamp on it. I winced, wondering morbidly where they would attach it on me if I ever fell into their hands, since mine had been removed at birth. Right now it looked more likely I'd face my own country's justice, in the form of a firing squad or a life sentence.

"That's gotta hurt," Danny commented, looking over my shoulder. He didn't usually show such an interest; I suspected he was imagining Arturo in the guy's place. Just as I was. As always, he'd locked his screen, which was all that saved him from being hit over the head, bound, and gagged.

"Yeah," I agreed absently. "And in a second they'll turn the electricity on. I need some air. Back in a few minutes." I dutifully locked my own screen and walked out.

A lot of guys went into the jungle when they needed to take a leak, since it smelled better than the latrines. As soon as I was out of sight of the camp, I pulled out my phone and sent a secure text message in Spanish: "We've got to move up the schedule. I may be compromised when they question Arturo. I'll stay and try to learn his location."

# # # # #

The next day I witnessed what I dreaded: a video of Arturo bound to a chair, still wearing nothing but boxers, being tortured with electricity. They began with his nipples.

Summoning up my meager acting abilities, I said, "Dude, come here! They've got him at Detention Center°5."

"That's not far from here." Danny came over. "Doesn't look so tough without the suit, does he?"

I thought my friend was being very tough, for a man with electricity running through his nipples. He must be in excruciating pain, but he had not yet even given his torturers the satisfaction of a scream, let alone pleas for mercy or any useful intelligence.

I glanced at Danny's station. It was displaying a picture of him and his shirtless buddies. Damn it, despite his excitement, he'd remembered to lock his screen.

"It'll be his balls next, won't it?"

"They usually take a day or two to get around to that," I said with unwanted expertise.

Now Arturo was cursing, using the usual scatological sacrilege that I'd heard other guys use casually but had never heard him reduced to. "Gotta translate," I said.

"Oh, sure. Sorry, man." He went back to his own workstation and unlocked his screen. I was sorely tempted to come up from behind and get him into a sleeper hold – less risk of brain damage than hitting him on the head – but if he slipped out of it or managed to call for help, everything would be lost.

# # # # #

"Dinnertime," Danny pointed out a while later. "You coming?"

"Still up to my neck in translations. If you wouldn't mind bringing me a plate again ..."

"You got it, buddy. By the way, as long as you're sticking around, do me a favor? I'm expecting an important package. Could you accept it for me if it comes while I'm out?"

"Of course. What is it?" I knew one of Danny's duties was to order medical supplies and ammunition, but he'd never personally taken delivery of any of them.

"An SCEIDU," he said. "Command wants us to tighten security. They got intelligence a couple of weeks ago that the rebels have at least one American working with them."

I really didn't want to watch the recording of what they had done to Diego to get him to rat me out.

He continued, "They got the idea he could try to infiltrate us. It's going to be a real pain, but better safe than sorry, I guess. Thanks, buddy."

He left, and I glared at his screen saver. I was beginning to hate those friends of his, although I'd never met them, even Bryce, the one who was still alive and around and still stationed here. They were all that was keeping me from learning where my friends were being held and getting out of here while I still could. There they stood, grinning smugly at me, knowing there was no way I could get past them.

On my own workstation, I brought up a search window to find out what the heck an SCEIDU was. It turned out to be my worst nightmare. I'd been on the right track when I'd worried that they could swipe my stolen ID card through a reader and look up the true owner's picture from central computer records. They did have wireless network units that could do that; they were linked to the page I found under "See also: WNEIDU." If that had been what Danny had ordered, I could probably have broken into the wireless router's firewall and made it conveniently fail to connect. A lot of things can cause a new unit to fail to connect to wireless, and the last thing that would occur to anyone was a spy with engineering training. But unfortunately for me, Danny had chosen the self-contained model that shipped with a snapshot of the entire database in read-only memory.

I sat there dazedly trying to decide whether to make a run for it while I still could, stay and desperately try to get information on the whereabouts of Detention Center°5 before they got around to checking my ID, or call Rodrigo on my secure cell phone for instructions. As luck would have it, the unit was delivered five minutes later, while I was still dithering. I scrawled an illegible signature with numb fingers and barely remembered to print my fake name below it.

I unpacked it, just to make sure it was what Danny was expecting and not a care package from his grandmother. It looked very sturdy, with components soldered together and nothing that could plausibly have come loose in transit. I sat there for a few minutes staring at the means of my destruction then made up my mind.

I tucked the box under my arm and headed in the direction of the latrines. On the way there, it occurred to me that before I disposed of it, I should be a good soldier and check in with Rodrigo. Couldn't have me thinking for myself, now could we? Everyone was in the mess hall at the other end of the base, but as I crouched down behind a large tent and fitted the headset around my ear, I still felt conspicuous. Even though it was dark. Even though I'd previously disabled the standard blue LED that would otherwise have shone like a beacon, proclaiming to anyone in line of sight that I had a connection open and was communicating with someone outside.

"Are you sure you can destroy it without compromising yourself?" Rodrigo wanted to know, once I'd explained the situation.

"Not at all," I admitted.

"Maybe you should abort the mission. You won't do us any good if you're dead. In fact, you'll be worse than useless and worse than dead if they turn you over to my government, but I don't think that's likely."

"No, they'll just shoot me or throw me in federal prison. But I can't leave yet. I'm in a perfect position to learn the location of Detention Center°5, where they took Arturo and Diego."

"And you're willing to risk your own life to give us a shot at pulling off a rescue?"

"For Arturo? Definitely. If it was just Diego ... yes, I'd probably risk my life for him, too."

"Are you sure? I have men in position if you want to ..."

"Just a minute. I think I hear someone coming."

I started to stand up, but then a strange sensation came over me and I sagged to the ground. I found I couldn't move.

"You'd better be right about what you heard," a voice said. "Do you know what they'll do to us for stunning a superior officer?"

"If the gadget in this box is what I think it is, we'll know soon enough if he even is a superior officer."

"Should I get the MPs?"

"No way! What if I'm wrong?"

"If you're wrong, we're screwed, sooner or later."

"If I'm wrong, we'll pour liquor down his throat until he forgets his own mother's name, and hope he doesn't remember anything when he wakes up."

"Did you understand anything he was saying? My Spanish isn't so great."

"Enough of it to be suspicious. Looks like he hung up before you stunned him."

"Let's get him into the tent."

I felt hands under my knees and armpits, and soon we were inside the tent I'd been crouched behind. I could blink, but not move my eyes, so I couldn't get a very good look at my captors, but I didn't think I knew them. They stretched me out. I was still completely paralyzed.

"There's a user's manual."

After a few minutes, he said, "OK, got it. Let's try our own cards and make sure our pictures come up."

After satisfying themselves the machine worked, they rolled me onto my belly to get the altered ID out of my back pocket. I lay there, knowing what it would tell them, but helpless to stop it, unable to run.

"Thought so!" one of them cried triumphantly. "No way is that him."

"We'd better make sure. Let's roll him over, so we can see his face again."

They rolled me onto my back. The paralysis was wearing off – it must have been a light setting – but I was still much too weak to resist. One of them held the device in front of my eyes. The screen showed a photo of a man with light brown hair, shoulders clad in a uniform like the one I was wearing – a man I'd last seen half naked, on his knees, bound and gagged and waiting for my dear old ex-bunkmate's tender attentions.

"Impersonating an officer! I'll bet he has no business wearing our uniform at all."

"I'll bet you're right. Let's get him out of it."

My voice was working just well enough now for me to softly moan "No" as one of them began unbuttoning my shirt and the other unlaced my boots.

"Better get used to it, pal," said one, flinging my shirt open. "They'll strip you naked in prison for the shower."

"Not to mention the cavity search," added the one pulling down my pants. "And those won't be the only times, if you know what I mean. You know what happens to young good-looking blond guys like you in prison, don't you?"

"Maybe we should give him a preview," his buddy snickered as he rolled me over to tug my arms out of the sleeves.

"No, we should turn him into the MPs."

"You want to carry him clear over to where the nearest one is posted? You know they're spread thin tonight. They can't spare someone to leave his post and come to us. They're afraid of an attack."

"You're right. Let's wait until he's recovered enough to walk, so we can march him over to them."

"Meanwhile ..." He slapped my ass through my boxers, suggestively. I mumbled a helpless protest.

"You know, pal, there are ways you can avoid that. If you're lucky enough to get a big strong cellmate who'll protect you, all you need to do is serve his every whim." He patted my ass.

I struggled to roll over onto my back, almost succeeding.

"Look at that. I think he's recovered enough to get up onto his knees."

They manhandled me onto my knees. "You really going to do this, man?" asked the one gripping my bare shoulders.

"Just hold him. I'll owe you one."

I still had trouble focusing on anything not right in front of my face, but the one guy's crotch was now right in front of my face, and he was unbuttoning his fly.

Just as he was reaching into his fly, he suddenly collapsed like a marionette whose strings have been cut. A split second later, the grip on my shoulders loosened, and the guy behind me pitched forward, knocking me over. The three of us wound up in a heap.

"Looks like we got here in just in time," someone whispered in Spanish. The weight was rolled off my back, and someone grabbed me by the shoulder and gently flipped me over, then gave me a friendly pat on the chest. I managed to focus enough to recognize Guillermo.

"You really got yourself into some trouble, my friend. Where would you be right now if you hadn't left your phone online?" He poked me in my ticklish ribs as I lay there helpless, and a laugh was forced from me involuntarily.

"Oops! We need to be quiet. We took out most of the sentries and sent a team to the mess hall, but it will be some time before the base is secure. We took a risk making your rescue our highest priority, but I'm sure we'll win in the end, even if we have some casualties. Aren't you glad we didn't save you for last?"

I still couldn't answer intelligibly, but in fact I wasn't at all sure I was glad that some of my comrades were going to become "casualties," as he'd so casually put it, just to save me from humiliation. Given the choice, I'd rather have been forced to perform oral sex than cost even one friend his life. But this was a different culture.

"We need to lay low for a few hours," Guillermo told me once I was recovered, "until the fighting is over." He calmly placed the stunner against each paralyzed man's spine and pulled the trigger. "That should hold them. How about if I guard the door and leave you guys alone? After what they were about to do to you, they deserve whatever you do to them. I won't ask."

I took him up on it. But he would have been surprised at the form my revenge took. I stripped them both naked, then began teasing each man's cock to erectness, first with my hand, then with my tongue, stopping when his cock was standing straight up, engorged and throbbing, and switching to the other guy. I alternated several times, stopping each time just short of letting them climax. When I finally let them ejaculate, I aimed each one at the other, and finished them off with my hand. Once they were both spent, I wiped my hand clean in the chest hair of the one who I'd been on my knees in front of, matting the hair down with a mixture of his own fluids and his buddy's. Then I hid the evidence by dressing them again. I considered asking Guillermo's help in lifting them as I pulled their clothes on, but decided I preferred a backache to an explanation. I gave them back their own uniforms, but deliberately switched their boxers and undershirts.

When the base was finally secure, Guillermo escorted me back to the communications shack, where I found Danny flanked by two guys that towered over him, Ernesto and Pablo, who each had a hand clamped around his biceps. When I walked in, I saw a flicker of unwarranted hope light his face for a split second, followed by disappointment when he saw that I had an armed rebel solider behind me. And then, finally, dawning comprehension as he took in our body language and realized I didn't seem to be a prisoner. It hurt to see that; I'd always dreaded facing this situation, second only to being discovered and arrested. Betraying my country for an ideal was an abstract thing, but betraying a friendly guy who had trusted me was another.

"John?" he said. "What the hell?"

"Sorry, Danny. My name's actually Josh. And I really am sorry. But ..." I took a deep breath, "I need you to tell me your password, so I can find the coordinates of Detention Center°5."

"How can you – you're an American, aren't you? Why are you doing this?"

"That's a really good question. I used to think I knew the answer, but it's not as black and white as I used to believe. All I know for sure is that two friends of mine are being slowly tortured to death, and I'll do anything to rescue them. I mean anything! I really don't want to hurt you, man. If you'll just ..."

"I'm not telling you anything!" he said defiantly.

"Take off his shirt," I said sadly in Spanish. I watched Ernesto strip Danny to the waist while Pablo held him. His chest looked very pale to me after all the golden brown skin I'd gotten used to seeing. The black hair between his pecs and bisecting his belly made an interesting contrast.

The poor guy looked scared and very vulnerable. If the stakes had been anything else, I'd never be doing this. I found myself wishing

Mateo were there, so I could defer to his expertise as an excuse to get out of doing it myself. Maybe I really was a coward after all.

"What are you going to do to me?"

"Nothing, if you tell me what I need to know."

"You know I can't give you my password." He screwed his eyes shut and said through gritted teeth, "Do you worst. You're not getting anything out of me."

I took an ice-cold bottle of beer from our little fridge and held it against Danny's left nipple. Not seeing it coming, he yelped, but when he opened his eyes and saw what I was doing, he said, "You're gonna have to do a lot better than that."

"I know," I said sadly. And I wasn't sure I could bring myself to do much worse to him. Maybe if I worked up to it ... "If you tell me your password now, you won't have to find out how much better I can do," I bluffed.

He shook his head.

"Hold his arms straight out," I ordered Ernesto and Pablo. It was scary how willingly two guys big enough to kick my ass followed my orders. I could think of things I'd much rather have them do, preferably to me or to each other, but ironically, I wasn't allowed to order them to do anything like that. But hurting another human being was a completely acceptable order.

With his arms forcibly held out to his sides, Danny stared at me wide-eyed, as though he thought I was going to bring the bottle crashing down on his arm, but instead, I stuck it into his exposed armpit, winning a sharp intake of breath.

With my free hand, I grabbed him by the back of his head and forced him to lean his head against my shoulder, a false intimacy with his forehead pressed again my false uniform. Then I began rubbing the ice-bold bottle on the nape of his neck. He shivered. I slowly moved it down his spine. He whimpered so softly that only I could hear.

When I finally looked up, having worked my way all the way down to the base of his spine, until the bottle fetched up against his belt, I found that Guillermo had returned from an errand I'd sent him on.

"They didn't have any of the really hot ones, just jalapeños," he said, his tone of voice suggesting that he didn't understand how someone could tolerate anything as bland as a jalapeño. "I did find bottles of olive oil and lemon juices, and a few spices like cayenne and cinnamon, and some rubber gloves."

"Thanks. Good work, Guillermo."

I took my time mixing the spices into the oil and squeezing some jalapeño juice into it. Maybe I was stalling for time, but after all, I was new at this. Finally I took a dab and smeared some on Danny's chest. He gasped as I deliberate rubbed it into his right nipple. At first that was all the reaction I got, but as his skin began to absorb it, he grimaced, then began moaning softly, then whimpering. I stood back at arm's length, doing nothing for as long as I could stand to do nothing. Then I grabbed a towel and wiped off the worst of it, then rubbed some pure olive oil in as a salve.

Ernesto caught my eye and jerked his head to indicate I should look behind me. Guillermo had been waiting to tell me something, not wanting to interrupt. He whispered a message in my ear.

"Good. Have them wait outside for the moment." One more try. In English, I said, "Now tell me the password, so I won't have to marinate your balls in the stuff."

"You wouldn't!" Danny said. "I don't think you've got it in you."

"Maybe not, but these men are trained torturers," I lied, "and they don't give a damn about you. They'll do anything to you I tell them to."

"And you'll just stand there and watch me suffer? I don't think you can do that."

I sighed. "You're right, Danny. I'm just not the kind of guy who can stand to watch a friend suffer. Well, maybe I don't deserve to call you a friend, but you're a nice guy. In fact, I'm absolutely sure that you're not the kind of guy who can stand to watch a friend suffer either." In Spanish, I said, "Bring him in."

Pedro and another guy whose name escaped me came in, holding the arms of a struggling man. His shirt, with lieutenant's bars, had been ripped open, the buttons gone. He had a tattoo matching the one in the screen-saver. I'd have recognized him by his face without having to bare his chest, but apparently all us white guys all looked alike enough to the locals that they had to be sure. I wondered if they'd ripped open the shirt of every officer they'd captured until they found the right one.

"Bryce!" Danny yelled.

"Looks like your skin is safe for the moment, Danny," I said in English, and then in Spanish, "Bring him over here so the lieutenant here has a good view."

"No!" Danny moaned. "No, please! Don't hurt him!"

I pointed at his buddy, Bryce. "Strip him," I ordered and began taking off my belt.

CORPORAL PUNISHMENT
By Logan Zachary

My hair flew back, and my open shirt flapped in the breeze like a cape as my bike picked up speed going down the hill. I was flying.

That was until the police lights came on, and I hit the brakes slowly, so I wouldn't flip over the handle bars.

Was there a speed limit for a ten-speed?

I'd soon find out. I pulled over to the side of the road and waited.

The tall, slender blond policeman sat in his car and looked up at me over his sunglasses. "Mr. Minnesota, what trouble are you coming up with today?"

"I'm on my way home from work."

Doubt was easily seen on his face, as I read his nametag, "Benton".

"And how long will you be staying in Santa Fe?"

"I'm not sure." I wiped the sweat from my brow before it ran into my eyes.

"I'm watching you. Ever since the Lady Gaga party, you've been on my radar. I just thought I'd let you know that your ghost writing hasn't gone unnoticed either. Good day."

What did he mean by that?

But before he took off, he poked his head further out of the squad car window and asked, "So who do you write for?"

I forced a smile. "I can't tell you that, he'd sue my ass so fast I wouldn't know what hit me."

Officer Benton pushed his sunglasses back up and put his squad car into drive and took off, leaving me in the dust and exhaust.

What was that all about? Who knew I was helping someone write a book? What else did he know about me? I was on vacation and helping out a friend, so why all these questions and concerns about me?

I pushed the bike back onto the road and pumped my hairy bear legs and soon regained my speed. I was renting an adobe home and loved the small fenced courtyard and tiled floors. The high desert made for cool dry nights and relief from the summer's heat.

I opened the gate to my courtyard, brought my bike in, and set the kick stand. I saw a stain on the wall where a glass of punch was thrown the night of the Lady Gaga party. The neighbors never complained to me about the event, and they had all been invited. The gala ended by midnight, so it wasn't too late of a night on a weekend. There were several outlandish outfits, the opera people loved to dress up, but no one was rude or nude.

Maybe Officer Benton was upset he wasn't invited. I grabbed my laptop and headed out the French doors to work at my table and enjoy the afternoon sun.

Benton was very hot and smolderingly sexy. His pouty lips were so kissable, and I imagined them doing so much more. What did he look like under that uniform? Sculpted muscles, blond fur over his chest, legs and butt. My body started to respond as my heart rate increased, and I felt a stirring in my shorts. A man in uniform always did that to me.

I couldn't work outside on the patio with a raging hard-on. Maybe Officer Benton would come by and do a strip search …

I pushed that thought out of my mind. I had my writing to do and couldn't focus when I was horny. I flipped my laptop open and found the file I had been working on. I glanced over the computer and noticed the sun shining off a windshield across the street. Squinting, it was a police car with a blond man sitting on the hood.

"So you know where I live." I went back inside and poured myself a huge glass of ice tea and evil intentions made me pour a second one. I sat down and raised my glass to salute him.

He pretended not to see me with his mirrored sunglasses.

I raised the glass to my forehead and wiped the cold, condensation against my sweaty brow.

Nothing.

I took off my open shirt and tossed it on the opposite chair before I ran the glass over my sweaty, hairy chest. Suck on this.

He unbuttoned his uniform shirt and opened it to catch a breeze. He wore a bulletproof vest and a wife beater. He took off his shirt and vest. Raising his arm to block the sun, Benton showed a hairy armpit. The dark hair was matted to his skin, slicked down with sweat.

As I breathed in, I swore I could smell him: Manly sweat, Right Guard, and something primal. His wife beater clung to his torso as a second skin, showing shadows of what lay beneath.

He knew exactly what he was doing to me.

Bastard.

I spilled some ice tea out of my mouth and felt it wash over my hairy chest and absorb into my shorts. I combed my fingers across my chest as my nipples rose into sharp peaks. Pinching one, I let my head fall back and enjoy the sensory overload.

When I looked across the street, he was gone, car and all.

"Ha, round one to me."

I looked at my laptop, but my erection hurt in my shorts. I adjusted myself and started to read the file I had been working on yesterday.

Damn. I couldn't concentrate now. My cock demanded attention. I stroked it through the denim, but that wasn't enough. I needed to slip into my soft shorts that were made out of T-shirt material. They were loose and allowed for air exchange and easy access.

I opened the French door into my place and unzipped my shorts. I pulled them off and walked into my bedroom. I tossed the shorts onto the bed and opened my dresser. The gray shorts lay on top of the pile. I pulled off my underwear and walked nude into the bathroom to take a whiz.

A sharp rapping on the front door startled me, and I ran to look through the peep hole, the shorts still in my hand, raging hard-on leading the way. Officer Benton stood outside my door, shirtless.

"What can I do for you, Officer?" my voice croaked.

"Open the door, now."

"I can't, I'm …"

"I don't care what you're doing. Open it now." I saw the gun in his hand.

What could I do? I opened the door and stepped back, covering my erection with my shorts. "I was changing."

He stepped into the house and closed the door, gun still drawn. His eyes scanned me up one side and down the other. His gaze burned as it rolled over me. "What are you hiding there? A weapon?"

FUCK.

"I'm covering myself for modesty."

"How do I know that?" He waved his gun at me. "Hands up."

"Trust me, I'm naked." My butt cheeks clenched as my bare feet tried to curl into the tiled floor.

"Hands up and prove it."

"I … I'm having a problem down there."

His gun pointed at me, and I raised my arms, shorts held tightly in one fist.

He looked down at me and stared. Slowly, he stepped forward and reached down and cupped my heavy balls. He squeezed them and rolled his thumb over them.

My cock jumped and grew another inch. It waved back and forth, as he pulled down on my hairy sac.

"They grow them big in Minnesota. Maybe that's why they have all those lumberjacks." His middle finger slid down between my butt cheeks and touched my hole. He pressed into it.

I gasped as he did.

"Do you have anything concealed? Do you?"

"No," croaked out.

"Maybe I should search, do a body cavity exam ..." His hand came out from between my cheeks and trailed along my balls up to my cock. He grasped it and stroked it a few times.

I closed my eyes, embarrassed at my body's response and afraid I'd shoot into his hand.

His finger explored the opening at the fat mushroom head, and pre-cum poured out. He brought the finger to his mouth and tasted it. "Nice. Let's go check out your bedroom."

"I … What did I do?"

"Just take me to the bedroom." He grabbed my arm and aimed me in the right direction.

We entered the room, and he motioned to the bed. "Drop the shorts. Kneel on the bed and put your hands through the headboard." He reached behind his body, took out a pair of handcuffs and motioned to the bed.

I did as he said.

He slipped the cuffs through the headboard and secured my hands. He slapped my bare ass. "Spread your legs."

I did as he said. I felt his hands spread my cheeks, and then he slid a hand down my crack. He slipped off the bed and opened the dresser drawers. He pulled out a bottle of lube and condoms from the third drawer he opened. He set them on the top. He rifled through the rest of the drawers, spending extra time with my underwear and jocks.

"Nothing yet, but a body cavity search may show something more." He pulled out a rubber glove and snapped it into place. He poured the lube over two fingers and knelt on the bed. "Relax."

I felt one finger slip inside me, and he twisted it. He pulled out and stuck another one in. He pulled my cheeks apart and pushed in deep. I felt his tongue lick my tender opening, and my cock slapped against my belly.

He tried three fingers inside, but I was too tight.

I arched my back and tried to enjoy his invasion.

"Maybe if I added some light …" He removed his mag flashlight from his belt and lubed its handle. "Take a deep breath." He inserted the rough handle in and pushed it into me inch by inch.

It filled me up, and when I didn't think I could take it anymore, he pulled it out and pushed it back in. The rough nubs on the shaft tickled my pucker.

"Maybe if the light was inside I could see more." He pulled the mag out and turned it around. He shined the light on my ass and teased my hole with the mag's head.

"Where's my Billy club? I bet I left it in the car." He stepped off the bed, but instead of leaving, he unbuckled his belt and slowly unzipped his pants. He kicked his boots off and removed his pants. He folded them and set them carefully on the chair. "This may take a while."

I looked over my shoulder and saw a huge wet stain on his cotton briefs. He sported a gigantic cock inside. His furry chest was amazing, and his hair darkened as it went lower across his belly. It was thickest and darkest at his waistband.

He climbed onto the bed and knelt behind me. He reached over my back as his pelvis brushed between my cheeks. His cock was thick and stretched my crease. It felt bigger than the mag light.

He rubbed along my back and reached under my arms as he explored my chest. He pinched my nipples and stroked along my ribs. As he worked down my sides, he hit the ticklish places at my hips.

I reacted, and he drove his pelvis into my butt, holding me close.

"Hold still. Let me check you out. Isn't that what you want?"

I held still and didn't know what to say.

"What do you want?" he whispered in my ear. "Tell me what you want. Do you want me deep inside you? Do you want to be deep inside of me?"

He was so fine and hot, I wanted both.

"Maybe I should take off my underwear and see what happens." He humped my butt a few times and let go of my body. He pushed his briefs down.

I heard his penis slap his belly as it sprang free from his underwear.

He lifted one leg and pulled them off.

He spooned my ass, and his hot flesh made contact. "Maybe next time, you'll invite me to the party."

Was that what this was all about?

"You've been a bad boy, and I'll have to punish you." He pushed up and slapped my ass with his hard cock. "You like that. Don't you?"

It felt amazing.

"Bad, bad boy." He struck each cheek with his dick. "What else can I use? Maybe if I lay you across my lap..." His hand slapped my glut.

My cheek stung where he used his hand. He kept his hand in place and squeezed, digging his fingers deep into my muscle. His thumb rubbed over my opening, and he teased it a few times, pushing the tip in and out, as if he was going to enter me again.

He picked his hand up again and slapped the other cheek. It stung and burned for a few seconds. "Are you enjoying that?" He reached under me with his other hand and found my erection. He jacked my shaft a few times and milked the tip.

Pre-cum flowed out of me and made his hand slide easier.

He slapped my ass and then inserted a finger into my butt as he milked my dick. He drove his finger in and out. His finger hit my prostate and pushed more cream out of my gland

I felt him pull out of my ass and slapped me again. Another slap, and he entered me again. My butt burned and stung with each blow, but my cock felt great, pleasure and pain.

The smell of sweat and sex, man and lube filled the bedroom air. The salty scent of semen tickled my nose, and I knew more was coming.

"Flip over and lay on your back," he ordered. He checked the handcuffs and made sure I wasn't twisted.

125

As my back hit the mattress, he pulled on my legs and stretched me out. He climbed on top and straddled my body, slowly he moved higher and higher, until his ass was sitting on my cock. He rode my dick a few times and slid my shaft along his crease.

I closed my eyes and enjoyed the ride. I felt more pre-cum ooze out of my dick and coat his crack.

He fell into a rhythm, but before I could shoot, he stopped and moved up my body. His dick rolled over my lips, and I tried to pull him into my mouth.

He moved higher and sat on my face. His tight butt hole positioned over my mouth. I could taste my juices on his skin. I licked and explored, as he pressed down on my tongue. I worked into his opening, and he rode my tongue.

Officer Benton jacked his cock as he spread his ass cheeks for me to dive in deeper.

Drool and butt juices ran down my face, and I wished my hands were free to touch him, to jack him, to fuck him.

He was a man of power, authority, and he had me at his mercy shackled to the bed, but if he wanted a release, he was at my mercy. His uniform was off, he was just a man now, and he'd have to work very hard to get that.

Sensing a change in me, he slipped off my body and reached over the side of the bed. He picked up his Billy club and ran his hand up and down the wooden length. "I don't know how many guys I've used this on. Some to subdue, others to obtain information …" He slapped his open palm with it.

My body cringed, but my cock stood straight up and proud.

He lubed the length of my cock and outlined my erection with the slick stick.

My dick sought out the club's wood, and pre-cum flowed, showing how much it welcomed the attention.

Benton noticed my body's response. "I wonder if another spot would enjoy this as much." He traced down my shaft, over a hairy ball, and down along my crack. He slipped it underneath me, and then pulled it back out. He added more lube. Leaning down, he took careful aim on his target and shot for the bull's eye. He hit it. Dead center. The lubed rounded tip pushed into my hole and sought entry.

My ass was tight, and the pressure increased.

"Relax, it won't hurt … much," he laughed. He pulled it out and drove it back in. The wet end entered quickly and stretched me wide open.

My sphincter tightened down on it, but before the pain started, Benton grabbed my cock and stroked. The lube and pre-cum mixed sending a calm over my body. My head fell back, and my ass relaxed, sucking the Billy club deeper inside me.

He pushed in and pulled out a few inches, sending more pleasure through my butt.

I felt my balls rise as my cock's nerves tensed up, preparing to shoot a load. Pre-cum poured out of me.

"Not so fast," his hand grasped the base of my cock and held tight, the explosion stopped and rumbled in my balls. "I haven't gotten what I came for, so you're not going to come until I get my satisfaction."

The pleasure that flowed over and through my body flooded my brain, and I struggled to remember what he wanted. Did he want to know why I didn't invite him to the party?

"Who are you writing for?" he asked.

What?

He wanted to know whom I ghostwrote for? Why?

127

"So why are you in Santa Fe?" Officer Benton inserted the club in a few more inches and tapped my prostate. He twisted it inside me.

My legs shot straight up as my whole body tensed. "Don't talk, just fuck me."

He stopped and slowly removed the Billy club from deep inside me. It exited with a pop. He set it down on the bed, before he grabbed his cock and stroked it a few times. Milking out a few drops of pre-cum, he moved further in between my legs. "Do you want this inside you?" He pushed his cock to my hole.

I closed my eyes and held my breath.

"Tell me what I want, and I'll fuck the living daylights out of you."

"What do you want?" I panted as I asked.

"Who are you writing for?" He twisted and pushed the Billy club deeper into me.

"Why do you want to know that?"

His eyes gleamed. "You don't need to know." A red flush rose in his face.

Did someone have something on him? Was he being blackmailed? An image from the paper flashed through my mind. I read the headline, "Local cop under suspicion."

"It's not about you if that's what you're worried about."

His cock slammed into me before I finished speaking. Benton grabbed my dick as he plunged into me.

It didn't take long for my balls to explode. He had been edging me for so long. Cum shot out of my dick and sprayed my hairy belly. As the warm goo flowed through his fingers, I felt his hips buck into me and stay imbedded. His fat dick pressed on my prostate and sent wave after wave of orgasm out of me. He pulled out and in slightly as another load erupted, filling my belly button.

Benton pulled out of me and rolled onto my bed, the sensation too much for him.

We lay side by side as our bodies returned to normal. Benton stood up and looked around the room.

I pointed to the bathroom.

He came back with a hand towel and wiped my belly dry. Setting it on the bed, he finally spoke to me. "So you're not writing a book about me?"

"No."

Officer Benton reached over my head and unlocked the handcuffs that still held my wrists.

I rubbed the circulation back into my hands and sat up at the edge of the bed. "I'm finishing up someone else's novel, and it's not your story."

Benton wiped the sweat from his brow and settled next to me on the bed. He smiled as he leaned over to kiss me.

The cold metal circled my wrist and snapped shut, again. Before I knew what hit me, my arms were pulled up over my head and secured to the headboard. "What are you doing? I told you I wasn't writing your story."

He checked the handcuffs and climbed on top of me, straddling my waist.

My cock nestled between his hairy butt cheeks and started to swell. I pulled on the restraints, but they wouldn't budge.

"I know, but now I want you to write it for me."

"What?" I said.

"And I'm not letting you get up until you agree to it."

My cock slipped into him inch by inch, and I knew it would be a very long time before I'd say yes.

COME WITH US
By Landon Dixon

Dixon's fiction has been published in many, many magazines and anthologies, including Men, Freshmen, Straight? Volume 2, Friction 7, *and* Best Gay Erotica 2009.

Colonel K slammed his riding crop down on his desk, muttered, "Blast it all! I must get more recruits for the front! Where have all the young men gone?"

Master Tom pulled the Colonel's cock out of his mouth with a wet pop, gasped, "That's what I'd like to know." He grinned cheerfully up at the grey-haired military man, from between the Colonel's legs, beneath the Colonel's desk.

Colonel K grunted, placed a large, authoritative hand on his secretary's blond head and redirected the lad's attention back to his ramrod straight cock. "You've got a dirty mouth, Tom," he mused. "That's what I like about you."

The simple country boy began eagerly sucking on the Colonel's cock again. He gripped the man's muscled thighs through the black worsted uniform pants and boisterously bobbed his head. Colonel K absently pumped his riding crop through the circled forefinger and thumb of his opposite hand, unconsciously imitating his secretary, urging the lad on to even more vigorous efforts.

The tall, bluff career Army officer had more on his mind than Master Tom's youthful mouth and figure, however. His command was homeland G sector, his responsibility as Provost Marshal to round up – by recruitment, if possible; conscription, if necessary – young, able-bodied men between the ages of eighteen and thirty-four for the war effort. Both his specific task and the overall war effort in general were not going well.

The Colonel knew there were still plenty of men in the rural valleys and woods and villages that made up his sector who weren't in uniform. If only he could find them. Otherwise, he might find himself in a trench by Christmas.

He suddenly bucked, like back in his cavalry days, as Master Tom took an extraordinarily deep pull on his pulsating cock, the lad's deft fingers fondling his tightened balls. Colonel K looked down again, anxious for the return of the staff officer he'd sent out to assess the missing men situation (and who, himself, had been missing for over a week); anxious now, as well, to come. He gripped Tom's head with both of his hands and pumped his hips in his fine leather chair, fucking the young man's pleasing face, as the lad sucked.

"Oh, no you don't, Colonel!" Master Tom yelped, abruptly jerking his head back, banging it on the oaken underside of the Colonel's expansive desk. "You're not spouting off in my mouth," he reproached the soldier.

The Colonel grimaced. "No one wants to swallow my orders anymore."

He shoved his chair back and got to his feet, helped Master Tom up. Colonel K briefly fondled the young man's sallow chest, pulling the lad's embroidered peasant blouse open and taking a quick pull on each exposed, puffy, cherry-red nipple in turn. Then he cleared a space for his secretary up on his desk, brushing aside the maps and population charts he'd been studying.

He held Master Tom's hand, and hip, assisting him onto the desk, onto his back. The lad pushed his felt pants down to his ankles, revealing the very erect tan penis, which sprouted up straight and smooth and true out of its nest of blond pubes.

Colonel K tugged Master Tom's pants right off the lad's slim, shapely legs, tossed them aside. Then the Colonel greased his own shining prick with some lubricant he kept conveniently on hand in his desk. He thrust his now gleaming sword in between Master Tom's taut cheeks, probing for an opening with the meaty tip.

"Oh, Colonel K!" the boy moaned.

As the Colonel plugged ripe, young pucker, plunged through, driving his steel-hard length deep inside Tom's superheated pink sleeve. They both groaned, sounding sexual union.

Master Tom hooked his slender ankles onto Colonel K's broad shoulders. The Colonel gripped the lad's prick, one of his thighs, shunting cock back and forth in Master Tom's anus. The desk creaked, flesh slapped briskly against flesh, Master Tom cooed, Colonel K puffed; another man clad in a ragged uniform stumbled inside the office.

"Captain Yannsen!" Colonel K ejaculated.

"Oh, Captain Yannsen!" Master Tom cried.

The disheveled officer staggered up to the desk, gasping for breath. His spectacles were knocked cockeyed on his long freckled nose, his cheeks, normally red as his flaming hair, were a ghastly white, drained of all color. "I've found the missing men, Colonel ..."

"One moment," Colonel K stopped him, holding up a hand lifted off Master Tom's slender, trembling thigh. "One thing at a time." Many battles, military and bureaucratic, had left the commander unflappable.

He returned his attention to his secretary, his hand, fucking the lad faster now. He banged into the blond with parade ground precision, pulling on the young man's penis at the same torrid pace. Master Tom plucked at his swollen nipples, rolled them, writhing around on the desk on the end of the Colonel's pistoning cock, own prick manhandled unmercifully.

Master Tom shrieked, Colonel K grunted. The lad shuddered, the Colonel jerked, the pair coming in fiery bursts of ecstasy; Colonel K spouting off into Tom's anus, jacking jets out of the lad's cock.

As Captain Yannsen straightened his glasses and pulled his tunic together, regaining some level of military composure.

"I'll hear your report now," the Colonel stated brusquely, pulling his cock out of his secretary's ass and stowing it back in his pants, buttoning. "That'll be all, Master Tom."

Tom demurely slid off the desk and put on his blouse and pants. He smiled at Captain Yannsen.

"I found almost a hundred military-age men stretched out flat on their backs underground – in the caverns along the west bank of the Josporus River, twenty kilometers south of Woormas," the Captain reported.

Colonel K gripped the slickened edge of his desk. "What!? Dead!?"

"No. Half-dead. Too weak to flee or fight, all but drained of their spirit. I know. I was one of them for a time!"

Colonel K's iron-grey eyes widened. "Who's holding these men captive? The enemy?"

Captain Yannsen smiled wanly. "Of a kind, yes sir. An enemy of life. But not our current military enemy." The man suddenly swayed, swooned, collapsing down into the chair Master Tom rushed to his backside.

"Water! Water, Master Tom!" Colonel K ordered.

He took a great gulp out of the glass his secretary handed him, then passed it on over to Captain Yannsen. "You're tired," he observed, some measure of concern in his rugged voice. "But I must have your report – quickly. So we can act. A hundred men could mean the difference between victory and defeat at the front."

Captain Yannsen drained the glass of water, gave it back to Master Tom. The lad's warm, caressing, brown hand on the officer's shoulder seemed to do him just as much good as the cool liquid. "My report," he spoke.

"I was on the road out of Woormas, feeling dissatisfaction at finding not a single service-eligible man in the village. Only worried, frustrated, tight-lipped women. It was midday, warm and sunny. When a man suddenly emerged from out of the woods alongside the road.

"He was one of the strangest creatures I've ever seen: short, well-fed, with a stocky torso and sturdy arms and legs, thick wide knees. His long blond hair was almost white, large pale eyes almost milky, and his creamy skin seemed just about translucent. He was wearing a simple white robe, see-through, and as he walked up to me on the road, I became hypnotized by his unblinking opaque eyes, mesmerized by the cloying scent he exuded, the utter lush redness and juiciness of his lips and mouth.

"He said nothing. Simply looked me in the eye, then the crotch. I followed his gaze, and was astonished to see that my cock was strikingly erect in my trousers, aroused so quickly and blatantly I hadn't even realized it. The man dropped to his knees in the middle of the road, at my penis, relieved some of the pressure and added much more, by taking it out of my pants and into his mouth.

"The glide of his overfull lips down my shaft was divine; his velvety mouth pure wet heated heaven engulfing my cock; his sliding tongue a silkily sublime instrument of otherworldly pleasure. Or so I thought at the time. Only later, did I come to know that that mouth and those lips and that tongue had more fallen angel than exalted angel about them.

"But, right then, I reveled in the man's wondrous cocksucking. He consumed me full throbbing length, sucked back up, stroked forward again, blowing me soft and supple and sensuous as the hot, humid summer breeze blows the trembling leaves on their hard wooden branches."

Colonel K and Master Tom exchanged glances.

"I'd never experienced a finer fellatio," Captain Yannsen went on, a strange shining light in his myopic blue eyes. "I just stood there in the open road, under the burning sun, looking down at the ethereal man, feeling his eternally erotic suck and lick and tug all through my exposed, wildly pulsing body and soul.

"Then I climaxed, suddenly, overwhelmingly, uncontrollably. Flooding the man's mouth. And he swallowed! Drank in my heated jack with a willing, voracious appetite, his milky eyes gleaming up at me, throat working with fearsome intensity. That was when I truly realized that this was no ordinary country-kin being – for they may suck, but nay do they swallow."

Colonel K raised his eyebrows at Master Tom. The lad petulantly crossed his arms on his chest.

"My suspicions, and fears, were confirmed. When he led me deep into the woods, down to the Josporus River, then below-ground, into the caverns. That's where I saw the other men – scores of them – lying on the ground, naked. Tending to them, turning them erect at the groin and then sucking and swallowing, were a dozen or so men just like the one who had led me astray.

"It was all so weird, so eerie, down in those dimly-lit caverns. The laid-out men, the other men servicing them. Just the sound of rapacious slurping, the weak grunts of climax, the eager gulping and gulping and gulping!"

Captain Yannsen sprang to his feet and grabbed onto the desk. "They were feeding on their bodily fluids, don't you see! Those men were being sucked of their very lives!"

He dropped back down into the chair, exhausted. "I was laid out and tended to like the others, hour after hour initially, then more sporadically, as I became more drained. I was held fast at first by the irresistible eroticism of the otherworldly men, by what they were willingly doing to my over-receptive cock. And then, when it was too late, I was too weak even to get up – except for it now and then."

Captain Yannsen buried his face in his hands, shuddering at the memory.

136

Colonel K and Master Tom stared at one another, their own faces drained of color by the disturbing report.

"Who-what are they, Colonel?" Master Tom breathed at last. "These cum-sucking sluts!?"

Colonel K sat down in his chair and folded his fingers together. "I don't know," he admitted. "We've all heard the legends of vampires roaming the countryside – but vampeters ... I've never heard tell before. Craving protein instead of plasma? The life-blood of young men who should be dutifully serving their country at the ..."

He suddenly sprang to his feet and wheeled around his desk, fastened his capable hands onto Captain Yannsen's slumped shoulders and violently shook the man. "You escaped their ball-draining clutches! How did you get away!?"

The Captain looked up into his superior's glaring eyes, taking strength from the other man's rough treatment. "My ... friend Karl rescued me. He's a eunuch, so he wasn't caught in the vampeters' velvet-lined trap. He beat the bushes looking for me when I failed to appear at a scheduled rendezvous with him, found me and dragged me out of there."

Colonel K stood upright, cupped his granite chin, scratched it. "Hmmm ... that provides me with a strategy – for getting those men back and up to the front where they belong. A-tten-tion!"

# # # # #

Captain Yannsen and his friend Karl guided the squad to the spot along the riverbank where a narrow path led through the thick brush to the underground caverns. Colonel K was at the head of the group of twenty-five soldiers, all of whom were outfitted with gasmasks the glass of which was deliberately distorted to prevent clear vision, and with steel chastity belts, which were firmly secured about all of their loins (the Colonel holding the only key). Thus, the squad was protected from the seductively intoxicating sight and scent and will-breaking suction of the vampeters.

"I want an orderly evacuation," Colonel K intoned, his voice as distorted as his eyesight by the gasmask. "First, we'll secure our men. Then the other 'men'."

Upon his order, the squad charged down into the caverns. As Captain Yannsen beat a hasty retreat back through the woods to the road.

On the road, was lined up a column of motorized troop carriers. Under the blackout canvas stretched over the rear of the last truck in line, was a steel cage, capable of holding a dozen or so prisoners. The soldiers manning the vehicles all wore gasmasks and chastity belts similar to the Colonel's assault force.

The vampeters rushed at the invaders, as they stormed into the caverns. There were twelve cum-swallowers, all told, a dangerous dirty dozen all alike in milky-white appearance. They fell at the booted feet of the squad, attempting to draw cocks out of trousers and throatily suck.

But their salacious counterattack was met with steely indifference. Cocks stayed locked, soldiers stayed focused.

The attack was repelled. The vampeters staggered to their feet with creamy expressions of terror. They fought hard against their capture, however, their strength almost equal to that of the oversized men under the Colonel's command. But sheer numbers, and Colonel K's indomitable spirit, soon turned the battle. He clapped irons onto the wrists of the vampeters, as his soldiers held them tight.

Ninety-eight men were taken barely alive and bodily-fluid-drained out of the caverns. To be rehydrated and rested. Then shipped to the front.

# # # # #

Master Tom glanced up from the Colonel's erection. "But what will you do with those – those vampeters?" he spat out, onto Colonel K's cock.

The Colonel shuddered, as his secretary resumed sucking. He stroked his riding crop contemplatively. "They will have to be destroyed," he said at last with a sigh. "Our scientists are working on a special 'rod' which ejaculates a toxic chemical when sufficiently heated and wetted and pulled upon. It's a shame they ..."

"They should be the ones sent to the front," Master Tom pouted, teasing a drop of pre-cum out of the Colonel's slit and slurping it up and swallowing it down.

Colonel K looked down at the lad squatting beneath his desk. Then he bolted even more erect, to his feet. "A capital idea!" he roared. "We'll send the vampeters to the front as part of a prisoner exchange with the enemy – twelve of our captured men for twelve of their captured men. They'll wreak havoc in the enemy trenches!" He stood tall, both vertical and horizontal.

Master Tom gripped the soldier's stiffly saluting cock with delight.

"The war will be over by Christmas," Colonel K pronounced.

COLD WAR HOT
By Landon Dixon

The bar was called Tally whackers, a notorious dive in the east end of London. Little more than a door off an alley, a dingy room scattered with tables and chairs inside, a bar that ran the length of one wall.

Jericho turned up the collar of his trench coat against the chill October rain and glanced down the darkened alley, along the misty lit sidewalk. The hour was midnight, the greasy street and sidewalk almost deserted. But there'd be action in Tally whackers, the man well-knew, especially in the thirst-slaking washroom and glory holes in back.

He took a last pull on his cigarette, then arced it down to the wet pavement, killed it with his foot. A couple of girls tap-danced by on their high heels, sodden newspaper held up over their heads, skinny white legs flashing beneath thigh-high miniskirts. Jericho touched the brim of his hat at them, and they giggled. He smiled coldly at the two mods chasing after them. Then he walked on down the alley.

A gale of high-pitched laughter and a gust of smoke-filled air greeted him as he pushed through the door. A quick count revealed twenty-three men having just a gay old time, how many more in the washroom, having an even gayer time, anyone's guess. Homosexuality was still technically illegal in Britain, but in the swinging '60s, the laws, like the times, were relaxing.

"Triple vodka," Jericho told the bartender, a big brute with a hard face and soft belly.

A man at the end of the bar raised his head, glanced Jericho's way.

The bartender slammed the glass down in front of Jericho. He lifted it, took a sip, grimaced.

Signals complete, the man at the end of the bar slid off his stool and approached Jericho, stood alongside him. "You don't like vodka?"

"Do you?"

"Not anymore."

"Jericho."

"Volga."

Passwords and code names exchanged, Jericho jerked his head to the left, at the hallway that led back to the washroom. Volga nodded, set down his empty tumbler of vodka and walked casually toward the hallway. A small, slim man, with shiny black hair and a shiny, pale, high cheek boned face, slitted blue eyes, a noticeable lisp to his speech along with the East European accent, a noticeable swish to his walk.

Jericho downed the rest of his drink in one gulp, shuddered. A big man, raw-boned, with a ruddy, handsome face and curly red hair, dimpled chin, grey eyes, a Cockney way of speaking and a cocky way of moving. He followed Volga down the dark hallway, through the swinging door labeled Gents.

Just another pick-up at Tally whackers, nothing unusual, happened a hundred times or more a night.

The washroom door was heavily padded, blocking out the noise coming from within. That noise wasn't chatter and laughter, the banging of glasses and sloshing of liquor; it was grunting and groaning, heavy breathing, the sharp smack of flesh against flesh, the slurping of tongues and sucking of mouths, the harsh cry of ecstasy. The sounds and smells of man-sex washed over Volga and Jericho, as they stood in the entrance to the brightly-lit, black and white-tiled room.

"Close the door, man." A huge black guy sitting on a stool, towels and condoms and lube stacked up at his elbow. He had the dirtiest job in the whole dirty joint – cleaning up, keeping order in sexual chaos. His grin ran as wide as his face.

There were six sinks along the near wall, three urinals further down, twelve stalls along the far wall. The doors were closed and locked on all but two of the stalls.

The two men walked down the line. Jericho pushed open the door of one of the unlocked stalls, revealing a young man sitting on the toilet. His pants were down around his ankles, hard cock straining up in his hand. He grinned nervously at the big man in the trench coat, stroking his clean-cut young cock in a come-hither manner.

Jericho turned away, bumping into Volga.

The second last stall from the end of the line was empty. The men went inside. Jericho shut the door, shot the bolt home. The sounds of frenzied sex all around swallowed up their voices.

"You're a translator at the Soviet embassy?"

Volga nodded, licking his lush red lips, rubbing the palms of his hands on his brand-new jeans. He wore a cheap leather jacket and high-heeled shoes, a white T-shirt. "You-you are with British intelligence, ya?"

"Yeah." Jericho thumbed back his hat, sending water trickling down to the floor. "You want to sell some information?"

Volga bobbed his head again, eagerly. "I see much sensitive information. I work for you, ya – for a price?" He grinned lasciviously.

Jericho grunted, took off his hat and trench coat. He hung them up on the hook on the stall door, then stripped off his sports jacket, striped tie, white shirt, dark shoes and pants. Until his powerful body gleamed naked under the bright lights, broad chest wispy with ginger hair, like his huge balls, cock hanging long and thick, semi-erect.

Volga watched, his slitted eyes gone wide, tongue sticking out from between his lips. Then he gulped, clapped his hands together, and dropped down to his knees. He grasped Jericho's cock and hefted the heavy slab, breathing hot and damp all over it. He shifted his sweaty palm up and down the already enormous, expanding length.

Long muscles tightened all over Jericho's body, mounded butt cheeks clenching in back. What Volga lacked in technique, he made up for in enthusiasm. Jericho's cock stretched out to its full bloated eight inches in the other man's pumping hand, shaft thick with engorged veins, hood mushroomed meaty. Volga stuck out his tongue and slapped Jericho's slit, making the big man grunt.

Emboldened, excited, Volga clasped Jericho's cock at the wide furry base with his left hand, grasped the man's heavy balls with his right, wicked his tongue around and around Jericho's knob, making the purple hood glisten. A man yelled down the line, repeatedly, in rhythm to his hot, salty discharges, no doubt. Volga slid his lips over Jericho's cap and sucked on the man's cockhead.

Jericho leaned back against the green metal stall wall, feeling the wet, hot, urgent tug of the other man, all through his groin. He slid his big hands up onto his muscle-humped chest, pinched protruding pink nipples with long fingers, rolled, pulled on the tingling jutters. As Volga sailed his one hand up and down the shaft, juggling balls with the other, pulling on Jericho's hood with his lips.

The big man thrust his hips out, spearing his cock into Volga's mouth. The kneeling man gasped, drooled saliva, staring up at Jericho, urging him to fuck face. Jericho pumped, gliding his cock in and out of Volga's sucking mouth, five inches deep, four inches back, shaft oiling between squeezing lips.

Until something suddenly pushed up against Jericho's buttocks from behind, and the redhead thumped his cock almost right down Volga's throat. Volga rocked back on his heels, gagging. Jericho turned and looked down. A long, hard cock protruded from the padded glory hole in the stall wall Jericho had been leaning against, obscene as a long, pink, shining tongue. Another dong knifed through the hole in the opposite wall, blading against the back of Volga's head.

Jericho helped the man to his feet, helped him strip, lube the cocks that had barged in on their blowjob, lube each other's assholes. Then the two men leaned forward facing one another, reached back and gripped the slickened hard-on's in behind them. Jericho and Volga kissed, twirled their tongues together, pulling the caps of the two cocks in between their cheeks and up against their puckers. The two men on the other sides of the walls groaned in unison.

Jericho pushed back with his rear-end, the glory hole cockhead popping into his manhole, followed by inches and inches of shaft. Until Jericho's big buttocks splatted against the green metal, strange cock embedded in his chute. Volga followed the other's lead, closing his eyes and moaning, taking cock up his ass right to the balls crowding the glory hole.

The two men gripped each other's shoulders and rocked back and forth, impaling themselves on the thrusting poles. Volga whimpered, shaking, getting reamed up the ass. Then he cried out into Jericho's face, when Jericho grasped his flapping cock and stroked in rhythm to the fucking both men were taking.

Volga grabbed onto Jericho's bobbing meat, frantically tugged, the two men bouncing on dong. The men behind the walls grunted and moaned, thumped against the metal harder and faster, fucking Volga and Jericho's hot sucking anuses as best they could.

"He's coming … inside me!" Volga shouted. Then jerked, jumped, his cock surging in Jericho's pumping hand, shooting.

Jericho heard the man in behind him swear, shriek, felt the man's cock spasm in his chute, spout hot seed against his bowels. And the big man let loose, letting Volga jack jets of superheated semen out of his seized-up cock.

# # # # #

The second meeting took place in a Soho massage parlor; Jericho the handler, Volga his spy to run.

They had a small room filled with a brown-padded table all to themselves. Volga handed a sheet of paper to Jericho, a coded communiqué from the Kremlin to the Soviet embassy in London. Volga had provided translation.

Jericho read, said, "The Russians are planning to attack Britain, have made a secret pact with the French and German not to intervene?"

Volga gravely nodded. "I'm sorry, but it is true." He began stripping off his clothes.

"What about the Americans?"

"That I do not know – yet." Naked, cock jutting up hard from his shaven loins, he handed Jericho a warm smile and a full bottle of baby oil.

The big man grunted, burned the piece of paper with his lighter, ground the charred remains and his cigarette out with his heel. Then he took off his clothes. Volga jumped up onto the table and lay back, on his back. Jericho poured baby oil on the reclining man's chest, rubbed it in with his strong, capable hands.

Volga groaned, his eyelashes fluttering, erection twitching up into the air. Jericho squeezed the man's thin, pale pecs upwards with his greasy hands, let his fingers slide onto the rigid pink nipples. Volga gasped, Jericho pulling his nipples up from his pecs until it looked, and felt, like they would be pulled right off. Then they popped out from between Jericho's fingers, sprang back down onto Volga's puffed-up chest.

Jericho rubbed lower, smoothing his hands all over Volga's stomach. He curved his hands around the hard-breathing man's groin, squeezing the balls, forcing the cock to leap higher up into the air, straining, stretching. Then he lowered his head and opened his mouth and consumed Volga's erection in one breathtaking gulp.

Volga jerked ram-rod straight, his cock gone, encased in Jericho's mouth and throat, squeezed agonizingly tight and moist and hot, pulsing with sensation in the super-erotic chamber of the other man's maw. He tried to pump his hips, but Jericho pressed down, forcing him flat. Then, after keeping Volga locked up for an anguished half minute or so, Jericho bobbed his head, sucking on the man's cock.

Jericho vacced with pneumatic precision and power, down to the balls and back up to the hood, over and over and over. Volga pounded the padded table with his little fists, craning his neck to see the big man's mouth pull on his beating cock. Then he flung his hands onto his oil-warm chest and desperately tugged on his nipples. His buttocks trembled violently beneath him, setting the entire massage table to shaking.

"Please! Please, you fuck me!" Volga cried, the wicked pressure on his cock driving him wild.

Jericho took one last long, hard suck and then let the rigid dong drop out of his mouth. Volga instantly flipped over on the table, sprang up onto all-fours. He waved his taut little bottom at the big British intelligence man like a white flag, anxious to surrender it.

Jericho climbed aboard, squatted in behind Volga's behind. The table groaned, then Volga, as Jericho pressed his baby oil-slick cockhead into the man's starfish, popped ass ring, plunged shaft into chute, pounded it home. The table creaked and Volga whimpered, Jericho sawing his huge dong back and forth in the other man's anus.

"Ya! Ya! Fuck me like Mother Russia fucking your country!" Volga squealed, gripping the edges of the rattling table with whitened knuckles, taking it hard and deep up the ass and loving it.

Jericho gritted his teeth and dug his fingernails into Volga's narrow waist, hammering his cock into the man's tight, heated chute. He did it with a ruthless, relentless efficiency, only the flush on his face, the gleam in his eyes, revealing the pleasure he was taking in driving another man's ass.

The brisk smack of corded thighs against rippling butt flesh filled the stuffy room, along with the sharp, short intake and exhaust of breath. Volga tore a hand off the table and grabbed onto his jumping cock, pumped it. Jericho upped the tempo to frenzy level, ferociously axing the man's anus, blood thundering in his veins and surging in his ass-cleaving cock.

"Oooooh … ya!" Volga screamed. His body spasmed and his cock spurted. He jacked line after thickened white line of cum out of his dick and onto the table, vibrating out of control on the end of Jericho's pile-driving prick.

The big man grunted, shuddered. His balls erupted and his cock exploded in the other man's gripping tunnel. He sprayed Volga's chute with scorching sperm, churning, coming.

# # # # #

Jericho watched through the drizzle as Volga and Marcel – a suave, moustachioed French intelligence officer operating in London – slipped inside the Cavalier Hotel, a well-known fuckpad for sexually repressed married men.

Then, two nights later, as he stood just outside the yellow halo of light shed by a streetlamp, in the rain, he witnessed Klaus, a stocky, shaven-head West German agent, welcome Volga into the backseat of a Mercedes. The tinted windows of the luxury sedan revealed nothing, but the rocking of the car on its springs revealed all.

"Hallo," Jericho greeted Klaus later that night. After the man had parked the Mercedes outside an apartment block just off embassy row.

The German felt something hard and round press into the small of his back, and he froze on the spot.

"What'd our man from Russia with love have to tell you?"

Klaus slowly turned around, smiled when he saw Jericho's erection jutting out from his fly. "He says the Soviets have decided to launch a first strike against Germany, have signed secret pacts with Britain and France not to interfere. Sound familiar, perhaps?"

Jericho grunted. Did so again, with more passion, when Klaus wrapped thick fingers and soft palm around the loaded barrel of his rod. "Maybe we should get together with Marcel – put our three heads together on this one?"

Klaus nodded, squeezing. "And our amorous Soviet spy?"

"He'll be peddling his yarns to the Americans next, would be my guess, along with his ass."

"To Dempsey? That awful, hulking, gay-bashing foreign agent?"

Jericho nodded. Then grinned, as Klaus led him by the hard-on into the Mercedes.

THE LAST MARINE
By Rob Rosen

Rob Rosen (www.therobrosen.com), author of several novels and has had short stories featured in more than 150 anthologies.

I stared out at the ocean from the cliff overlooking the dock. Perfect spot to zone out and enjoy the summer breeze, to inhale all that fresh air, get a bit of sun on your face. Which is just what I was doing when I spotted it: a ship, big and gray on the horizon. Military, had to be. I looked from it to the parking lot down below, which was all of a sudden filling up, cars streaming in, even a bus soon enough, the band piling out, banners waving.

I knew what this meant, of course: a troop was returning home. Happened more and more lately. Though I'd never actually seen it happen, except on TV. My eyes scanned the parking lot, at the people emerging from their cars, posters in hand, flags, cameras, babies in their mother's arms. It was an impossible event to pass up.

And so, I didn't.

I hopped back into my car and sped down to the parking lot below, finding one of the few spots that remained before I joined the massive group that had gathered down the length of the dock. Hundreds of people, families, loved ones, neighbors and friends, news crews. Everyone smiling big and wide, their welcome home signs raised high, flags even higher, fluttering in the ocean breeze. It was a sight to see. Made your heart go pitter-patter.

And then the ship was drawing near, the length of her now visible, every spare inch with a marine standing tall at attention, identical uniforms running from stem to stern. And with that, the cheers went up on all sides of me, sending Goosebumps up and down my arms, the contagious smile now plastered onto my face.

The cheering reached its ear-shattering crescendo as the ship docked, horn loudly blowing her welcome as the plank got attached. In mere minutes, marines came charging down, running at full gallop, their packs and bags flung over their shoulders, hooting and hollering as they made their way toward us, to the families waiting with open arms, faces already streaked with tears, present company included.

I stood there, apart from the rushing throng, watching as one by one they were all reunited, all with hearty handshakes and eager kisses, with arms wrapped tightly around necks and waists, with smiles so bright as to put the sun above to shame. I watched it all, taking it all in, feeling the joy emanate from one group to the next. It was tangible, really, breathtaking.

And then they started to disperse, to head to their cars, which quickly began to leave the parking lot, taking them back to the lives they once new. I, too, headed for my car, the glorious scene at last coming to an end.

But that's when I spotted him.

Everyone had matched up already, in pairs, in small groups, in large ones. Everyone except him. He merely stood in the center of it all, his massive duffel at his side, smiling as he watched the happy reunions. And I, in turn, watched him, waiting for his. Only, judging by the lack of new car arrivals, his didn't seem to be happening any time soon.

Thirty minutes after I'd arrived, it was just me off to the side and him still standing there. By then, his smile had vanished, and the sun was clearly having its effect on him, sweat pouring down his handsome face, pit stains forming beneath his underarms. I started to leave, but then thought the better of it, choosing instead to make my way toward him.

"Um, hi," I said, from a few feet away. "Do you ... do you need a ride somewhere?"

He squinted and flashed me a grin. "Not sure," he replied, closing the gap between us.

Up close, guy was dazzling, too. Clean-shaven, square jaw, eyes so blue you wanted to dive the hell on in, tall and broad and movie-star handsome. Meaning, my stomach gurgled and my crotch pulsed at just about the same instant. "Not sure?" I echoed. "So your lift still might show up?"

He nodded. "Friend of a friend. Made the plans last week. Haven't heard from either of them since. Guess I was hoping for the best."

I stared around at the nearly empty parking lot, then back to him. "How about second best?" I reached out my hand. "Geoff."

He did the same, palms sweaty, grip like a vise. "Matt," he said. "And I think I might take you up on the offer. Too hot out here to wait. Too much like Iraq."

I gulped upon hearing him say it. See, I'd never met anyone who had served there before. "That, uh, that where you came from?"

He nodded and shrugged. "Two tours of duty. Fucking hellhole."

Then I nodded. "Well, welcome home then. And I, I, uh, really would like to give you a lift."

His smile gleefully returned, those butterflies in my belly, too. "Your car got air-conditioning?"

My smile echoed his. "Cold as an ice chest in less than a minute flat."

He grabbed his duffel and winked. "Then lead on, Geoff."

And so that I did, both of us soon hopping in before I started the engine and cranked the air on high. He sighed when the cool blast hit his face. "Better?" I asked, pulling out of the parking lot.

"Much," he fairly moaned, which made my crotch go boing.

"Good," I said, with a chuckle. "Now where are we headed?"

"Motel 6," he told me. "Or someplace cheaper."

I couldn't help but laugh. "Cheaper than a Motel 6? What, like a park bench? Doesn't the military give you money to get home?"

"Some," he replied. "But I need to save up until I can get a job, get settled." He turned to look at me, and me to him, his gaze locking in on mine, causing me to suddenly swerve the car. He chuckled, his hand quickly on the steering wheel, three of his fingers covering two of mine, sending a white-hot flash up my spine. "If I make it there alive first, I mean."

A flush of red spread across my cheeks. I paused, weighing my options, but decided to go for broke. "Um, I have a pool house you can crash at. And free is definitely cheaper than a Motel 6."

He paused and I figured that I wasn't the only one weighing their options. "But you don't even know me."

I shrugged and lowered the air some, before icicles started forming on the car's ceiling. "You're a marine; how much more trustworthy can you get?" Again I turned his way, his profile just as stunning as the head-on shot. "Besides, place is rarely occupied by anyone other than family, and it does have a private bathroom. Might as well put it all to good use."

"And a pool house means a pool, right?"

I grinned and nodded. "And a wet bar."

He slapped the dashboard. "Sold!"

Twenty minutes later, we were pulling up in my driveway, and I, suffice it say, was suddenly nervous as all hell. I mean, I had just invited a perfect stranger, emphasis on the perfect, to stay with me. And a marine, no less. One that could snap my neck and down a bottle of beer at the same time, without even blinking.

Still, it was too late to renege. In other words, we were in the pool house all too soon. He dropped his duffel and looked around. Then he turned and smiled, flashing me a perfect set of pearly whites. "I, uh ... thanks," he said. "This is awesome."

I smiled in return. "Make yourself at home, Matt."

He laughed, rubbing his hands together. "That mean that pool of yours, too?"

My heart skipped a beat. "I'll, uh, I'll go get you some trunks." And with that, I quickly turned to leave. Suddenly, being alone in that small room with him was just too much to bear. Me and my prick both.

And speaking of bare, the other spelling, that's just what he was when I returned, already in the pool, floating on his back, eyes shut tight, cock rising and falling in and out of the water's surface. He popped open his stunning blue peepers when he realized I was standing there. "Sorry, couldn't wait. Been years now since I went for a swim." He went vertical, treading water. "Hop in; water's perfect."

Sweat was now pouring from my brow, and not because of the broiling overhead sun. "Um, sure. I'll just go get a bathing suit."

He laughed and pointed to my hand. "You're already holding one, dude." He swung his arm up and sent a crashing wave of water my way. "Or just hop in. Trust me, I've seen my fair share of naked dudes before."

Me, too, I thought, but none that looked anything remotely like you. Still, I did as he asked, kicking off my sandals before sliding out of my shorts and boxers and whipping off my T-shirt. Then I dove in fast, just in case my midsection suddenly decided to salute him. I popped up a foot away, both our heads bobbing above the water.

"Perfect," I said, only slightly meaning the pool.

"Amen," he agreed. "First time I've relaxed in months." His smile returned, eyes sparkling like the water beneath us. "Thanks again, dude."

"My pleasure," I said. Gross understatement. And then I noticed his shoulder, the scar that ran circles around it, marring his otherwise faultless flesh. It was jarring to look at. Out of place. "Sorry," I added, when he noticed me staring.

"Sniper," he said, by way of an explanation. "Two bullets." He pointed to the holes' remains, the scar thicker where the bullets entered. Then he turned around and showed me the other side, at two more identical marks out the back. "I was lucky. No major damage. And a six month leave to boot." Odd to call that luck. Then again, he was alive and floating nearby, so maybe he wasn't too far off the mark. "Trust me," he said, swimming to the edge of the pool. "It could be worse."

And then he hopped out, all six feet of dense muscle of him, face impossibly tan, the rest of him impossibly pale, the scar especially. Then he plopped down on a lounge chair, legs wide, hands dangling over the sides, dick nestled in the center of it all, his body dripping with water, stunning. "So much better than a Motel 6," he said, with a loud sigh.

Tell me about it. "Yup." It was about all I could muster.

I tried to look away. And failed. Seriously, I was like a moth to a flame, my eyes glued to him. He broke the silence, though. And scared me something fierce in doing so. "So, you're gay, huh?"

I coughed, my face blistering red again. "Um, what?"

He laughed. "Bette Midler at the Coliseum poster in my room, Geoff. Dead giveaway."

It was the word dead that pierced through. "That, uh, that a problem?" I knew that marines were the least accepting of gay guys.

All that machismo crap and all. Still, he didn't look mad or anything. In fact, he was still smiling.

"A problem?" he repeated, clearly weighing his answer, densely-packed chest suddenly rising and falling a bit faster now, glistening beneath the sun. "Get's a bit lonely out in the desert," he replied, somewhat cryptically.

Still, I took the bait. "So you've, uh, experimented?"

His eyes locked onto mine, smile thankfully still wide. "A bit," he replied. "But just a bit. What the surroundings and the occasion would allow."

And it seemed that his bait might've been for a bigger fish. And I for one wasn't about to make him struggle for the catch. "Nice surroundings here," I pointed out. "And a homecoming is one hell of a great occasion."

He chuckled, the sound running down my body like a runaway train, his cock suddenly stirring, coming to life, moving to the side as it swelled, both of us watching as it made its gradual ascent. Until it stood there at full attention, seven thick inches of it, the head fat, balls dangling way down in all that heat. "Seems to be the consensus," he said, eyeing the beast and then me.

I grinned and walked up the steps that led out of the pool, my steely prick swaying as I made my way to him. Then I pointed at my boner, which was now pointing, as it were, at him. "Seems to be."

He lifted his hand out and held my cock in it, giving it an easy, gently stroke as a million volts of electricity shot through all four limbs, all while I groaned and stood their dripping. "That about all the experimenting you've done?" I asked. He nodded, eyes wide now, the gulp noticeable, his swollen cock more so. "Feel like a little more then?" His nodding merely continued, but the smile grew even brighter. "Then flip over, son. And be quick about it," I ordered.

Needless to say, he was good at taking orders. And fast. Meaning, he was now straddling the chair, chest to the seat, alabaster butt jutting up and out. I walked around and stood behind him, ogling the spectacle. Never had I seen a more beautiful sight, a more perfect ass, the crinkled, hair-rimmed center winking out at me, balls dangling so low they might as well have been in a different zip code.

I moved in closer and gave the right cheek a smack, the red rising in an instant. "What do you say, Marine?" I rasped.

He moaned when another slap landed on the opposite cheek, then another. "Thank you, sir; may I have another?" he barked, sweat now trickling down his back and impossibly broad shoulders, cock bouncing beneath him as I landed another hard one on his upturned rump. "Fuck," he moaned, legs trembling as I gave one more thwack and a yank on his nuts. "Marine's can take a lot more than that, sir," he grunted.

I grinned and pulled back harder, his nuts stretched to their limits, inches behind his ass now, then up, high, his cock pulled down with my efforts, almost as thick as my wrist. I gave it a light smack with my free hand, sending it swinging. Still, this marine had had enough pain in the last several years, and it was time for some pleasure.

I crouched down and ran my finger down his hairy crack before I zoomed it around his satiny hole, around and around , spreading it open with two of my fingers, wide enough for a tongue to slip on in and back. He moaned, loudly, when it made contact, louder when it dove in, my hand now working his cock while I reamed him out. "Fuuuck," he repeated, slamming his ass into my face, balls banging on my chin, cock so thick in my grip it was near impossible to keep a hold of it.

When I'd had my fill, I hocked a loogie at his ring, watching the spit drip down before it got tangled in his hairy nutsac. Then I gently slid a finger inside, slowly, evenly, all the way in, feeling the smooth, muscled interior of him. He clenched, sucked in his breath, and then relaxed, allowing for a second slicked-up digit to worm its way inside. "Hold your cheeks apart for me, Soldier," I commanded.

He reached around, quick as a wink, and did just that, asshole spread out wide, allowing for a third finger to penetrate, until all three were buried deep up his ass, his moans and groans rolling through his solid as a rock body and up through my own. "Harder, sir," he grunted, body wet yet again, now from sweat instead of from my pool.

"Harder, Marine?" I barked back.

"Harder, sir!" he grunted, loudly, shaking the chair beneath him.

I withdrew my fingers from his hole. "On your back then," I ordered.

"Yes, sir!" he said, flipping over, staring up at me expectantly, blue eyes sparkling, face sweat-soaked, his expression eager as he watched me, with him panting all the while.

"Feet up, legs wide, Soldier!" I told him, stroking my cock as he did as he was told, hands on his feet, legs wide, asshole again in view. And it was then I noticed something extraordinary about my marine. "Your dick, Soldier, seems to nearly reach your chin."

He grinned and stared down at the tip of his cock, now slick with sticky pre-cum. "Seems to, sir. Yes. How about that, sir."

"Hold the position, Soldier," I rasped, now stepping to his side, the flat of my palm on his upper back, pushing him forward, until the tip of his cock was touching his lips. "Now suck your cock, Soldier!"

And, lo and behold, he did just that. I was surprised that someone so dense with muscle was also so limber. Three cheers for our armed service's training. Then he helped me out by placing his feet behind his neck, his cock head now deep inside his mouth, with him sucking away as he watched me, spit dribbling down his thick shaft.

I moved around to the front of the pool chair, again crouching down. Then I pulled his cock from his mouth. He was panting even harder now as I took my turn with it, downing it in one fell swoop, until a gagging tear cascaded down my cheek. Still in his twisted position, I handed it back to him. Again he gave it a suck, working his mouth down and around it as best he could before popping it out again.

My face was an inch from his, eyes locked, his cock the only thing separating us. "Welcome home, Marine," I whispered.

"Good to be home, sir," he whispered back, licking the tip of his cock.

I put my lips around the front, his lips around the back, until we were both going at it, up and down and all the way around that fat sucker, tongues slipping and sliding, until our mouths, at last, met just above the head. He moaned, loudly, as he kissed me, so hard it hurt, but still I kissed him back, faces so flush it was impossible to tell where he ended and I began.

"How long can you stay like that?" I asked him, when our mouths reluctantly separated.

"As long as you tell me to, sir," he replied, again sucking the tip, balls bouncing, chair squeaking beneath us. He tipped backwards a bit, leaning on the rear of the chair now, cock embedded in his mouth, asshole pointed up at me, cheeks wide.

I hopped up. "Hold it, son," I said, running into the house, cock swinging. When I came back, he was as before, watching me as he sucked his cock, body dripping, that scar of his lit up, making me ache for him all the more. "Ready for the invasion, Marine?" I quipped, sheathing up my cock before lubing up his stretched out hole.

"Mhm," he mumbled, cock even further down his throat now, the sound of his sucking swirling around my head like a swarm of bees.

I slid my cock inside of him, every nerve ending in my body shooting off fireworks, until his moans drowned out every bird and lawnmower in a three mile radius. I pulled out, my cock hanging midair, then slammed it on in. All the way out, his hole gaping, then all the way in. "Feel good, son?" I groaned, head tilted back, sweat dripping down my face in a torrent.

"Mmmmm," he moaned, popping his prick out for a second, in order to catch his breath. "Yes, sir," he said, taking it in again, all the way down, almost to the base. And then I let him have it, rocketing my cock up his ass, as far as it would go, pummeling his prostate until I very nearly felt faint.

And then he came, his massive frame quivering and quaking as his cock exploded inside his mouth, ounce after ounce dripping out and down, coating his shaft in a stream of white spunk, his chin dense with cum.

A split second later, his hole gripping my cock, I shot and shot and shot, filling his ass and that rubber with one heavy load after the next, until I thought for sure that chair would come crashing down beneath us.

Fighting to catch my breath, I eased my way out of him and helped him get prone again. The cum dripped down to his heaving chest as he fought for air. "Better, Marine?" I asked.

He grinned and wiped the remaining jizz from his mouth. "Thank goodness we didn't experiment like that in Iraq or I might've signed up for a third stint." He reached his hand out and pulled me on top of him, holding on tight in case I slipped off. Then he kissed me, slow and easy, gently, like he had all the time in the world now. Which he now did. "Thanks again, Geoff," he eventually said.

"Welcome home, Matt," I said, yet again, smiling down at him.

He wrapped his arms even tighter around my waist. "Home," he hummed, his forehead rubbing against mine, hand sliding further down, until a finger was gliding inside my sweaty asshole. "Oorah," he moaned. "Ooh-the-fuck-rah."

BARRACK BUDDIES RISK IT ALL
By Jay Starre

Residing on English Bay in Vancouver, Canada, Jay Starre has pumped out steamy gay fiction for dozens of anthologies and has written two gay erotic novels. Contact: Jay Starre on Facebook.

I trotted behind Mark as we yelled out the chant the Drill Sergeant had ordered. Sweat dripped from every possible body orifice, and my head was pounding, but one thing kept me going under the hot Georgia sun. My eyes remained glued to the rhythmic cadence of Mark's butt-cheeks ahead of me. Up, down, roll, swell. God! I could see the crack between those compact mounds outlined perfectly by the olive-green of Mark's uniform. I could smell him in front of me, a sweet sweat that sent an aphrodisiacal thrill through my nearly exhausted body.

I managed to hang on for the next half hour as we ran up and down hills and valleys. Mark's ass undulated before me, pulling me forward, urging me to catch up, so I could reach out and grab a big handful of lush flesh. The crack was soaked with sweat, and I imagined my hand crammed up that crack, feeling the satiny-slick valley and the secret pucker buried deep within. I imagined tearing down that uniform and shoving my hard dick between the rolling cheeks, fucking and fucking and fucking.

By chance, I spotted Sergeant Hernandez watching from the wooded sidelines. His usual menacing glower was missing. He was smiling. Worse yet! He only smiled when he was about to make one of his young soldier victims squirm somehow.

He looked directly at me, and then at Mark running in front of me. His smile grew broader.

Fuck! I was sure he'd noticed how my eyes had been glued to the sexy pump of my pal's hot ass. The bastard sometimes seemed able to read minds! I flushed bright pink but managed to look away and pretend nothing was amiss.

He didn't call me out, thank God! I stumbled onward, turning my attention back to Mark's round butt and the sweaty crack between those pumping globes.

We stumbled into the barracks, released finally from the sadistic Sergeant's torture. What did Mark do? He fell face first in his bunk beside mine, his thighs spread and that beautiful butt in full view, jutting up from the hard mattress. His butt rose and fell rhythmically as he labored to catch his breath.

"I gotta lie here and rest, RJ. I can't even undress. I'll just unbuckle and fall asleep. You can go to town with the rest of the fuck-heads if you want," Mark mumbled.

"I'm fucking beat, too. I just want to lie down and die," I replied with a groan.

I fell on my bed and rolled on my side to watch Mark. I may have been totally exhausted, but I still had enough energy to stare at Mark's hot ass. As I gazed at it, Mark reached under his belly and undid his fly with fumbling hands. He lifted his butt as he did, the rounded hills of his butt-cheeks writhing just slightly as he opened up his pants.

His olive green pants slid down just enough so that the crack of his butt showed in a tantalizing line. White flesh against the tan of his back marked the beginning of that amazing ass. His tight beige T-shirt had ridden up so that there were a few inches of naked flesh for me to stare at. I could see sweat beaded along his waist and a line of it running down into the furrow of his crack.

My cock was as hard as the steel of my bunk's railings. I shivered and sighed as I stared greedily at Mark's perfect butt and dreamed. I fell asleep amidst the sound of the other soldiers scurrying around to get ready for a Friday night out on the town.

I awoke on my side still facing Mark. It was night. The barracks were mostly dark, with one glaring light bulb in the far hallway. That light illuminated the swell of Mark's ass. He was still on his belly, his breathing quiet and steady as he slept peacefully beside me. I rose on one elbow as I shoved a hand into my pants and idly massaged my dick.

As my eyes grew accustomed to the dim light I realized we were alone. The others would still be in town drinking. My dick swelled into an instant boner as I noticed that Mark's pants had slid down so that half his ass was bare. His underwear had somehow shimmied down with them. I was staring directly at Mark's deep crack.

There's something about a dude in uniform, a hot young soldier with muscles and a cock and balls and a butt all hard and tight, something that is so fucking sexy I just can't get enough of it. The army seemed to be an ideal place for me to spend a few years. With that in mind, I'd joined up. But enduring all the brutal exercise, the cold-hearted Drill Sergeant, getting my thick black hair buzzed off, and the excessive discipline, had me thinking I'd maybe made a mistake.

Then there was Mark. He was a platinum-blond Ukrainian-American and with his large nose and plump lips, he was damn good-looking. And he had the whole package, muscles, cock and balls and a butt – a really hot, sexy butt.

I sat up on the bed, my fly open and my hard prick in hand. We were rarely alone, and looking at my watch, I realized we still had at least a couple hours of that rare opportunity before a bunch of drunk and puking soldiers returned in the barracks shuttle. I pumped my stiff meat and stared at Mark's half–exposed butt. He'd moved a little so that one thigh was pulled up toward his chest, which was why his pants and underwear had ridden down his ass. That crack was deep! Fuck!

I spit down on my dick and began to rub the goo into it, wondering if I had the courage to reach out and touch that bare flesh. The slick sound of my fingers pumping up and down seemed loud in the quiet barracks, but I didn't give a shit. I was hot and horny and only nineteen fucking years old. At that age, a day was an eternity, and a hard cock just couldn't be left unattended too long or you risked insanity.

Mark stirred, one of his arms sliding behind him over his can. I kept on jerking off, wondering if he had heard me sit up and was listening to me jerk off. That was a steamy notion. I spit some more and pumped. Mark's hand was on one butt-cheek against the olive-green of his uniform.

Something fucking amazing happened. That hand moved up slowly and slipped under his pants. I bit back a gasp as that hand moved around under his pants in a slow massage, obviously digging into the crack to scratch an itch or some fucking thing.

I shook all over, just imagining my own hand under those skivvies and searching around in the sweaty crack. Then, Mark's hand pushed at his pants, shoving them down so that his entire butt was exposed. He was facing away from me, and I was offered a perfect view of his naked ass! I gawked, my hand riding up and down over my dick faster and faster. Mark's hand cupped one round cheek, his fingers half in his crack. Fuck, that ass was so white and smooth!

At that point, I was fairly certain Mark wasn't asleep. He was either offering me a piece of that white can or he was teasing the hell out of me. The thing was he joked around a lot and most of the time it was about sex. So did a lot of the other dudes, seeing as we were all young and full of cum. But Mark did it more than anyone, winking at me and groping his cock and balls in the showers every fucking day. Still, it was just the usual horsing around – or was it? Was he just yanking my chain now?

I had to stop jerking off, or I'd blow a load right then and there. Instead, mustering up more courage than I thought I possessed, I fell to my knees and crawled across to Mark's bed, only a yard away. My entire body was shaking.

It was risky. Very risky. Not only could I offend my best friend by coming on to him, but also risk getting caught by someone unexpectedly entering the darkened barracks. I believed we were safe for a while from that. But honestly, I didn't care anymore if it was risky or not. I just had to have that soldier butt!

His ass was right in front of me, his fingers in his own crack. I got a glimpse of his balls nestled down in the lower end of that crack, squeezed into a hairless, swollen sack. I was breathing in heavy pants by then, and if Mark couldn't hear that he had to be dead to the world.

His hand moved again. This time his fingers clasped the cheek of his butt and pulled it slowly open. As I stared in awe, he opened up his crack and showed me his asshole. I was looking right at his sweet little pucker! I stared at a wrinkled slot, pink against ivory, flushed and a little swollen as the lips actually fluttered right there in front of me. Mark's fingers pulled his crack open farther, and his butt humped upwards just a little, as if he was dreaming. Dreaming of getting his asshole plugged?!

I couldn't help myself. Weeks of yearning boiled over. I leaped on his bed, grabbed his butt in both hands and spread it wide open. It only took a second, and I was straddling him. As soon as I had my hands on the searing flesh of his naked ass, I went nuts. I dug into the crack and spread it apart. The hole gaped lewdly. I leaned over and buried my face in his ass.

"Eat my ass, RJ. Eat a hot soldier's butt-hole."

I barely heard Mark's lusty growl, my ears surrounded by his rearing butt-cheeks as I snuffled in his crack. My tongue was out lapping greedily, slurping up salty sweat that had dried on his butt. I ran it up and down the deep valley, passing over his steamy hole and swabbing it with a few teasing swipes as I did. Mark reared up into my face as much as he could, with my body weight pinning him to the bunk.

There was no question any more about whether he was teasing me or not by that time. He was obviously as serious as me about some soldier butt-play.

I squeezed the taut mounds of his butt with savage glee, holding them apart as I rummaged around in his crack with my mouth and tongue. There was no hair to speak of in there and just a down of it on his big butt-cheeks. The hole was alive with little palpitations as I teased it. He humped up into my mouth with small groans when I settled on it and began to work it over.

"Oh fuck, yeah! Eat me out, RJ," he repeated

Mark had his own hand in his crack beside mine, and his fingers moved to either side of his asshole, pulling the lips apart for me. I experienced a dizzying moment of realization that he was as hot and horny as I was, but then the thinking part of me disengaged. I was just a soldier, eating another soldier's sweet, convulsing pucker-bud. Nothing more, nothing less.

I rammed my tongue into the satin center of that open slot. The flesh parted as the sphincter relaxed. Mark writhed and his asshole pushed up to meet my invading tongue. I stabbed with the tip, pushing into him. He groaned under me and wiggled his butt in my face. I vibrated my tongue up his asshole, pushing back.

"Oh my fucking God," he gasped out.

The heat of his ass-cheeks burned my own cheeks. He seemed to be on fire. His asshole was even hotter. I tickled it with my tongue then clamped my lips over it and began to suck. I poked and sucked at the same time, forcing his rim to open up and gape outwards. My tongue drove far up his hole. I felt his squishy insides throbbing around my tongue.

I reared up. "I gotta fuck that sweet hole!"

"Do it. Fuck this soldier up the ass – hard!"

I still had my hands on Mark's butt, and his own hand was down there, too. The alabaster white of his ass flushed around my fingers and his. His crack was slick with spit, and his hole puckered outwards with a swollen look of battered hunger. While I stared, he wiggled his butt sensually, and his asshole twittered with beckoning spasms. It was all gooey with my spit, wet and wide open.

My cock reared out of my open pants, throbbing and jerking as I stared at soldier ass. I was more than ready to jump him. He was ready, too. His fingers were on his own asshole, pulling it open. To top it off, those fingers lewdly began to stroke and pet the hole as he humped upwards. That was unbelievable.

"Fuck this soldier hole. Fuck it good, RJ. It's all yours."

Of course I knew we needed some kind of lube. Spit just wasn't going to be good enough. There was a solution, buried in the trunk at the foot of my bunk. I leapt off Mark's bunk and scooted over to my own while he watched me and laughed.

"I know what you're getting. Some of that nasty ass cream you keep hidden in there. I've seen you try to sneak it out to the can. Do you finger your own hole with it? I bet you do, RJ. I bet it will work good on this soldier's hungry hole."

He was fucking right! I'd used it in the can late at night to jerk-off with and finger my own hole, dreaming of his. I had the lid of my trunk open and was staring at my own face in the mirror I had fastened to the inside of it. My face was flushed and my wide mouth coated with my own spit. My blue eyes were wide and excited. My buzzed hair created a dark cap while it emphasized the narrowness of my face. I looked kind of like a hawk with my hooked nose, and the wild look on my face suited that picture. I had my prey in sight! Mark's snug, eager soldier hole.

I found the lube, flushing a little with embarrassment as I thought of Mark snickering behind my back as he noticed me trying to sneak it into the can only last night. But maybe that's why he had decided to stay behind in the barracks tonight, to see if I was game to use the stuff on his ass.

I was back to his bunk in a second, only this time I kicked off my pants before I jumped back on him. I was dressed in my beige T-shirt, and socks and that was it. My body, honed from all the brutal drilling our asshole Sergeant put us through, was strung tight and quivering all over. My cock jutted up from my waist, dark purple and oozing a dribble of pre-cum.

Unable to control my shaking hands, as soon as I had the lid off the bottle of lube, I squeezed it. A spray of the slippery cream arced out to splash his rearing white butt and that spread crack. There was a lot of it.

Mark laughed. Then he stuck a finger up his own asshole. I watched in awe as he piston-poked the wet thing in and out, writhing around beneath me and moaning. As he finger-fucked himself, my spit and that gooey lube squished around and spurted back out.

I needed no more encouragement. I scooted forward, while yanking his olive-greens down to his ankles and tearing them off along with his skivvies. I leaned into him and pointed my cock at his crack. The pole strained in the air, like a big purple missile about to launch. My cock has a huge head with a flared flange that really opens up a hole before the thick shaft follows. Good thing we'd lubed him up.

I didn't even wait for him to pull his finger out, thrusting forward with my cock-head at his mushy slot and driving with my hips.

My knob slammed into him. He grunted like a stuck pig and reared backwards. Convulsing, hot asshole swallowed me up. I cried out and shoved deeper. He pushed back to eat more of me. Together we humped and squirmed until I was buried to the balls up his fuck chute.

His finger was up there beside my cock, trapped in his asshole as it clamped around my shaft like a tight glove. He groaned and I gasped as we both reveled in the sensation of cock in ass. For a moment we remained motionless, his asshole throbbing and my cock pulsing. Then I gripped the firm flesh of his ass-cheeks and began to fuck.

"Take soldier cock up your soldier ass," I mumbled as I plowed into him.

"Fuck my soldier hole. Fill it with cock … uhhhn … yeah!"

Our words degenerated into grunts as we fucked. Pent-up lust spewed out of us. We banged all over the bed, his ass humping up to meet my drilling cock. I pushed up his T-shirt to his shoulders and trapped his arms above his head in it. I kicked his pale thighs wider apart and shoved my cock far up his tender ass, spitting down on it and adding more slippery lube from the bottle as I fucked harder and faster. He writhed beneath me, his balls mashing against my knees as mine slapped rhythmically against his sweaty butt-cheeks.

I stroked and pinched those alabaster globes, unable to get enough of the feel of them. They were so damn smooth and tight. He had a firm butt, yet it jiggled with every thrust of my cock up his hole. He arched his back and squirmed against that driving digger, wanting more and more and harder and faster. I pounded his prostate relentlessly, and he grunted with every furious drive.

The friction of his mushy hole was taking its toll on my cock. My knob felt like it was on fire. The slick lips of his asshole gripped my shaft as it pumped faster and faster. The slap of my hips against his sweet butt-cheeks was almost as loud as our grunts. I didn't want to come; I didn't want the amazing fuck to end. But I was at the mercy of my passion. As the heat intensified, I just pounded faster. My cock was being incinerated by his heaving butt-hole.

I blew. My cock slammed in and out so fast the eruption spewed half in his asshole and half out of it. Goo oozed and bubbled around my pounding pole. It dribbled down his ass-crack as I pumped my balls empty and cried out in the midst of a drowning rapture.

I fell on top of him, still pumping him full of erupting goo. The stuff was a squishy lubricant, coating his crack and my shaft as I began to slow down. My head spun, but his solid body was a welcome mattress, and I flopped over him, my cock still up his ass and my body shaking all over.

I would have passed out like that, Mark's awesome muscles my pillow, but he wasn't satisfied quite yet. He squirmed out from under me, moving forward so that he was on his knees and my face was in his ass. There it was again, that soldier ass. His ass dripped sweat and was smeared with cum. His balls hung down between his beefy thighs, then his hand appeared from in front to push down his stiff cock. He began to pump it furiously while I stared at his ass-crack. The hole pouted and oozed as he whacked off. His tight can squirmed. Then he crammed his other hand up into his crack and shoved two fingers up his just-fucked asshole.

He shot all over my face that hard cock pointed backwards.

I snorted in the smell of that cum, loving it. I tasted it on my lips and tongue. It was amazing.

He still wasn't through. He scooted back over me, grabbed my shoulders and rolled me over onto my back. His soft blue eyes boring down into my own big blue ones, he leaned down and kissed me.

Even though we'd just fucked and he'd shot a load all over my face, this kiss seemed to be the most taboo. Practically any horny young soldier would fuck a hole if it was offered, but kissing was something else. Something more important, something ultimately nastier and more exciting.

His solid body, naked except for his T-shirt and socks, sprawled over mine. I reached down and cupped those firm ass globes I'd just been pounding so savagely. Our tongues slid into each other's mouths. It was incredible.

"What the hell is going on, Privates!"

Sergeant Hernandez! If blood could curdle, I'm sure mine would have at that moment. The bastard had snuck up on us while we were so focused on our steamy fuck.

I blurted out the first thing that came to mind as we both reared up from our embrace to face him. "Sergeant, Sir! It was all my idea, Sir. Mark was just going along ..."

My words hung in the air as both Mark and I gasped with shocked surprise. Sergeant Hernandez stood at the foot of Mark's bunk, his dark glower as piercing and intimidating as ever. But there was something more. His fly was open and a fat brown dick reared from the opening.

A really fat brown dick. Really hard and really fat.

"Privates, it's clear you need a lesson in how a soldier fucks. That wimpy little pussy-pounding you just offered your buddy certainly doesn't classify as a real Army fuck. Time to show you how the men do it. Get on your goddamn back Private, and show me that soldier hole. Your buddy can hold your legs up and sit on your face at the same time, since it's goddamn clear you like to eat hole as much as fuck it. Now! I mean fucking right now!"

We were used to obeying the big Sergeant's every command. This was no different. It took only a moment for us to position ourselves. With Mark's alabaster butt-cheeks covering my face, I couldn't see what came next, but sure as hell could feel it!

Fortunately my buddy was cool-headed enough to snatch up the lube off the bed and spray my ass with it before the Sergeant's cannon of a cock rammed deep into my gut. He was right about one thing, the pounding I'd given Mark paled in comparison to the savage pummeling Sergeant Hernandez gave me.

I have to admit it felt good. The very savagery of it served to open me up right away, and the slippery lube created a smooth friction as he slammed balls-deep, yanked all the way out, and drove home again, and again, and again.

I sucked my own jizz out of Mark's tenderized hole, sympathizing with him now as I experienced the same relentless fuck I'd only just laid on him. He'd taken it without a hitch, so I could only do the same. The thick meat ramming in and out rubbed my ass-lips and mashed my prostate with such intensity I couldn't help myself and actually shot a second load.

Hernandez unloaded up my tenderized butt as he offered us his cruel laughter. He was an asshole, as usual.

He pulled out and hopped off the bed. He left us there without another word. Mark got off my face and turned around to stare down at me.

"Are you OK?"

I started laughing, and he joined me. We rolled around on his bunk in a fit of hysterics. From relief, mostly. It seemed like we'd risked it all, but got away with it.

Not exactly, it turned out. The big Drill Sergeant didn't treat us any different after that night. He was just as nasty and mean and savage as ever, but nothing was said about what had happened. Of course Mark and I took advantage of every opportunity to lube up each other's soldier holes and stuff them with soldier cock. It seemed we couldn't get enough of that.

It was just before we completed our basic training when the other shoe dropped.

Sergeant Hernandez called us into his office. We knew something was up when he pulled down the shades over the windows and locked the door behind us. We looked at each other and nodded. There was nothing to do but be bold.

"Sir! Our soldier holes are yours," we chimed together.

Whipping down our olive-greens and underwear along with them, we leaned forward and bent over his desk, bare-assed and side-by-side. The sound of lube squirting and then being pumped up and down over stiff cock set our minds at least a little at ease before the battering began.

He fucked the hell out of us. Without missing a beat, he plunged that thick brown cannon up my ass, then yanked it out and rammed it up Mark's. The hot pole reamed us both non-stop.

"Let's see another little kiss, Soldiers! Come on, you pussies know you want to. Goddamn it, right now ... and I mean right ... fucking ... now!"

His grunts punctuated his command. We obeyed. Mark's plump lips mashed against mine as officer cock slammed balls-deep up my poor ass.

He creamed us both, yanking his spewing cock out of my hole and then burying it in Mark's. We thought he was through with us then, but no. He made us fuck each other while he sat behind his desk and smirked.

He finally let us go. I guess that was our graduation gift.

Mark and I survived our basic training, and two years in the service after that. Lucky for me, we're still best buds, and I get a steady supply of soldier hole to satisfy my needs, even it is former soldier hole now!

I guess Sergeant Hernandez is keeping an eye out for any shenanigans in the barracks to this day. Good luck to him. I'm sure he would agree, there's nothing better than soldier hole.

SOLDIER OF FORTUNE
By Jay Starre

Sergeant Dayton Riley was from Ohio. He'd grown up beside corn fields and blue skies. Now he was in a camp on the edge of the Congo in Africa. He was no longer playing games with his boyhood friends, but was now a real soldier. A soldier of fortune.

He was a mercenary.

Lieutenant Everett was black and big and had a reputation for being tough as hell and mean as fuck. He wasn't friendly with his unit, but he was smart and direct. He kept them alive, and they trusted him.

Dayton trusted him, and he was the most experienced of the soldiers who served in the mercenary unit. The Brits and the Americans were behind them, though no one was supposed to know. They weren't exactly special forces, just grunts with a mission they were paid to accomplish.

Pay. That was their motivation. Glory, patriotism, revenge or hoping to save the world from the bad guys, that was for regular soldiers. Dayton had been one of those. He'd enlisted at nineteen, fresh-faced and full of all those nobler motives. He'd served in Afghanistan and come home alive.

He'd been good at war, but he wasn't exactly thrilled with the pay. Now he was getting more of what he was good at and more money, too. It was a choice, for good or bad, he'd made. At only twenty-three, he wasn't too concerned about getting killed or making something of his life. He was young enough to believe it would all turn out in the end.

Sandy-haired with plump pink cheeks, a dimpled chin and an easy smile, he looked and acted like an Iowa country boy without a mean bone in his body. Which he was – except when there was an enemy in his sights, and then he was a killing machine.

Everyone liked him. Everyone except Lieutenant Everett who didn't seem to like anyone. Dayton meant to change that, and he thought he knew exactly how.

It was dusk, and the jungle sounds nearby were peaking as the daytime creatures began to settle for the night, and the night time creatures were preparing to prowl. He'd just come in from a patrol with a pair of Aussies and the lone African of the unit, a black from Botswana.

With his AK-47 on his hip, he strolled over to Lieutenant Everett's tent. Set away from the others, it was sufficiently isolated to offer the taciturn officer his peace and quiet. The glow of a pair of lanterns bled through the canvas, but otherwise the interior was hidden. That all suited Dayton's purposes perfectly.

"Lieutenant, Sir. Have I your permission to enter?"

"What the hell do you want, Sergeant? Come on in if you gotta."

He hadn't expected a warm welcome so wasn't surprised by the gruff response. Wiping a smirk off his face, he ducked and entered through the door flap.

The officer lounged on his cot, a book in his hand and a lantern on the small stand beside him. A massively built dude, one muscular arm was folded behind his head while the other rested on his powerful chest with book in hand.

"Any sign of Abu Kalil and his evil gang?"

The deep voice sent a little shiver through Dayton's spine, which he was unable to hide. That was fine, though, as he was about to show the big Lieutenant more than a little shiver. He had a hunch the officer wouldn't object either.

"No sign, Sir. I'm sure we'll pick up their trail soon."

Abu Kalil was a Ugandan guerrilla leader who was more interested in theft, rape, and murder than actual revolution. Worse yet, he had terrorist ties to Arabs in North Africa. Everett and his men had been commissioned to seek him out and take him out.

"You've been giving me that line of crap for a week now. Tell me something I want to hear, Riley, or get the hell out."

Now Dayton allowed himself to smile. It was one of his best assets, although it might not do much to alter Everett's foul mood. The truth was, the two had a lot in common. They were the only two officers and the only two Americans. Dayton was counting on one more similarity.

"I'd like to suck your big black cock. Is that something you want to hear?"

Now the big officer smiled. A very rare sight indeed, it looked pretty damn good on him, too. He had a large mouth with big straight teeth and a really plump lower lip. Dayton's cock stiffened under his camouflage fatigues as he stared at that grinning orifice. His imagination ran riot thinking of what he could do to that mouth, or what it could do to him.

"Hell, Riley, I've been wondering when the fuck you'd get around to offering. Strip off those fatigues and come on over here."

He'd guessed right! With the alacrity of a trained soldier, he swiftly deposited his weapon, ammo belt, sheathed knife, and helmet on the rickety camp table beside Everett's cot. The officer watched, his smile growing broader as the blond soldier kicked off his jungle-muddy boots and then his fatigues, and finally his skivvies.

"Nice cock for a white boy, but show me that ass, Riley. I intend on raping it good with my tongue before I fuck it with that big black cock you want so much."

Dayton felt a warm rush in his gut, and a quivering response in his asshole at the promised rape. He hadn't seen Everett's cock, but others in the unit had and told tales of its enormous girth and length.

And the sight of that big mouth grinning up at him certainly had his cock stiffening and his asshole pouting. He strode forward, pink hard-on bobbing in front of him. When he reached the lounging Lieutenant, a huge hand whipped out to seize one cheek of his white ass and halt him in his tracks.

"One thing, Sergeant. I am the top here. You do exactly as I say. Play the passive, pretty bottom boy and all will be well. Do you fucking understand?"

Dayton had no problem with that. "Yes Sir! Absolutely fucking understood!"

"All right then, Riley. Step over my cot and sit your sweet fucking ass on my face!"

Shaking all over now that he was close enough to smell the musky male stench of the officer, Dayton did as he was told with athletic ease. He lifted one muscular thigh and bare foot to step over the narrow cot and straddle the Lieutenant's face.

The book was tossed to the ground and two hands seized his ass-cheeks. As they spread them wide open, Everett emitted a low growl, almost a purr, as he took stock of the offered butt.

"Fucking pretty as a peach, Riley. Smooth and lily-white and nice and chunky. I like my butts big. That hole looks hungry, too. Show me how hungry it is."

Dayton's cock lurched as he obeyed the lewd command. His butt crack was wide open in that position especially with Everett's hands spreading it, so his hole was on perfect display. He couldn't help letting out a low moan as he pushed out with his ass-lips and wriggled his butt against those clasping fingers.

"All yours, Sir! All fucking yours!"

"You bet it is. Sweet fucking slot. Looks like it wants a good tongue-bath. Come on then, Riley. Sit on my face."

The growled command sent another wave of shivers rippling up and down his spine as he obeyed. With feet wide apart on either side of the narrow cot, he sat down directly over the Lieutenant's face.

Big wet mouth met his smooth crack. Plump lips clamped directly over his pouting asshole. He let out a gasp as they sucked briefly, then a grunt as tongue began to swipe at his hole.

It must have been a huge tongue. It lapped across the puckered rim with wet slurps before settling on it and beginning to probe. Dayton felt himself melting into that tongue, squatting right down and wriggling all over the Lieutenant's face.

He stared at the officer's crotch, noting how the bulge in his fatigues was swelling, and swelling! How big was it going to get?? He ached to reach out and uncover it, but knew Everett's command to do only as he ordered couldn't be ignored if he knew what was good for him. The officer had no patience with disobedience.

Instead, he placed his hands on his own muscular thighs, gritted his teeth and wallowed in the Lieutenant's tongue drilling. And it was quite a drilling! The tip of that monster tongue tickled the entrance to his hole with darting flicks, then pointed at the pink center and stabbed. It forced its way past the sphincter and twirled around inside.

"Fuck! Sir, that feels so fucking good! Eat me out, please Sir," he mumbled.

Everett's answer was wordless but unequivocal. He thrust that fat tongue far up inside Dayton's gooey slot. His giant paws squeezed the Sergeant's pale butt so hard it flamed pink under his black fingers.

Dayton was tall and well-built, with long limbs and smooth pale skin. His muscles rippled as he tensed from head to toe in that squat, while his asshole did the opposite, relaxing as it turned inside out over that probing tongue.

His eyes locked onto the immense bulge in Everett's fatigues, imagining the promised rape to come. He wriggled over the invading tongue and willed his asshole to gape open in preparation for the fuck he'd been promised.

Everett pulled his mouth off just long enough to growl out a welcome command. "You can take it out and feel it, but you can't suck it."

Now that he had the go-ahead, both his hands whipped out to seize the Lieutenant's belt buckle and fly. In a flurry of greed, he tore open the officer's fatigues and shoved down on them. Everett co-operated by raising his butt off the cot enough to get his pants and underwear down to his knees.

There it was! Big black cock. Really, really big black cock. Uncut, the foreskin had peeled down just enough so that the oozing piss slit showed. The outline of a mushroom-shaped crown showed beneath the flap of skin.

He longed to swallow it! But he'd been ordered not to. Instead he grabbed hold of it with both hands. It was long enough for both fists to surround the fat shank. He began to pump it.

The sprawled Lieutenant lifted his hips to hump those fists while he purred deep in his chest. His tongue danced deep inside Dayton's spit-dripping hole. The white Sergeant squeezed that black cock with his hands and slowly pumped it, amazed at how much pre-cum was forced out of the piss slit as he did. He could barely restrain himself from diving for that dripping knob and gulping down the shiny goo.

Everett momentarily distracted him from his fixation on the slippery cock-head. He pushed up on Dayton's ass and growled another order. "I know you want to suck it, but I got something else for those pretty lips of yours. Get back here and kiss the mouth that's been eating your ass."

He was quick to obey. Extremely agile, he only had to move his feet slightly back and raise his ass in the air, place his hands on the officer's massive chest, and bend down to plant his mouth over the Lieutenant's. Huge lips parted wide and sucked in his tongue. The mouth that had just been clamped over his asshole now clamped over his mouth.

That wasn't all. While the steamy orifice swallowed his tongue, the giant black hands on his ass moved into his crack and blunt fingers began to stroke and tease his spit-gobbed asshole. They pulled the hole open and rubbed the distended lips, tickled the sensitive entrance, and tapped at it with fingertips. The kiss was sloppy and noisy while the hole-rubbing was as maddening as it was enjoyable.

He groaned and wriggled, aching to have something shoved up his pouting hole, those fingers, that tongue again, or best of all, that huge black cock. But the officer was not done toying with him. He broke the kiss with a smack of his big lips.

"OK, Sergeant. Time for some more ass-eating. Get that pretty butt back over my face. Now!"

"Yes Sir!"

He moved forward enough to sit back down on the mouth he'd just kissed and grab hold of that humongous cock again with both hands. As he felt the pulsing girth of that thick meat in his hands, lips surrounded his asshole and tongue drilled inside him.

"Hell yeah, Sir! Tongue-fuck my ass!"

The fat tongue probed him deep as big fingers pulled his hole wide open for it. He squirmed and groaned as the black officer ate him inside out, and he pumped the giant cock with both hands.

Everett continued to dig around in his hole with that twisting tongue but removed one hand from his crack to reach under the cot. That hand came back up with a bottle of baby oil. Dayton grinned as he imagined what the big Lieutenant had planned to use that oil for. No doubt he'd put the bottle there for easy access when he wanted to jerk his huge cock.

Everett flipped open the bottle with his thumb, then upended it over Dayton's bobbing pink cock where it rose up from his crotch above the black Lieutenant's throat and chest. A stream of the clear oil coated it. The bottle was casually tossed onto the cot between the officer's spread thighs as the hand that held it snaked out to seize the oily cock and start stroking it.

"Oh my fucking god! Hell yeah! Fuck yeah! Please, Sir, don't stop!"

He meant it. The tongue drilling his aching hole and the big hand pumping his aching cock were twin sensations that only multiplied the pleasure of each. He ground his solid round ass into that mouth and tongue while he humped the slippery fingers stroking his pink cock.

He wondered if he should grab that baby oil and lube up Everett's cock with it, but he hadn't been given permission to do so. Instead he continued to pump it with both hands and watch the flow of sticky pre-cum ooze from the piss slit. His endeavors did work to peel back the foreskin. He got a good look at the flared crown he hoped to get up his ass soon.

Meanwhile, he was going nuts over the digging tongue and stroking fingers. He wasn't sure how long he could hold out. His entire body quivered and jerked, his mouth gaped open, and drool coated his lips and chin. His hole felt as if it was being consumed by a wet heat that pulsed way up into his gut.

Everett must have sensed his imminent orgasm. The hand he had in Dayton's smooth crack abruptly drove upward along his spine, propelling him forward and downward. He didn't need to be told what to do as that hand reached the back of his neck and huge fingers splayed over it to force his face into the officer's lap.

He opened wide and gulped in that monster black cock.

It was enormous. His lips stretched over the flared head and sucked it in. But the hand on his neck forced him lower, and he was eager to surrender to it. With his own cock on fire from the slippery hand pumping it, and his asshole gaping around the tongue raping it, he drove down to swallow half that giant cock. His throat yielded, and he had the head lodged in his gullet.

The young Sergeant gurgled noisily as he wriggled over the mouth that ate him and the fingers that stroked him. With that pulsing meat deep in his throat, he lost control. He shot.

Everett was merciless. He continued to drive his tongue into Dayton's convulsing asshole while he stroked out a spray of cum from the soldier's pink cock. His steely grip on the back of Dayton's neck forced him to gulp and snort over the giant cock in his mouth as he thrashed around in the throes of his orgasm.

But the big officer was hardly done with him.

The fingers on his neck tightened and then pulled upwards. He was yanked off that hot cock and then shoved forward even as he was still spurting cum. The hand on his cock moved back between his legs to propel him toward the foot of the cot. At the same time, the black officer sat up and leaned forward himself.

Dayton found himself crouching on the edge of the cot with his head down almost on the ground and his ass in the air, bare feet still planted on either side of the canvas bed. Everett was quick. He seized the bottle of oil and upended it over Dayton's raised ass.

"Fuck yeah! Open up that pretty pink hole so I can fill it with oil," he demanded.

That was easy enough. He'd been eaten inside out, and breathless and shaking from the orgasm that still rocked him, his asshole pouted wide open as a stream of oil squirted down into it. The clear liquid filled it then overflowed to run down his crack and balls and cum-dripping cock.

"Fucking sweet! Now you're getting that big black cock you wanted so bad!"

It happened so quickly Dayton was caught totally off guard. That enormous knob slammed down into him from above as Everett rose up and flung himself on top of the bent-over soldier.

All he could do was let out an explosive grunt and take it. The blunt head drove deep into his oil-and-spit-filled gut. It was incredible. He'd been warmed up by that devouring mouth and then relaxed into a quivering limpness by the powerful orgasm he just experienced. His asshole offered absolutely no resistance to the monster meat slamming into it.

Everett gutted him. He slammed deeper, yanked out, and rammed right back in, even deeper. With both hands on Dayton's shoulders, he leaned over the soldier and fucked him by driving down with his powerful hips. Buried under the heavy black officer, there was nothing he could do but take the drilling punishment.

The final drops of cum were driven from his balls as that giant cock forced its way into him. He gripped his own ankles and held on as Everett pummeled his ass with increasing force.

"Yeah! Fuck yeah! Love that sweet white ass! Love that gaping pink hole! Love ... fucking ... love it! Here comes my load!"

He must have been as turned on by the ass-eating as Dayton, because that furious fuck only lasted about five minutes before he was driving balls-deep and shooting.

Dayton relished the loading while he found his cock returning to full mast with a renewed urgency. He wanted more!

It was a risk, but he couldn't help himself. He grabbed the edge of the cot and with all his strength, he pushed upwards and backwards. The hefty Lieutenant was dislodged from his perch and propelled backwards. Before he had time to react, Dayton had whirled around and was crouching between his beefy thighs. He immediately seized the backs of the Lieutenant's knees and shoved them up and back. Without pausing, he dove into the officer's crack.

His pink mouth clamped directly over the dark hole between those big black cheeks. He began to eat it.

"Hell, Sergeant. Don't mind if you do! Eat that big black ass! And if you eat it good enough, I just might let you fuck it."

Dayton's risky ploy worked. He was going to fuck Everett!

He tore off the officer's fatigues, dragging them up and over his boots as he slurped and sucked on the pouting black hole. He remembered exactly how it felt getting eaten out only a few minutes earlier, and now he was determined to return the favor. He hoped the Lieutenant would get just as heated up as he had and want his white cock up his hefty black ass.

And it was a big ass. The Lieutenant was three inches over six foot tall and weighed in at nearly 250 pounds. He was solid muscle, too. His butt was gigantic, black as midnight and smooth as satin. The hole itself was pink with a big rosy rim and a surprisingly sloppy center. Dayton was sure the officer had a big old dildo hidden somewhere in his tent for those lonely nights after a hectic fire fight in the jungle.

He shoved his tongue into that gaping slot and dug around. Everett responded by reaching down between his massive thighs and seizing the back of the Sergeant's head with both giant hands. He held him in place with a firm grip as he raised his legs higher and spread them wider apart.

Dayton smacked his lips as he ate that hole with gusto. He had to do a good job of it if he hoped to fuck it. And it tasted damn good, too. The hole yielded easily to his stabbing tongue, which he believed was a good sign. But what he wasn't prepared for was the way that hole began to kiss him back.

Everett had claimed he was a top, and now he seemed to be proving it. He wasn't merely laying back and allowing the Sergeant to eat his ass, he was eating back. The lips of that black hole began to clamp and quiver around Dayton's tongue, gripping it and pulling it deeper with little snapping convulsions. It was absolutely amazing.

187

And he couldn't escape it. Those powerful black hands held his pink face in place as he snuffled over the convulsing hole. He snorted for air, inhaling the rank stench of ass and balls and cum.

He fucking loved it.

"All right, Sergeant. You proved yourself. Now mount me up and give me a good fucking drill! Let's see if you know how to fuck with that pink cock of yours."

The hands released their steely grip. He pulled back just in time to miss the copious squirt of baby oil Everett fed his own yawning dark hole. Just like it had in Dayton's, the clear liquid pooled in the open pit and then overflowed.

Dayton didn't wait for any change of heart and leapt atop the sprawled Lieutenant. His cock was stiff and still dripping when he shoved it balls-deep in that well-oiled black ass cavern. It swallowed him with ease, even though his shank was thick as hell.

"I could take your goddamn fist if I wanted to. Maybe next time, Sergeant. For now, you just gotta give me what you got, and hard!"

There was no need to urge him on. He was on fire. His own hole was well-stretched and drooling from the pounding fuck Everett had laid on it, and now he craved retribution. He gripped the Lieutenant's ankles and pushed them back toward his head, settled between his splayed thighs and fucked like a madman.

Oil squirted and squished. The hole fought back, but it was pretty much a no-win situation as Dayton gave it a such a savage pounding it could only surrender and gape wide open for the duration.

Still, the Lieutenant hardly seemed as if he was on the losing end. He urged Dayton on with nasty comments while gripping the round cheeks of his pale butt and driving him forward with them. It was almost as if he was fucking himself with Dayton's cock!

188

Either way, they both were getting exactly what they wanted. The sandy-haired Sergeant plowed black butt like there was no tomorrow while the sprawled Lieutenant took it all with a big nasty grin and a constant stream of snarling abuse.

The Lieutenant held Dayton in place on top of him with his burly arms and giant hands. He heaved up into the pounding cock with his giant ass and powerful hips. The fuck lasted and lasted, now that both had shot their loads once.

But surprisingly it was Everett who lost it first. With his black fingers spread over the reddened cheeks of Dayton's thrusting white ass, he reared up into the cock drilling his ass and let loose with a second spray of nut juice.

His asshole, instead of snapping shut with his powerful release, instead seemed to yawn even wider open. Those giant hands held him in place as the Lieutenant thrashed around on the cot with Dayton's cock up his ass and blew a huge load all over his stomach.

Trapped in those massive arms, his cock buried in hot and juicy asshole, he couldn't hold out any longer himself. He let out a grunt and unleashed a second torrent of cum.

Everett was laughing as he rolled them over and held Dayton in place beneath him. Still shooting up the Lieutenant's warm asshole, he could only gasp and moan.

"Now I got you where I want you. We got a few hours before either of us have to take our turn on night guard. I expect another good fuck or two out of you before then."

What had he unleashed? The Lieutenant was a sex maniac!

Dayton smirked happily beneath the sweaty bulk of the officer's massive body and said nothing. What was there to say anyway? I love you? Hell no. We're best pals now? No way.

It hardly mattered. He'd gotten what he wanted, and was going to get more of it before the night was out. He wasn't going to argue with that. Tomorrow, they'd be back in the jungle with the enemy lurking somewhere in the dim vastness, so tonight best to get all the ass and cock and tongue he could.

MARINE MANEUVERS
By Donald Webb

Donald Webb has had short stories published in numerous gay magazines and anthologies. He lives with his life-time partner in Victoria, BC. andon402@shaw.ca

It's going on 11:00 am when I decide to take a hike down the beach from Navarre toward Fort Walton Beach. I slip into a white thong and white jogging shorts, throw a beach towel, a couple of bottles of cold water and – ever hopeful, some safes and lube, into a backpack. My camera goes in next. I take a quick look in the mirror. Sun enhanced golden strands enhance my dark-blond hair. I shaved my chest yesterday, so I'm buffed and ready to go.

The sun-warmed beach burns the soles of my feet, so I jog between the sun worshippers and cool my feet in the frothing water of the Gulf. Water churns around my ankles as rollers break on the beach. I set off down the coast. When I step over a broken-down fence, that marks the boundary of a military installation, I remove my shorts and place them in my backpack. The sun feels good on my exposed butt. When I reach the dunes, naked bodies – both male and female, are stretched out on towels. One straight couple, lying between two smaller dunes – oblivious to their surrounding, are in a tight embrace. I can see his big dick and hairy nuts as he slowly fucks her thigh.

I keep walking. I'm not interested in straights. I removed my thong and stuff it in my backpack. Further down the shore I reach the gay section of the beach. Heads turn as I walk by. One guy calls out, "Hey, cutie. Come over here and let me suck on that big dick." My cock becomes fully hard, but he doesn't interest me, so I keep walking. My cock sways back and forth, from thigh to thigh, as I keep going. Later, when I've covered a fair distance, I round a bend and see the front end of a military Jeep parked between two larger dunes. My body goes into full alert. Usually, the patrols ignore trespassers, but sometimes they can be assholes. What'll they do to me if they see I'm naked, flashes through my mind? I quickly make a detour into the dunes and then, to reconnoiter the area, I slowly creep to the top of the dune closest to the Jeep.

Usually there are two Marines to a Jeep, but today there is only one Marine in the Jeep, and he's not doing a good job of patrolling the area. More urgent things seem to be occupying his mind. Dressed in his utility uniform, he's flat on his back, lying across the two front seats. His shirt is open and his olive green T-shirt is pushed up above his hairy nipple line. The sleeves of his shirt are rolled up to his bulging biceps. His trousers and Jockey's are pushed down to his knees, and his widely splayed legs are bent. One foot is cocked up on the dash, and the other foot dangles over the back of the passenger seat. He's working on his meaty cock. He spits in his hand and lubes his shaft. I watch him stroke for a while and then take a few snapshots. I need to be closer. I want a close-up of his asshole.

After backing down the dune, I move stealthily around the base. When the Jeep comes into view, I drop to my knees and crawl forward. I'm hoping the noise of crashing waves will cover the sandy crunch of my knees as I approach the passenger side of the vehicle. When I'm crouched below the entrance, I sit back on my haunches and slowly raise my head. His face is hidden from view by his rumpled trousers, but his exposed butthole is only inches from my face. Big hanging balls bounce as he jerks on his rod. I can't see the head of his dick, but I can see his hand working up and down the hefty shaft. I move my face closer and take a deep breath. His aroused body gives off a distinctive male aroma. I remove my camera from my backpack and take a few shots of his butch Marine butt.

I stow the camera and then play with my skin for a while. I spit in my hand and stroke my dick. I'm hoping he's not ready to spunk because I want the experience to last. I nearly gasp out loud when his hand sneaks around his left butt cheek, and his shiny middle finger probes his moist butthole. I quickly move my head back when his butt slides toward my face on the vinyl seat cover. When he pulls his finger out of his chute for more lube, his hole, surrounded by a coating of dark hair, remains open as though begging for cock. I'm tempted to move forward and lick him but am able to control myself. What could he do if I did? I'd be well away from him by the time he had his trousers up and gave chase. And if he caught me, what would he do? I can see him reporting to the CO, "This guy licked my asshole, sir."

Two lubed fingers reappear and slide into his gaping hole. He grunts and pushes back against the invading digits. This guy's no stranger to ass play, I think as a third finger slips into his chute. I ease my backpack off my shoulders and retrieve my tube of lube. I coat my big throbber and stroke myself as I watch him finger-fuck his Marine butt. When his hand goes for more spit, his hole is agape and begging to be fucked. I slowly come to my feet. His eyes are closed, and he's sucking his fingers. I push forward, and my lubricated knob slides into his well-primed hole. His eyes open in shock, but I can feel his silky chute massaging my shaft as I shove it home.

"Dude!" he bellows. "What the fuck!" I've got his massive thighs in an iron grip when I push hard against his upturned butt. His chin lifts, and his mouth opens in a long drawn out wail when I start pummeling him. His hand slides up and down his huge shaft, his knees draw up to his chest, and he cries out, "Fuck me, dude." I obey, and fuck him hard and fast. He's twisting around on the seat and groaning as if he's getting the best fuck he's ever had when my cock erupts deep inside his clinging channel. A massive load explodes from his dick. Volley after volley of thick jism hits him on the face and neck.

He smiles at me when he's through shooting. "Fuck, dude. It's been a long time since I've been reamed. I really needed that." He turns his forearm around and glances at his watch. "Dude!" he shouts, "It's thirteen-hundred hours! If I'm not back in five minutes, they'll send out a search party." He springs out of the Jeep. After he's cleaned himself with my towel, he dresses, hops into the Jeep, sticks his utility cap on his head, winks at me and then gives me a snappy salute.

"You'll be back here sometime?" I ask as he starts the motor. He thinks for a long moment, and then says, "Yeah. Same time, same place tomorrow." Sand sprays up from all four wheels as he puts pedal to the metal.

I take a leisurely swim then slip into my shorts and head back to my hotel room.

# # # # #

Sure enough, when I get to the same place the next day, he's in the same position. Today, for the first time, I notice his last name is Miller. A name tag is stitched to his uniform above his right breast pocket. I'm naked when I stand between his legs. I don't waste any time. He groans when I shove his legs up to his chest and lick his hairy perineum. The aroma of his sweating body spurs me on. The lips of his asshole are gaping when my tongue moves further down. He growls when I chew on his hole and sink my tongue into his chute. I pull his dick back between his thighs and deep-throat his meaty shaft.

"Dude," he says. "That's awesome. Wish I could smuggle you into the barracks."

He seems to be getting close – which I definitely don't want, so I stand up and fish out my lube. I'm getting ready to lube his chute when he says, "Not today, dude. Today your ass belongs to the Marines."

I'm all for it. I can't wait to feel his Marine dick in my channel. We swap positions. He lubes his dick and then smacks a dollop of lube on my hole. There's no foreplay with him. I guess Marines fuck, and some get fucked, but that's it. He gives one big shove, and he's balls beep in me. I squeeze my nuts and stroke my dick as he pile drives my receptive chute. He looks up at a dune and smiles. I look in that direction. A Marine, dressed in full utility uniform, is charging down the dune like he's after the Taliban. I'm shocked. I try to unseat Miller, but he holds onto my ankles and keeps pile-driving me. Now I know why Miller didn't want to be fucked. He'd never do it in front of another Marine.

The other Marine, by the name of Kennedy, comes to a stop next to Miller. They high-five like they've just won the lottery. When Kennedy drops his trousers, opens his shirt, and rolls up his T-shirt, a huge dick – a good ten inches long with a massive knob, pops into view. Red hair covers his upper chest and, below his six-pack abs, a love trail of red hair drops to his pubes. Kennedy walks around the Jeep to the driver's side and pulls me toward him so that my head overhangs the seat. I open wide to give him a direct shot at my throat. He doesn't disappoint. It's a tight fit, but he manages to shove all ten inches down my gullet. I'm choking on dick when he starts pounding my throat. I'm beginning to think he's going to dislocate my jaw when he thankfully backs out and feeds me his nuts. I gobble on the tasty orbs for a few minutes then he pulls them from my mouth, turns around, spreads his muscular asscheeks, and lowers his butt to my mouth. I grab his thighs, pull him tight against my face, and breathe in his heady aroma. He wiggles his ass when my tongue darts out to assault his tiny pink pucker. I'm at it for a while, but when I try to insert a finger, he slaps my hand and steps away from me.

Kennedy joins Miller. He lubes his big fist then strokes his shaft. "Okay, buddy," he says to Miller. "It's my turn." Miller pulls out and Kennedy immediately moves into place. His big boner opens me up like I've never been opened before, but I feel only pleasure because Miller has done a good job at preparing me for his buddy. They keep switching, taking turns to ream my chute, and I'm in heaven. I've never had it so good. I wish they could do it all day. But all good things must come to an end. When Miller shoots his spunk deep in my body, and Kennedy takes his place, I grab my dick and keep pounding till I drop a load. Kennedy is quick to follow.

We're using my towel to wipe the splooge off our bodies, when I ask, "You guys gonna be 'round tomorrow?"

Miller shakes his head. "I'm heading out from Hurlburt tomorrow."

I'm disappointed when they leave. Now that I've had a taste of Marine cock and ass, I want more, but what's a guy to do? I take a swim. On the way home, I reminisce about the two studs. I wish I could get together with them again, but that's not going to happen because they're leaving tomorrow. But then I remember, Miller said he was leaving. Maybe Kennedy will still be around? I'll check tomorrow. I'd love to take a crack at the humpy redhead's rear-end. Maybe he'll be less uptight if I catch him on his own?

I bring my towel to my face. I can smell Marine sweat and cum on it. I'm not going to wash it. I'll use it and the photos of Miller at my next jerk-off session.

MARYJANE: THEN AND NOW
By Michael Bracken

Michael Bracken is the author of several books and nearly 1,000 short stories. He lives and writes in Texas.

"Wear the uniform again, Tommy." Stephen lay on the bed, a thin sheet his only cover, watching me rummage through the closet. "You know I love the uniform."

The last time I had worn my uniform, I'd barely been able to button my shirt and fasten my pants, and I'd done little since then to rein in my once-taut abdomen. "Not now."

"Why not, Tommy? Why not wear it for me?"

"Maybe tonight," I repeated. I selected a short-sleeved, green-and-white-striped seersucker shirt, tan chinos, and a pair of brown cap-toe oxfords, and I dressed in front of the open closet while Stephen continued to watch me, and I remembered the day we'd met.

#

I had just returned from Vietnam, having served my time without being outed, and I was only a few days away from discharge when we met. Fresh from the Ft. Hood barber, my black hair cut high and tight, I wore my uniform – all razor-sharp creases and mirror-polished boots – to visit friends in Austin who took me to a house party where my uniform brought sideways glances and caused some attendees to vacate any room I entered.

Stephen, a draft-dodging undergraduate at the University of Texas, wore faded purple bell-bottom hip-huggers, a colorful dashiki, love beads, and leather sandals. He'd parted his blond hair in the middle, and it hung plumb straight to his shoulders. The only thing we seemed to have in common was the haze of marijuana smoke that enveloped us.

I had smoked my first doobie in country, sharing it with an Alabama redneck so white he glowed in the dark and a coal black Negro from Chicago, the three of us unlikely to ever meet if it weren't for the draft, our insignificant high school GPAs, and our parents' low socio-economic standings.

"The poor are always cannon fodder in a rich man's war," I told Stephen as I passed him the doobie a braless brunette had handed me few minutes earlier.

For sure, he said, already several tokes beyond the ability to hold rational conversation. He said, "That's righteous thinking, man." Then he drew a long drag, held the smoke in his lungs, and passed the doobie back to me. Only the roach remained so I ate it.

I don't know where my friends had disappeared to by then, but I didn't care. Stephen was stroking my thigh and telling me how groovy I looked in my uniform. As my cock lengthened and stiffened, I realized that we had more in common than a relationship with Maryjane.

Then Stephen decided he was hungry. He braced himself on my shoulder and pushed himself to his feet. After I stood, he took my hand and led me into the kitchen, where a random assortment of snack foods had been spread across the counter. He pawed through everything until he found an unopened bag of Chips Ahoy!

"Far out," he said when he showed the package to me. He stuck it under his dashiki and led me out of the kitchen. Our next stop was an upstairs bedroom in the back of the house, and we sat on the floor with our backs to the bed, staring out the sliding glass door and down at the backyard as we devoured every chocolate chip cookie in the bag. Stephen even licked the cookie dust off the inside of the bag, and I thought he looked so funny I laughed until I blew snot out of my nose.

"You're cool, man," Stephen said as I wiped my nose with the back of my hand. "You're like, what, a colonel or something, right?"

I had never been anything more than a private, had never aspired to be anything more than a private, had wanted only to serve my time in country and get the hell out, and I told him so.

"Private?" he said. "I like privates. They take orders, don't they, colonel?" He patted his pockets and said he wished he had another smoke, something he could put in his mouth and suck on. Finding nothing in his own pockets, he began patting my pockets, and my cock began respond to his touch. Stephen noticed. He stopped patting my pockets and concentrated on my crotch. "What do you have in there, soldier boy?" He unzipped my trousers, reached through my government-issue boxers, and wrapped his fist around my tumescent cock. He pulled it free of the confining material and then buried his face in my lap. I couldn't see what he was doing because his long blond hair blocked my view. but I could certainly feel it when he wrapped his lips around the swollen head of my cock.

I'd not had a man's mouth around my cock since a brief encounter in a San Francisco bathhouse during a two-day layover on my way to Nam, and I couldn't restrain myself. Stephen had barely taken half my length into his mouth when I came, firing a thick wad of hot spunk against the back of his throat.

He swallowed and then licked my softening cock clean before he pulled away. He patted my thigh before he stood up and said, "Wait here, I'll be back in a minute."

I tucked my cock back inside my government-issue boxers, zipped my fly closed, and waited. In the back yard, two women had removed their tops, and one of the men had removed all of his clothes. They and half a dozen others danced to music that had no discernible beat.

Stephen returned with two bottles of Lone Star beer, a container of Crisco cold from the refrigerator, and another doobie. He popped opened both beer bottles and handed one to me. Then he snuggled up next to me and lit the doobie. We passed it back and forth between swallows of beer.

"You were there, man," he said, "and, like, what were you fighting for?"

"My life," I told him. The Vietnamese didn't want us there, and we didn't want to be there, and every day in country made me more aware of my own mortality. The Alabama redneck had his face blown off by a sniper when he was standing so close that bits of his brain splattered my face, and the Chicago Negro had his throat slit during his turn at watch while I slept next to him in the same foxhole. In the backyard, one of the girls wrapped an American flag around her shoulders, and I said I fought so she could do that.

Stephen followed my gaze. "So why'd you go, colonel?"

"I didn't have a choice."

"Everybody has a choice, man." He put one hand in my lap. "Canada's a choice."

"Nobody from my small town ever went to Canada, not before me and not after me."

"A bunch of good little privates, huh, colonel?"

"Cannon fodder," I said. "Nothing but cannon fodder."

We finished the doobie, and Stephen popped the roach into his mouth. Then he twisted around and kissed me hard, his tongue found mine, and before I realized it I had the roach in my mouth. I swallowed.

I had unbuttoned my jacket when we were in the living room, so it was easy for Stephen to unthread my tie and unbutton my shirt. I pulled the dashiki over his head as he kicked off his sandals. He peeled his purpled hip-huggers off and wasn't wearing anything beneath them. By then my cock stood at attention, a good little soldier surprisingly ready for action so soon after his first encounter with an opposing force, and Stephen helped me shed the rest of my clothes until he wore only his love beads, and I wore only my dog tags.

He opened the Crisco, scooped out a fistful, and slathered some of the still cold shortening on my cock, causing it to temporarily lose rigidity. He reached beneath his erect cock and between his legs and smeared some Crisco up the crack of his ass.

"You've wanted me ever since we met," Stephen said as he turned his back to me. I had, and I grabbed his hips. I pressed the head of my shortening-covered cock against his sphincter and pressed forward. Maryjane had relaxed Stephen, and I entered him with minimal resistance.

I pressed my entire length into his ass and then drew back, pressed forward and drew back again. As I fucked Stephen, he wrapped his Crisco-covered fist around his own cock and pumped hard and fast. He came first, firing a stream of cum across the jumbled pile of our clothing, leaving a stain on my uniform jacket that I would pay hell explaining if my sergeant saw it before I had my jacket cleaned.

At that precise moment, though, I didn't care. I drew back and pushed forward, pumping harder and faster until I was slamming into Stephen's ass, my desire compounded by a year spent hiding my true sexual desires from the cooze hounds of my platoon and confused with my anger at returning home to a country where the people I thought I had been defending were spitting on my uniform. His love beads bounced against his chest while my metal dog tags jangled against mine. I wasn't just having sex with Stephen; I was fucking everything he represented, from draft-dodging college students to country club politicians who sent poor kids to fight their battles while their own sons played solider in National Guard units.

And when I came, I came hard, slamming into Stephen with enough power to knock him off balance, and I fired wad after wad of hot spunk into his ass as we collapsed on the bed.

We've been together ever since, what binds us together more powerful than anything that might have driven us apart.

# # # # #

We were old men now, Vietnam a distant memory, cancer our newfound enemy, and one friend from those days still welcome in our home. When I returned that evening, I put on my uniform, leaving one shirt button unfastened over my abdomen, and sat on the bed next to Stephen. I rolled a doobie from the lid I'd purchased while I was away, lit it, and passed it to him.

The first toke began to take away his pain.

OF SERVICE
By R. Talent

"Lance Corporal Roderick Stevens was that man."

Captain Ronald Goodwin halted briefly, listening to the agreeable grunts of fifteen or so servicemen of color, mostly commissioned officers, who stood out of uniform naked in the enclosed circle slow-jerking their dicks around the fire dancing out of the barrel on a star-lit beach. Captain Goodwin attempted to hold back a simper from his otherwise stoic face. He tried his damnedest like a Marine should, but couldn't stop those memories from flooding back.

He wasn't alone. There were about four or five others that did the very same thing, only less subtle, with one office choosing to pump his hand faster in honor of the lance corporal.

Each man had their own special memory of the lance corporal, but none stood out more iconic than the lance corporal in that dark room whimpering with his head in the crook of his arm as he fitted another cock in his tight rear.

"If the boy was a bitch, he would've been pretty. Orange brown skin that glowed like smoothed clay, a brilliant bald head that shined like a light post, and a body of a nineteen-year-old just proving its worth."

"He had the hope of America right in there in his eyes and helped us serve this country just a little bit better," offered the master gunnery sergeant.

"And he was just for us," beamed one of the colonels, with a sophisticatedly youthful face.

"Huh?"

"Black and brown servicemen only," the master gunnery sergeant offered to the second lieutenant that was just transferred onto base.

Captain Goodwin took over, and added, "Most of the white sluts around here will take care of one or two black men at a time without being forced to. Other than that, the rest of us have to fend for themselves elsewhere or resort to other means. Of course, that is nothing new to the Corps, it just that some officers don't like sharing their toys and want to bitch about it through official means."

Captain Goodwin reflected bitterly. If he had known these lessons beforehand, he would have proudly have been a general of some kind instead of being demoted from his former position as a colonel.

"That's what made the lance corporal so special? He was on of ours?" The second lieutenant asked.

"That and more," said Captain Goodwin with a smirk, "that and so much more."

# # # # #

Captain Goodwin was sitting at his desk when he received the call. He was glad to hear that in his short absence that the third and fifth in command spearheaded the effort to draw in more recruits for his specialized training program; training that set itself apart from the official guidelines of the Corps for its covert operation. He didn't expect the program to fall short of expectations since he wasn't there to oversee every detail as he had been continuously doing for years. He was just delighted that his men had fortitude to work harder in his absence to make him proud, scheduling him to report by twenty-three-hundred to be introduced to his newest inductees.

He looked forward to the stress relief later on that night. He needed something to take his mind off of his current work and the havoc his recent vacation proved to be on his psyche.

Captain Goodwin had just returned from overseas. He wasn't there to enjoy the Christmas holiday with his family so much as he was there to walk his youngest daughter Reagan down the aisle. He thought his job was extremely simple: Show up and dress in uniform. Not so. After having to come out of pocket an extra ten grand after he specifically gave his daughter and affable ex-wife a reasonable set budget, he was force to meet with his daughter's fiancée's hippie parents that tried everything in their power to hurl every insult they could at his profession and his beliefs. If that wasn't enough, he had to hear them badmouth the extravagance of the wedding while underhandedly only adding to the expense without offering to contribute a dime. His only morsel of joy that came out of the ordeal was this heavy cat-and-mouse game he played with one of the younger groomsmen on the sly. He swore on the honor of his country that he was going to make sweet love to that tauntingly high bubble ass. A mission he failed at accomplishing because his ex-military wife interfered with a sexually-suggestive agenda of her own. It didn't matter anyhow. It seemed that every other family member wanted to cook him every home cooked meal under the burning sun. He spent so much time catching up with everybody that he wasn't able to sneak in a side trip to a local bathhouse that he liked to visit whenever he was back in the States. He fancied the place because of its historic grandeur or its replication of one. He fancied it even greater because every time he stepped foot in the place, he was treated like royalty. Men ran to dry him off after a soothing soak. Other men generously offered to pay for his massages, if only they could watch the expensive oils being slathered onto his flawless biscuit-brown flesh.

His body was just that magnetically magnificent of course to warrant such admirable attention. Taut definitions like his couldn't have been attempted by some of the finest sculptors out of Italy. Some could chisel the muscles from the photos but never do them quite the justice nor get the intricate details of the snaking veins that slithered across his hardened body like lightning bolts; great storms of it in some places, simple but commanding strikes in others. All work harnessed by more than three decades of a bodybuilding regimen.

Everything about Captain Goodwin was worthy taking in. If he had a particular prize, it was his clean shaven face. Hard with clear cut lines that didn't lend itself at all to a slight feminine beauty. It was immovably masculine in its rawest form.

It was the face above that magnificent body that made every man take notice when he stepped into the usual space that night, a dark wide place with a low ceiling and high window, filled with the dizzying almost suffocating heat of shirtless military men everywhere. Marines that were predominately black and brown in color with hues of red and yellow dotted in between.

Captain Goodwin was quite pleased with the spectacle array. Against one wall were several men standing at attention. Their nipples clipped to a long gray bar that ran above their heads to a pulley wheel controlled by a commanding officer relishing in their contorted expressions. Another wall promised a different scene, men being bounded and whipped along a variety of wooden posts and steel platforms enduring the torture leveled against them. And a third was buffered by a dark thin curtain that showed the clandestine actions of some of his graduates wolfishly molesting some of his newest recruits.

But of course his main focus was garnered underneath the sole light that illuminated from the middle the room. Directly underneath it was a beefy reddish-brown man that looked to be just a few reps away from being an ultimate cage fighter in another life. Here he was just a maggot dangling from the ceiling by a wooden plank with the tip of his feet barely touching the flat wooden post. His balls tied to an old-fashioned pale bucket below with a steady cascade of water and piss washing over his bald head from the showerhead above. Captain Goodwin was anxious to see where this might lead although he had seen the end result of these kinds of exhibitions too many times to really count. So when he wasn't terribly disappointed when his third in command pulled him to a side room. It was there that he saw his newest star pupil bent double over a padded horse with his legs spread and a long rubber tube shooting out of his rear. It was connected to a valve that was connected to a barrel of oil.

"What's this one's story?" Captain Goodwin asked of his subordinate, unfazed the young man in from of him happened to have his limbs chained to the floor. And unlike the bald-headed man underneath the light, this bald-headed kid was compact and wiry and appeared to be younger by a full decade.

"Lance Corporal Roderick Stevens, sir. Nineteen years old. He came to the Corps looking to be toughened up. He's got heart and skill, but can't seem to keep his cocksucking eyes off of others Marines in and out of uniform."

"No, sir, not true, sir," Lance Corporal Stevens spoke.

"Speak when spoken to Lance Corporal," the other officer barked.

"Yes, sir," Lance Corporal Stevens answered in defeat.

"Willing or unwilling," Captain Goodwin inquired.

As the Captain's training program went under the radar with a large number of top brass, it was infamously known amongst other Marines. Many outside of the tight-knit group of pledges really didn't know much about it, only hearing that it was considered a part of special operations and possibly a fast track up the Corps later, bringing a slight smirk to any Marine given a secret invitation to join. That is right before learning the scope of their sacrifice in order to become a part of their brotherhood.

"Like the rest of them. Willing, but wanting to renege on his honored commitment after he learned of his specific requirements were going to be from here on out."

Captain Goodwin understood his fears. He was brief about the specialized collective and jumped through enough hoops to feel like he belonged. He did everything right, above and beyond the call of duty. He assumed that he was being separated from the pack because of his ability, not because something more sinister was in mind.

"Doesn't sound like the heart of a Marine, maggot." Captain Goodwin dutifully noted. "Not the heart of a Marine at all."

"Sorry, Sir," Lance Corporal Stevens said with a slight sob in his voice.

Captain Goodwin motioned for his lesser command to shut off the valve of the barrel and removed the tubing out of the cheeky rear of the bowed Marine while he undid his belt to reveal a long slender penis that beautifully pointed downward with an unflattering tip that angled up.

"I guess your drill sergeant let you slip through the cracks, maggot. I guess as your Captain I have to show you what a Marine's heart is all about. I'll start by teaching you how to take it like a Marine!" Captain Goodwin retorted, rearing behind the lubed Marine for the very first time with no leniency.

# # # # #

"Stop running from it, maggot! Take this dick," barked the master gunnery sergeant, holding tight to the ankles of the nineteen year old in the wheelbarrow position, face down on the cot.

The master gunnery sergeant was pummeling his tender hole this way, getting a good squeal out of him with every plunge. Alternating between thrusting as hard as he could with his long stodgy dick to putting his hands behind his head and letting the young Marine bounce off of his crotch with his pinched cheeks.

"That's it. Rub those nutts. Make me feel real good in front of these fine men. Show all these Marines how you can be of service. Your fellow countrymen count on this great ass and throat." The master gunnery sergeant said for the benefit of the fifty-two naked Marines standing around waiting their turn.

Captain Goodwin had spent the better part of three months keeping the best kept secret, Lance Corporal Stevens, under wraps between him and his most trusted commands. He was reluctant to share such a wonderful gift with the rest of his operations after training him so well to the pleasures of men. His student was a natural, and he had to accept that he awakened an insatiable beast inside of the boy that went far beyond the limited scope of him and his handful of men.

Lance Corporal Stevens started out crying like a little maggot, crying that his commanding officer had raped him terribly. He wasn't a fag. He had a girlfriend somewhere expecting his first child in a few weeks. Captain Goodwin comforted the young man like he comforted other young men before him, telling him that the way he chose to use the young man had nothing to do with him being gay or not. He was just the most viable option to service his men in the tightest of spots. These words brought very little comfort to the ears of the lance corporal, just a great amount of soreness throughout his frame, even things that should have never hurt to begin with, after the fact.

The tide soon changed.

Lance Corporal Stevens began to resent the way his body turned. He hated that he got hard thinking about something long and hard teasing outer lips of his butthole or that his mouth knew what to do well when a dick stood at attention before it. He hated that his body thirsted for every glob of gunk that spewed out of it and did whatever it took to get it, and the sheer number ceased to matter.

"You're getting this nutt, Stevens. Open up! Open that ass up." The master gunnery sergeant howled, pumping a few times more.

He surprised his audience by not unloading into the kid, but rather spinning him on his dick where he lay flat on his back.

The master gunnery sergeant made sure that the bed was rocking again pinning the kid behind his knees over to his side, spreading him wide enough to let every man know that he was greater than his given rank.

"Thought we were done, maggot? You're getting this nutt … just not this second."

The master gunnery sergeant pulled his dick far enough out for the neighboring men around to watch the puckered asshole twitch open and close starving to be filled again.

"That's it. Talk to me, Stevens. Talk to me real good," the master gunnery sergeant said choking his dick in and out of the throbbing gap to get the same result for the obscenely impatient crowd.

Lance Corporal Stevens was holding back his own leg while stretching out another behind the master gunnery sergeant urgently thrusting faster and more calculating between them, driving in deeper and harder.

"You're getting this fucking nutt, maggot. You're getting every drop of it!" The master gunnery sergeant howled again, only this time staying in the same place and spreading his hot seed into the sodden muddle of the fifteen or so other colored men before him.

The master gunnery sergeant pulled out of that hole with a sickening pop, with no warmth or a thank you afterwards, as a commissioned officer quickly took his place.

The sight brought a huge smile over the man overseeing the whole event, Captain Goodwin, standing there at the end of the cot stroking his meat and smelling the distinct deposits of so many horny Marines snaking out from the bottomless pit that it was quite dizzying.

Lance Corporal Stevens took it every way possible on that cot, sometimes being forced to take it on both ends at the same time like a human rotisserie; on his front, his back, and his side in constant rotation. With so many men using him so, it was next to impossible for him to keep a soft dick. Forcing him to holler grunts and scream obscenities and squirt involuntarily all over the place as each man proved to be a different fit and his prostate tender to them all.

Captain Goodwin had to give it to the Marine. He showed a lot of heart. He was as good as he got when he started, men desperately wanting to be the one to rip him a new one. He held out longer than anyone expected, especially when one Marine sported a wine bottle that sprang out of his stinky crotch. He looked fatigued nearly halfway through, finding burst of energy nearing the finish line. He looked like he was about to give up as the final five took their place.

It was one by one by then. His mouth too tired to really work anybody over with decent head other than a soggy opening to muffle the incoherent noise still rattling out of it. Even that wasn't extremely necessary with his throat being sore from screaming the acclaim of half a hundred men and shamelessly chugging down a canal of Marine cream in between.

His mouth was finished, and so was his used rear. Slimy and sore, crusty and bruise, there wasn't much of a show to give them other than a certified cumbucket stretched far beyond belief. The men would've had a tighter more satisfying grip using a missing door knob opening. But, it wouldn't have provided the warm center that the power bottom had built up in his guts fucking all those piston-forced men.

"C'mon Marine," Captain Goodwin offered tiredly stroking his meat, after listening to two other men rapidly slosh inside of the slutty Marine as a third tried to get his balance.

Lance Corporal Stevens looked as if he passed out again. Though, he hadn't. He was still in the game barely, and was down for the count. He was going when the fourth man took his time emptying his load and was practically gone by the time the first man finished with him.

Captain Goodwin wanted to laugh, looking at the boy rolling his neck back to the cot stuck with his legs wide open from the last position he had been so thoroughly fucked in. He was so far gone that he probably didn't see that his dick was hard and running a cloudy stream from the arched tip. Captain Goodwin took a bit of it onto his fingers and ran it over the lips of his fully stuffed lay. Captain Goodwin only thought the Lance Corporal was tired as the nineteen-year-old licked and sucked them hungrily like he did every dick shoved into his mouth that night. When he slowed down after cleaning them of the salty spew, Captain Goodwin stuffed his fingers down into the well used hole covering them in gummy goo only to be rewarded with the same result.

He did this a few times to see how much the kid was going to take before his dick stayed hard. He had jumped in and out of line a few times that night, so he thought he was too spent to do anything else.

He guessed he was wrong.

Captain Goodwin did as he did several times before, and like the other men before him, drilling his dick back into that saturated hole.

Lance Corporal Stevens whimpered.

Captain Goodwin was a bit bewildered that the kid had closed up enough to feel his walls, which meant he felt his dick inside of him. The Lance Corporal grinded his hips on him doing none of the work that were often expected of him in their private sessions. The Lance Corporal felt warm and good and naturally sticky, fully understanding the dirty joke about warm apple pie for the first time.

"I'll tell you what, Marine," Captain Goodwin offered. "If you can make yourself cum just like that on my dick without grabbing yourself, I'll let you stand in line with the rest of the Marines to initiate the next recruit for my program."

Lance Corporal Stevens looked up at Captain Goodwin and gave him a slight smile for introducing him into this world.

"You're going to come for the Captain?"

Lance Corporal Stevens slowly rolled his hips again, this time in a hard rocking motion before picking up the smooth speed like a raging twister fully concentrated.

"You're trying to come for the Captain?" Captain Goodwin huffed, putting his hands behind his back trusting that his star pupil had him covered.

Lance Corporal Stevens did, shifting gears to get at the spot that had him going a few times that night. He was tired as fuck, and under any other circumstances wouldn't think he had it in him. But he had to give more than the best to the first man that ever plowed him, his commanding officer.

"Take it deep." Captain Goodwin coached. "Breathe, Stevens."

Lance Corporal Steven moaned, letting the black pipe scrape against his spot bringing about a renewed sensation that he hadn't felt since earlier that night. He wanted to slow down and savor it. Not so much savor it, but scared to death to ride that feeling over its edge again. He heard stories of people not being able to reach certain peaks anymore after such sensory overload. He had done it a few times for the first time that night already. It hadn't escaped his mind in the least the number of men he fucked that night or that some had automatically made him do exactly what his captain was requesting of him. He just didn't want it to be a requirement that he had to take that many men at once to ever get off again.

Even as he turned over in his mind on what to do, his body took the wheel edging the feeling tempting to go over it, and holding back just enough. He looked over at his captain shirtless and muscular and couldn't help but to feel honor that a man like him still wanted to use him like this after everything he saw.

"Owwwwwww. Ahhhhhhhhhhhhhh. Nnnnghhhhhhhhhh!" Lance Corporal Stevens shouted his lights out.

It was only short of a miracle that the kid shot anything short of a ghost load, but he sent a very narrow ribbon of white slime back at his face. It looked more like a line from a spider's web than anything else.

Lance Corporal Stevens barely had a second to recover when he felt the dick inside of him pump rigorously a few minutes more. He looked up to find his captain scrunching his face.

"Uuuuurrrrrrrghhhhhhhh!" Captain Goodwin screamed louder than he shot, probably adding no more than a drop into the hole.

It was over, both men thought.

Captain Goodwin eased his sore dick out and slapped Lance Corporal Stevens on the thigh, leaving him to sleep just like he left him with his legs proudly pulled back to his sides.

"What became of Lance Corporal Stevens?" The second lieutenant asked.

Captain Goodwin sighed along with some of the others.

"He proved to be of service elsewhere." Captain Goodwin spoke with tearful honor, holding onto the last memory of walking in on the young Marine steadily sawing into a top brass official using what he learned from the program to work his way up the military ladder.

"Once a boy learns how to stud, he doesn't bend over ever to take it again so well."

MILITARY HANDSOME
A Novella by R. W. Clinger

> *R. W. Clinger is always up for some rough play with a military man. He is currently at work on a gay mystery and can be reached at* kentiorico@verizon.net.

1. THE NEIGHBOR

We meet on purpose. I hear noises in the empty Cape Cod next door, which sits approximately two hundred yards beyond the line of narrow woods that separates the two properties. No one has lived in the Cape Cod for the last three years since Helen Rutger died of a heart attack on Christmas Eve at the age of seventy-three. I knew she was childless and willed the house to her sister, Evelyn Rutger. I met the sister once, who wasn't impressed with my lakeside town of Edson, which sits next to Lake Erie, hidden in the Pennsylvania woods.

"What the hell?" I say to myself, listening to hammering, a drill, saw, and other tools at work on the Rutger property. I exit my study, rush through the house, and step into the beating sun.

We meet at the end of July in the middle of the afternoon. The temperature feels like one hundred degrees. It's sticky without a cloud in the sky. Rain isn't expected for another two days.

I bolt to the property line, step into the woods, and surround myself with tall oaks, lush maples, and slim birch trees. Again, I hear tools at work: more hammering, a circular saw, and a rumbling drill.

I see the Cape Cod through the woods: smallish in size, dilapidated with broken windows and missing shutters, weathered because of abandonment. Beyond the Cape Cod is the green-blue lake: motionless and beautiful, at peace during the hot day.

We meet …

I see the stranger working on the three wooden steps that lead up to the Cape Cod's portico and bleached red front door. He's massive with suntanned skin, an onyx-colored crew cut, 240 pounds of all muscle, six-four frame, tapered waist. I estimate he's thirty-three years old and not a native of Edson since I've never seen him before. He wears khaki green shorts, shin-high socks, and military boots with black laces. He slams nails into freshly cut oak boards, wipes his brow because of the heat, and turns around to fetch a canteen of water.

I view his bare torso and face for the first time, which causes my limp package of beef between my legs to stir with excitement. The man is beautiful: onyx-colored eyes, stubble on his rugged cheeks and chin, slightly crooked nose because of a few breaks. His torso is ripped with abs and dark hair. The man's nipples are the size of plates, and his navel is perfectly dented and furred.

I stop in the woods approximately forty feet away from the handsome stranger. Here, I watch him take a drink from his military canteen, one chug after the next. Now, he tilts his head back and pours water onto his chiseled face. The liquid rolls down and over his forehead, cheeks, and the cords that line his neck. Zigzag tracks of the water roll over his sculpted chest, over all of his abs, and into his khakis.

"Jesus," I whisper, open-mouthed and now completely hard between my legs. I can't remember the last time I saw a man who was so handsome, masculine, and unbelievably sexy. Without a single thought in mind, excited in the woods, I push the erection down, heavily breathe, and decide to close the gap between our heated bodies.

When I step out of the woods that separate the two properties by the lake, the stranger immediately reacts. He quickly drops the canteen to the dusty ground next to the refurbished steps, spins to his right, clasps his right palm against a M9 Beretta and swings it to his left, aiming it at my chest. The stranger yells, "Don't move, and no one gets hurt, buddy!"

The sidearm is just as sexy as its handler, and everything I want to write about for the magazine I work for, *Guns & Target*. From a distance, I study its sleek beauty: a double-action, semi-automatic that holds 15-NATO standard 9mm rounds. The truth of the matter is simple: I don't know which I want to hold more, the man or his handgun. Instead of deciding, I raise both palms above my head, and yell back, "Don't shoot! Lower your weapon! I'm unarmed!"

We finally meet, as expected. The bulky and handsome stranger eyes me from head to toe, studying me with an avid concern: Rufskin T-shirt snug against my chiseled torso, navy blue Diesel shorts, bootie socks, running shoes, a pencil above my right ear. He calculates every detail of my body with dubious care: sweep of blond hair, fern green-colored eyes, six-one frame, 200 pounds of muscle from daily workouts, thirty-two waist, thick thighs, semi-swollen package between legs, and thirty-one years old.

Does he take me for a magazine writer? Does he realize my infatuation for men and guns? Can he pinpoint my likeness for sex with men who just happen to look exactly like him?

"Who are you?" he calls out, dropping his weapon to his side. The steel barrel brushes against his sexy hip. He makes eye contact with me that states: *Don't fuck with me. I'm not afraid to use my sidearm.*

I slowly lower my arms and reply, "I'm the neighbor. I live on the other side of these woods."

The massive man seems to relax a little, blinks, rubs his left temple with his free hand, and inquires, "Were you my aunt's neighbor?"

"Helen Rutger?"

"Yes. My mother's sister."

I carefully nod my head and answer with a direct surety, "I was very close to Helen. She was like my own aunt, and I miss her dearly."

"I'm Keith Rutger," he says, setting aside the sexy M9 Beretta exactly where he retrieved it. "I'm Evelyn's son."

217

I step closer to him, bridging the gap between us. Still cautious, I reach my right hand out for him to shake.

Within seconds, he man-handles my right palm with a firm shake and asks, "What's your name, pal?"

"Greg ... Greg Islip."

"Nice to meet you, neighbor." Again, the stranger checks me out from head to toe.

I steer my gaze to his right and see the M9 Beretta next to his toolbox. Saliva enters my mouth with the need to touch its glinting steel.

"Don't get any ideas about my sidearm. I'm pretty quick about reaching it and plugging you with a round."

I shake my head and admit, "It's a beauty," and I rattle off facts regarding the handgun: Italian made, from the 92 series, overall length is 217mm, muzzle velocity is 1,280 feet per second and ...

He drops his massive paw from mine and a grin of seduction and likeness forms over his model-like face. He says, "How do you know so much about my sidearm?"

I tell him what magazine I write for, and my editor's name, Hilliard Dawning. I add, "Your aunt helped me with my articles when I was younger. She was an amazing English teacher at Edson High."

Rutger seems impressed, nods his head, and says, "I'm familiar with Dawning. And yes, my aunt was a stickler for dotting i's and crossing t's."

"She and I wrote a lot of articles together. I was always looking up to her for help, and guidance."

"You looked seduced by the M9, Islip."

"What can I say? I like men and their guns."

He smiles from ear to ear at my playful quip, and adds, "It's nice to meet you, Greg Islip."

"The pleasure is all mine," I respond, eye up his sexy frame again, but concentrate on his sidearm even more.

I learn that Rutger is only visiting Edson for the summer. He tells me that his mother, Evelyn, practically begged him to make the drive from Annapolis to Erie and attempt to mend the Cape Cod. He tells me he's good with his hands, likes to work with tools, and enjoys carpentry. I tell him I'm good with words, sentences, and paragraphs.

Twenty minutes pass in his company, and he asks me to share a beer with him in the shade. I want to stay, but don't. "I have an article to finish."

"What's it about?" He has a spark of interest in his black eyes.

"Sniper rifles."

A smile warms his face yet again. "Which ones?"

"The AW50 and the L115."

"I'd like to read it when you finish it, Islip."

"Not possible. I don't share my work until its published."

He nods his head and comments, "I can respect that. If you change your mind … I'd still like to read it, though."

"I'll make a footnote of that," I reply before shuffling away. "If you need anything, I'm just a few hundred yards away."

Again, he nods his head, thanks me, and continues with his carpentry.

2. POST-MIDNIGHT

I Google Rutger later this evening and find the most interesting facts about him: he spent two military terms as a corporal in the "Dark Horse" 3rd Battalion, 5th Marines; graduated at the top of his class with honors in 2007 from the School of Infantry – East Division; granted the Legion of Merit award this spring; obtained the Marine Corps Good Conduct medal; suffered a hip casualty in Now Zad the previous winter; father unknown; attended Bessimer High School in Annapolis, Maryland; attended two years of business school at Medesta College; no children; no wife; honorably discharged from the military with many ribbons and medals.

My history is nothing like Rutger's. I attended Temple in Philadelphia for four years, majoring in English and minoring in world literature. My grades were fair, the product of too much partying. Following my degrees, I started writing for *Guns & Target*, being the low man on the totem pole. Now, I am a full-time writer and assistant editor at the magazine. I publish 10,000 words a month, which usually equals two nonfiction pieces, and work from home: 7219 Mossdale Road. Sometimes I travel to gun shows or private gun collections for research, but recently I have just become a homebody/recluse.

The Tudor on Mossdale belonged to my parents, who are now deceased; lung cancer was obtrusive in their lives and snatched the pair away from me when I was twenty-two years old. The Tudor has two bedrooms, a small bathroom on the second floor, and miniature-size rooms on the first floor: living room, kitchen, dining room, a study, and a tiny foyer to hang jackets or kick off summer sandals.

The back of the property slopes to the lake. There's a tomato garden to the left, small plot of woods to the right, and a cobblestone patio off the smallish stoop where I sometimes barbecue, sit and read or edit. The place is comfortable, paid in full, home for one; my likeness.

# # # # #

July 31. The night is sticky and hot. Thunder rolls overhead as heat lightning blisters the dark heavens. I sleep in nothing more than a pair of damp boxer-briefs the color of oil. I toss and turn for an hour ... two hours ... three hours ... and eventually fall asleep. A dream carries me back to the previous day and meeting Keith Rutger for the very first time. Again, he is bare-chested in the steeping sun, perspiration-covered, and surprised to see me. This time he does not sport a gun. Instead, he unzips his khaki shorts, pulls out a ten-inch slab of veined cock, and chants to me with an ear to ear smile, "Blow it, Islip. You know you want to. Shove all ten inches of it down the back of your throat. Eat my seed. It's time you and I get down to some man-to-man business."

A masculine scream wakes me in the middle of the night. I immediately sit up in my queen-size bed, feel a layer of sweat glaze my chest, and listen to the soft sounds of thunder in the distant clouds. The abrupt scream resembles that of someone being murdered. The noise is horrendous, resonant within the night. Its origin wafts from Rutger's Cape Cod, through the plot of woods, and enters my Tudor's open bedroom windows.

Here, sitting up in bed, sweat-covered, and still, I turn my view to the digital alarm clock by my bed and see that it is 3:45 in the morning. The night is pitch-black beyond my windows. The time when light sleeps like humans.

And here, I decide to climb out of bed and investigate the unnerving scream at the Cape Cod. Hastily, attired in nothing more than my ink-colored boxer-briefs, I carefully navigate my trek through the wooded area between my house and Rutger's. Branches try to tear out my eyes and scar my bare chest. Although dangerous, I continue to be cautious, nimble within the maples, oaks, and birch trees. Above the black-green canopy thunder speaks, warning me of endangerment. To no avail, I proceed with my investigation, curious of the scream, a possible emergency at hand concerning my delicious looking next door Marine, Rutger.

Yellow-gold-white light shines inside the Cape Cod's kitchen window. Once reaching Rutger's property, I make my way up to the back stoop, find myself at the rear screen door, tap on its pine frame, and announce my arrival, in hopes of not being shot for trespassing, particularly after dark, "Rutger ... It's me ... Islip!"

The young Marine answers the door with sweat covering his naked brow and chest. He too is wearing nothing more than a pair of underwear: white cotton briefs with an Aussiebum label. He breathes heavily, wide-eyed and open-mouthed. His right hand holds a glass of water with three ice cubes. "Islip, what are you doing here?" he questions, raising an eyebrow, stunning me yet again with his chiseled handsomeness, and an unstoppable desire to connect our lips, nicely sculpted chests, and cotton-covered cocks together in lust.

He welcomes me inside the Cape Cod after I explain my unannounced presence. He offers me a glass of icy water, which I kindly decline. Here, we stand together in his kitchen, partially naked, practically face to face, both of us drenched in July sweat and terribly wide-eyed. "I'm intruding," I say, unsure of what the hell I am doing inside his kitchen at four o'clock in the morning.

"You're keeping an eye on me," he ambiguously says.

I do a once-over of his body and feel my internal organs rumble with pleasure. Cock-spew leaks out of the deflated joint between my legs and dribble decorates their snug cotton. "You scared the shit out of me," I confess. "I thought you were being murdered."

"Sorry about that."

"Anything I can help with?"

"I'm good. Thanks. It was just a bad dream."

I want to ask him what kind of dream but decide it's none of my business. Instead, I make the decision to leave, having already interfered with his night.

As I apologize for my unexpected visit, he stops me from leaving. Rutger calls out to me, "Hey, Islip."

I spin around at the kitchen's screen door, make eye contact with him, and say, "Yeah?"

"Thanks for coming over to rescue me."

"Any time," I reply, provide him with a wide smile, and continue with my exit.

# # # # #

He watches me from the screen door as I walk away from the Cape Cod and find myself back at the edge of the woods that separates our properties. Intuition kicks inside my head, between my temples, and I clarify with myself that he studies my bare back, naked thighs, and cotton-covered ass. Rutger visually takes every inch of my masculine mass in, perhaps enjoying what he views.

I spin around at the edge of the woods for no apparent reason. In doing so, I capture something of the absurd. My own view takes in the Marine, who stands at the full-length screen door. His right palm is flat against his muscular and hairy stomach. Fingers and palm roll down and over his sculpted abs, bypassing his dimpled navel. There, semi-hidden by the screen, the tips of his four fingers on his right hand glide into the rim of his white cotton Aussiebums, stop, and mix with the tangles of his pubic triangle.

I vanish into the woods and head for my Tudor. Upon this short journey, I imagine the Marine toying with his ten inches of beef inside his briefs because he finds me handsome, something to sexually feed on. His military fingers cause the tool to grow into its maximum size between his stern legs. His gun is palmed for the next ten minutes, its excess skin jostled up and down. Fit breath is caught, released, and caught again as Rutger masturbates within the night at the screen door. I imagine his hairy balls swinging to and fro because of his self-excitement. More perspiration builds on his plane of chest as his palm-friction continues and … white goo is released from his spike, which splashes against the screen, and hangs there in splotches as spent-time for the Marine is discovered, and post-sexed enlightenment.

3. NONE OF MY BUSINESS

It happens again the following night, except this time Rutger's scream is much louder and more prominent. In fact, a string of screams is heard, immediately waking me from a Rutger-dream, which entails our naked and soapy bodies connected in my upstairs shower. Challenged by the neighbor's horrifying yelps, I am pulled out of the intoxicating dream, gasp for air, open my eyes wide, and begin to collect my composure.

Now, because I am naked, uncomfortable with clothes due to the summer's unkind heat and humidity, I find a pair of boxer-briefs from the top drawer of my dresser, slip into the fabric, and have every intention of investigating the Marine and his night terror yet again.

It's another terrifying dream, I imagine. Keith Rutger is somewhere in Afghanistan in search of the evil Taliban: bombs drop; women and babies scream at the top of their lungs; an AH-64B military chopper explodes over a desert; a sandy menagerie is everywhere; Marines cry out for help; gunshots echo within his mind … phat … phat … phat; red-yellow-gold-orange explosions fill the night; a Marine's bloody torso in in another Marine's lap; the strong scent of bittersweet blood hangs in the dusty air; another explosion occurs; another masculine scream ensues; more gunfire; flesh is seared open by flying metal; landmines explodes; a Marine is missing his arm; open-eyed corpses of fellow members of the "Dark Horse" line the desert sand; young men are being torched and …

I bolt out of the Tudor, over the side lawn, and through the woods. An oak tree's branch almost slays my right arm and attempts to scratch its skin's surface. I rush through the night in search of Rutger, ready and willing to save him from …

From what? What am I saving him from? Post-traumatic stress from his two years in the Middle East? A rescue from his horrible nightmares? His flummoxed mental state following his days in Afghanistan? How am I to help the Marine? What safety can I offer him? Why am I concerned so much? Who do I think I am? What kind of person am …

Again, the Marine is in his kitchen with a glass of icy water. This time I witness him taking three pink pills, swallowing them down with a hearty gulp of water. Again, he is dressed in nothing more than a pair of cotton briefs. Again, he heaves for breath and is perspiration-covered. Again, he is ...

He has tears in his eyes, which tells me he woke up screaming and sobbing. The man's beautiful onyx-colored eyes have flecks of reddish fire within their pupils. Tears ebb at their corners. A bubble of snot hangs at his left nostril.

"Afghanistan nightmares," exits my lips in a helpless manner; immediately I want to swallow the words back, but they already escape my mouth, unintentionally.

He shakes from head to toe in the kitchen. He places his glass of icy water on the quartz counter, leans into the counter's edge, lowers his head, closes his eyes and ... continues to tremble.

"What can I do?" I ask, scared for him ... and me. I really don't know what to do for him.

"The pills," he whispers, "let the pills do their thing. It takes a few minutes."

Anxiety pills? Post-traumatic stress pills? Anti-Taliban pills? Afghanistan Nightmare pills? Survive the Middle East pills? Social disorder pills? Post-war pills?

I close the gap between us and step up to him.

He applies a palm between my pecs, pressing it into my skin. "Away ... Back away. There's nothing you can help me with, Islip. The pills will help."

Truth is his palm feels wonderful against my chest. The tip of one fingertip is applied to my right nipple. Tingles of elation ski up and down my spine, and between my legs. I want his entire body to compress itself against my own. I want tonight to swing into something relentlessly sexual between us. I want …

"It's none of your business," he whispers, looking at the white, marble tile on his kitchen floor. "You should go home."

"I can help you," I explain in a most soothing manner. "I really don't know how to help you, Rutger, but I can."

He slowly shakes his head and informs, "Go home. I don't want you here. Stay where you belong. My problems cannot be your problems. Respect that."

I turn away from him, removing my chest from his comfortable touch. I back into the screen door with caution and say, "I understand … Honestly, I do."

He doesn't reply. Instead, he grips the edge of the quartz countertop with both fists, clasps his eyes and lips closed and stands still. Sweat falls off his nipples and drips to the tile floor. His legs tremble and his shoulders seem to quiver.

I escape the Cape Cod, just as I did the night before. This time, though, the Marine doesn't watch me from the screen door, and nor do I imagine him playing with his junk until he comes. Instead, he leans his bare torso over the counter and shudders in state of needed repair.

# # # # #

I can't sleep the rest of the night. My mind races with Rutger's screams … the consumed pills … and his trembling at the counter. I can't get the man and his problem out of my mind. The severity of his post-war condition (isn't my business) is inexorable. Rutger obviously suffers from his Middle East days at war. Afghanistan plunders his dreams after dark and inhabits his mind with dangerous events/memories. The man agonizes dearly, I believe.

My writing calls for me, but I can't write. I have an article due by the end of the week on the MAG-58 machine gun used by the

Rhodesian Army. A second article is due next week on the West German G3 rifle, which I'm almost finished writing.

Unfortunately, words are lost as I sit in front of my HP laptop. The white page continues to be white for the next hour ... two hours ... until dawn.

As a warm sunrise welcomes a new August day, I sit in my leather reading chair inside my small study and decide to clean my Smith & Wesson Model 686: a six or seven shot double action revolver that also fires .38 Special cartridges, 2-1/2 inch barrel length as a standard model, owned by my father in 1980 and willed to me, cylinder with extractor, ejector, and internal parts. An hour passes, almost two hours at work, and eventually I begin to yawn. The sun is a ball of yellow-orange in the distance, rising with speed, adding heat to the day, summertime gold.

I find my bedroom and queen-size bed, slip onto the mattress in the buff, close my eyes, and dream:

Rutger is next to me on my bed, bare-chested and hard between his legs. Ten, steeping inches rise from his middle. Bubbles of pre-shoot accessorize the pole, which I lick away with my outstretched tongue.

"Suck it," he whispers. "It doesn't bite. Make me shoot more of it out."

I lean over his still body, open my mouth and push three ... six ... all ten inches of his post inside my throat. I rock my head up and down, gag, moan with pleasure, and swallow his peg clear down to his balls.

I wake from the dream when he explodes his thick and creamy juice into my mouth. Suffocation is discovered and ...

It's shortly after noon when I open my eyes. The spot between my legs is hard, damp, and sticky. The wet dream is over. A smile surfaces on my face of happiness, longing, and of spent emotion. I reach between my heated thighs and find the sticky leak from my hard shaft, draw the fingers up to my lips, take a bittersweet taste laced with urine, and whisper a single name in lust: "Rutger."

4. BEHIND ME

I set up target practice in my backyard where there is plenty of space for no accidental injuries. Here, I display a Birchwood twenty-four-inch in diameter target next to the lake, opposite Rutger's summertime abode. Approximately fifty yards away, I use a Ruger MK III and pop off a shot with a one-handed grip. The shot breaks ring seven. I pop off a second shot and break ring nine. A third shot hits the X on the target and a feeling of deep satisfaction surfaces on my skin.

The heat is almost unbearable, but it doesn't prevent me from carrying out one of my favorite hobbies. Having the Ruger in my right palm feels similar to a cock: sleek, powerful, and daunting. I pop off seven more shots, become pleased with my results, score big, and decide to practice for another half hour in the afternoon sun.

Rutger discovers me in the afternoon's throbbing heat as I pop off a few more shots at the Birchwood target. He finds his way through the narrow strip of woods that separates our privacy, arrives shirtless because of the heat, sports a pair of canary-yellow A&F shorts against his suntanned thighs, and smiles from ear to ear. His nipples are hard on his chest, his smile is broad, and his biceps of steel gleam in the day's warmth. Upon his arrival, he informs, "When a Marine hears shots, he has to find out what's going on."

I pull the Ruger down, put its safety on, hold it at my right side, turn my attention directly to him, and say, "I actually love to shoot. I find myself out here all the time."

"Nice piece," he says, smiling.

I wonder if he's talking about the pistol at my right hip or the fleshy package between my thighs. "Thanks," escapes me, a small smile that feels heavy with lust for his body to compress against my own, allowing me to perform a blowjob on him like the dream I had at lunchtime.

He rubs his nose with his right fist and rattles off, "Islip, I want to talk about last night if it's alright with you."

I nod my head in agreement but keep quiet and still.

The Marine clears his throat, blinks, and says, "I didn't mean to kick you out of my house. And, I didn't mean to say what I said about my nightmares not being any of your business."

"They aren't my business," I reply quickly, honestly. "You live over there ... and I live over here. The woods keep our business private."

He steps up to me now, allows two feet between us, and reaches for my right shoulder with his right palm, grasps the shoulder, pleasantly rubs its muscular mass with his fingers and palm, and coddles, "I was overreacting. The nightmares are hell. Afghanistan haunts me after dark. I really appreciate you checking up on me, Islip. I'm sorry about my reaction. Honestly, I am."

He tells me he suffers from post-traumatic stress from being in the Middle East, and that he's getting help for it. "I take a few drugs to calm me down. Sometimes they work. Other times they don't. I see a shrink twice a week. Her name is Suzanne Ewing. She has an office in downtown Edson."

"I know her," I say.

He seems surprised by my information. "You do?"

"I do. We played together as kids. Went to the same high school. Graduated in the same class. Edson is small. Don't be surprised that she's popular."

Does he wink at me? I'm really not sure. I think he winks at me. Or, I want him to wink at me. No matter if he winked or not, he becomes comfortable with my presence and begins to open up to me ... just how I want him to, of course.

He continues his confession regarding his post-traumatic stress condition, and chatters, "I've had nightmares ever since I returned to the States. Children blowing up. Marines losing limbs. Bombs exploding. Shit like that. Tough stuff. Horrible things. Some Marines are worse off than I am, though. Some have lost their legs or arms. A few come back blind. Many fail to come back at all. Suzanne helps me with my condition. The drugs work, too. I'm making baby steps through it."

"Thank you," I whisper, nod my head, and sound sincere.

"For what?" he inquires with wide eyes and interest.

"For being an American and risking your life for our freedom. For having your ass mentally kicked and …"

"It was my job, Islip. My duty. I took an oath, and I lived up to that oath."

"I respect you for that, Rutger. I just want you to know that. It takes a lot of courage and strength to go over there and do what you did. I get that. Anyone who protects our country from terrorists is a hero in my opinion."

His onyx-colored eyes light up with gold sparks. He says, "You're good therapy for me, do you know that?"

I shake my head and reply, "Nope. I'm just your neighbor. Nothing more. Nothing less."

"Whatever," he prattles, beams with a smile, and welcomes me into his world just a little more.

# # # # #

A minute later, I pop off another shot at the Birchwood target but miss. A sigh is released from my chest and exits my mouth.

Rutger steps up behind me and says, "It's all about your grip."

"How so?"

"Let me show you." He presses his bare chest to my naked back and instructs me, "Your grip is weak. Lift your right arm."

I listen, following out his instruction.

"Take the pistol's safety off." His warm breath lines the side of my neck and tickles my right earlobe.

Done.

"Show me your hold." His hairy chest feels wonderful against my back, almost naughty. He smells of sweat and a spray of morning cologne that drives me mad.

Done.

"See how your grip is a little to the left. This is why you're missing the target." He applies his bulky and muscular arm against my arm and repositions my right hand. "Hold still. I'm going to back away and you fire. I bet you hit the target."

I want him snuggled behind me like this for the next five decades, just the two of us, man connected with man. Instead, the Marine pulls away, and I fire the Ruger MK III.

I'm hard between my legs as the bullet flies out of the Ruger and hits the target approximately fifty yards away. The lead nails the target's bulls eye dead on, which adds a jolt to my sexual excitement.

Calmly, Rutger says, "Put the gun on safety and spin around."

Done.

Surprisingly, he holds out his left hand for a congratulatory shake. In doing so, I rattle off, "I was hoping for a hug."

The Marine laughs, and jokes, "Maybe next time. Try another shot."

Our shake ends and I turn back around. Two more shots are popped off; both of which nail the bulls eye.

He wants a go at the target after my turn. I pass him the Ruger after I slide the safety on, and say, "Best of luck."

"Luck is having you as a neighbor."

"Why do you say that?"

He loads the gun with a fresh round of bullets, takes his stance, and replies, "You could be an asshole if you wanted."

"Why would I want to be that?"

"Some guys are."

"I'm not like some guys," I respond, watch him raise his right arm and quickly pop four bullets into the bulls eye next to the lake. Following his work, I say, "Shit, you know how to shoot."

"Most Marines do."

"The few. The proud. The Marines. Right?"

"Semper Fidelis," he turns around, sporting pride on his face.

"Always faithful," I translate for him.

"Nicely said," he adds and passes the Ruger back to me.

My eyes stray to his rocky chest again: pointed nipples decorated with black fur, ab-lined stomach, tapered waist, dented navel, and massive biceps. I lick my lips, wish our bodies would connect and …

"What are you looking at, Islip?"

"Nothing," I whisper with a bubble of saliva at the left of my mouth, which proves that he causes me to drool.

"I don't believe you."

"You should."

"I don't."

I want to tell him to stop playing sexual games with me and ... fuck me. My balls aren't this big, though. Instead, I just gawk at him as if he is a Hollywood actor who just happens to get off on guns and target practice ... and next door neighbors.

He leans into me, cradles his palms against my hips, brushes his sweaty and firm chest against my sweaty and hairless chest, allows our nipples to touch with ease, and he whispers, "You're hard."

I say nothing in return, unable to utter a single word. The writer in me becomes absolutely wordless.

Rutger leans closer to me, brushes the tip of his nose to my nose, almost meets our lips together and ...

Our heartbeats connect, pumping blood together. Blended sweat on touching chests stings. Our pulses race with unstoppable velocity.

I become dizzy, unsure of my stance, and windblown. Pre-leak squirts out of my cock's tip and decorates my underwear. I feel traumatized by our mix, and unsure exactly what is going to happen next between us.

A kiss never transpires between us. Instead, he awkwardly pulls away from me with speed. The Marine fakes a cough and shakes his head. Immediately, he brushes a palm across his lips, heads for the woods, and calls over his right shoulder, "I have some things to do, Islip. See you around."

Here, I stand frozen in the sun with the pistol at my right hip, and feel the coldest I have ever felt in my life, knowing that I have scared him away.

5. SEXY

Gay? Straight? Bisexual? I really don't want to put a label on the sexy Marine, but can't help it. I honestly want him to be queer for selfish reasons: to hold me against his skin again, to endearingly kiss me, to wrap his legs around my body, to do everything unthinkable with him against a wall, on the floor, in the shower and …

I study Marine comradeship on the Internet and the closeness Marines obtain, an unbreakable bond between adult men in battle. What was his association with the other "Dark Horse" members? How close did he become to those men of war, caught in the Middle East? Is he the type of man who likes the company of another man?

I wonder.

I will only wonder until Rutger … touches me again.

A goal of mine is to learn if the Marine likes cock. Does he want it inside one of his large palms, buried in his mouth, or against his tight rump? Would he ever find pleasure having his furred chest drizzled with my gooey cream? Does he have the potential to lean over the solid rock between my legs and lap up the sap that I ejaculate out of its cap? Could he pinch my nipples with fingertips and …

# # # # #

I decide to invite him over to the Tudor for steaks on the grill, summertime corn on the cob, and beer. I illuminate the back patio with candles, set out a cooler of Blue Moon beer and bowl of sliced oranges, and play some light jazz on the rock speakers.

Of course he accepts my invitation. "What time, and what should I bring?"

I'm honest with him and say, "Seven o'clock and two shot glasses. I have this new whiskey I want to try with you."

"Marines are always up for whiskey."

"So are writers," I reply, and tell him not to be late.

# # # # #

"How did you get into guns?" he asks after our steaks on the patio.

We share Blue Moons and sit across from each other on Polywood outdoor chairs around a matching table. I reply to his question with: "My father had a lot of guns. I was infatuated with them as a young boy. My interests grew in writing, and with guns. I decided to mix the two after college."

"You're amazing," he replies, and toasts me.

"I wasn't fighting terrorists in the Middle East. That's amazing, and heroic."

"You're going to make my head swell, Islip."

I joke, "Who says I was talking about you?"

He finds a stuffed outdoor pillow on one of the spare chairs and tosses it at me. I catch it in mid-air, laugh, and suggest, "Let's try the whiskey out for size. What do you think?"

"Bring it, writer man," he answers, happy as my guest.

We have shots of Bush Mill Irish whiskey. I say it goes down pretty smooth. Rutger says that he prefers the Blue Moons over the whiskey. For the next two hours we drink and he tells me about Afghanistan and his war stories. At one point, I have to stop him because he is just about ready to cry, which now prompts me to say, "Let's make a toast."

"Absolutely."

"To your survival, Rutger."

"To my survival."

We drink for another two hours. I become sloppy, and he seems perfectly fine. Marines are built to consume a lot of alcohol, I learn. Rutger does a number of shots and consumes most of the beer and doesn't even seem to be affected by either.

"You're not human," I rattle off, completely blitzed.

"I'm a Marine."

"You're beautiful," I spit out. "You need to know that. From one man to another."

He merely stares at me from his seated position on the opposite side of the table: motionless, perhaps numb by my comment, overtly surprised.

Now, he stands, pulls me out of my chair, leans into me, cradles his palms against my hips, brushes his sweaty and firm chest against my sweaty and hairless chest, allows our nipples to touch with ease, and whispers, "You're hard."

"I like you ... too much."

"How much did you drink tonight?"

"Too much." A giggle escapes my lips. "A dozen or more shots, I'm sure."

"Why do you like me?" His face is so close to mine we can kiss. His warm and beer-scented breath cuddles against my face.

"You're dangerous," I admit, wanting to kiss him, hold him, drag my tongue along his hairy chest, and between his thighs ... whatever he wants from me.

"How am I dangerous?"

"Sexy dangerous, that's how."

"That's pretty dangerous," he confesses, winks at me, teasing me, and pulls abruptly away.

The night is breathtakingly sticky, hot, and sensual; summer at its splendid peak. The sky is a blue-purple darkness. The moon is half-hidden behind dark clouds. How melancholic but lovely it feels, just right.

"We need to put you to bed. You're really drunk," he says. His right hand grazes my right cheek in a soft manner for just a second and hastily pulls away, dividing us by two feet.

"Do you like me, Rutger?" I inquire, blitzed out of my mind, wobbling, happy as a queen in a gay bar, and ready for another shot of whiskey, but decide not to have one for fear that I will pass out.

"Of course I like you." He sounds confident, sure of his answer; bless his soul.

I nod my head, and ask again, "Yes, I know. But, do you like me?"

He blushes. The Marine's cheeks turn a bright red hue in the candle's moderate yellow-white light. A glistening sparkle in his left eye presents a bashful look. "What are you saying, Islip?"

"Do you want to kiss me?"

"I don't know."

"Why don't you know?"

"I just don't know," he admits, shrugging his left shoulder.

"Are you straight?"

"No," he replies, quickly.

"Are you gay?" I interrogate him; shame on me.

He doesn't answer me. Why should he when he has already said too much?

"Will you hit me if I lean into you and kiss you on the mouth?" It's the alcohol speaking. My head spins with my stomach. Half of me feels elated regarding this current moment with the Marine; the other half feels sickened that I am behaving in such a ludicrous manner.

"I would never hit you, honestly. You're hardly dangerous."

"I'm not going to kiss you, just so you know," I admit, maybe breaking my own heart.

He nods his head, smiles again, and takes a drink of his beer. "You're really drunk. Do you know that?"

"Maybe. I don't know." The outside world spins between my temples. I see five Rutgers instead of one and I mumble, "Can you do me two favors, please?"

"Yeah ... sure. What favors?"

"When you want to kiss me ... go ahead and do it. I won't stop you."

"I will," he answers, maybe soothing me because I'm blitzed, tanked, completely inebriated. "What's the other favor?"

I heavily sigh, enjoying our Walt Disney moment together this evening. Invisible, warm, and delicate butterflies float up and down my arms. "Will you take me upstairs and tuck me into bed?"

The Marine softly laughs, caresses one of my cheeks again with two of his fingertips, and shares, "Of course I will, Islip. I'd be glad to help you out like that."

He carries me into the house, up the narrow stairs, and into my bedroom. Here, he places me on my bed, helps me remove my summer shorts and sandals, dropping them to the hardwood floor. Rutger stands over me as I lay on my back. He visually takes an interest in my body and studies my swollen pecs, comma-shaped navel, and the package between my legs. He reaches out his right hand, grazes fingertips against my right thigh, pulls his appendages away, and sighs heavily.

"You can stay if you want," I murmur.

He shakes his head, licks his upper lip in possible frustration, and says, "I really have to go."

"You don't."

"Honestly, I do."

"Why?" I inquire, wanting him to spend the night with me, even if I'm smashed on whiskey.

"I could fall for you if I stay," he confesses, continues to shake his head, and vanishes from my side, the bedroom, and my world for the night, suddenly.

6. HIS KISS

I vomit in the toilet at twenty minutes after nine o'clock the next morning, feel the porcelain bathroom spin around and around and around, decide to take two aspirin, and slip back into bed ... sleep ... dream.

I swear, during my period of light and drunken sleep, the Marine stands over me, and checks on me after my previous night's binge. I feel his presence within the bedroom, positioned at the foot of my bed and peering at my partially naked body.

When I wake from a dream and look down at my feet in hopes to see him there, he isn't, which really isn't a surprise at all.

I shower, dress in shorts, no shirt, no bootie socks, and find myself in the small study where I decide to write, or at least try to write. Here, I work on a new article for my editor, attempt to find words, fail miserably, and decide that a cup of coffee is in order.

Once at the kitchen sink and hovering over a fresh cup of coffee from my Kreuig I hear a hammer pounding, a table saw cutting boards, a sander, and other carpentry tools. I try to ignore the head-pounding noise by studying the day: hot again, almost one hundred degrees, cloudless with a dry-blue hue, no wind, and exhausting; summer slapping Edson with a mighty palm.

Twenty minutes later, and the Marine finds his way through the narrow woods that separate our properties. Again, he is shirtless and sports his hairy chest, bulky frame, thick thighs, and a pair of khaki-colored shorts splotched with white paint. Summer perspiration lines his forehead, cheeks, chin, mounded pecs, and tight abs. I watch him through the kitchen window as he makes his way up and over the cobblestone patio. Once at the back door, he sees me in the kitchen and lets himself in.

"You can't stay away from me," I say, enjoying his presence, again.

"I came to see how you are feeling. That was a mighty drunk you threw last night."

Helplessly, I consume his chiseled torso with hunger. The urge to lick every drop of sweat from his skin is relentless. My desire for the man is nothing less than superior; something that will most likely never be fulfilled.

"I could swear you were watching me sleep earlier today," I share with him.

He shakes his head and says, "I was in town grabbing supplies. I'm fixing the foyer's coat closet. How are you doing?"

I decide to tell him the truth. Why lie? What do I have to lose by being honest with him? "My head is pounding and my stomach feels like I have the bird flu."

He laughs at me, drawing a fist up to his mouth to conceal his grin.

"You think it's funny?" I inquire, glad that he's smiling from ear to ear.

"I'm sorry, Islip. My apology."

I scold him in a playful manner, "I'll let you get away with it this time. Don't laugh at my hardship ever again, though."

"I promise not to."

"Pinky swear it," I say, holding out my left pinky for one of his pinkies to wrap around it.

He chortles, "Marines don't do pinky swears."

"Pinky swear it anyway."

To my surprise, he does. Rutger lifts his right hand, extends its pinky, and wraps it around my pinky. "Done," he says, grinning.

Our connection is just beginning, I think, but smartly choose not to express this out loud.

"About last night, Rutger," I say after our pinkies unwrap, "I was really drunk. Obnoxiously drunk. I just want to say I'm sorry for being forward."

He shakes his head in a cordial manner and recites in his sexy-deep voice, "You don't have to apologize. We all get that blitzed sometimes."

"I was out of control."

"Whatever. You were harmless."

I fetch him a bottle of water from the Kenmore because he looks hot. Once I pass the plastic bottle to him, I say, "I haven't been that drunk in a long time."

He opens the bottle of water, drains two inches from its plastic, swallows the liquid down, wipes the back of his left palm over his mouth in a rugged manner, and says, "If you feel guilty about hitting on me last night, you can make it up to me."

My eyes grow wide with interest and I wonder if he's toying with me. "How?" I challenge, ready for his addendum, if there even is one.

"Help me with my foyer closet. There's some wood I need you to hold while I use the table saw on it."

A smirk surfaces on my face, and I nod my head in agreement. Now, I reply, "I'd be glad to help you with your wood any day, Mr. Marine," and follow him outside, through the woods, glowing and horny and happy and ...

# # # # #

Although I suffer from an insufferable hangover from the whiskey shots the night before, I manage to be like Jesus and help revamp Rutger's foyer closet. Together, we work with the oak wood, which we measure, cut, and nail into place. An hour turns into two hours ... and I'm about ready to drop dead from exhaustion.

Rutger says, "You need a break."

"I won't tell a lie. I do."

"Thanks, Pinocchio," he chides, and lights up his handsome face with a wide grin.

We drink bottled water in the shade, next to his summerhouse. Here, nestled under a maple's privacy, I ask, "Do you like living next door to me?"

"It's horrible, Islip. You constantly play loud music. I'm always calling the cops on you. And, I think you're making meth in your basement," he quips.

"Must be hell for you, huh?"

"Completely. I can't stand it anymore."

"You think you'll stay here after summer or head back to Maryland?"

"Haven't made up my mind as of yet, but when I do, you'll be the first to know."

"I like that idea," I respond, tilt my bottle up to my lips again, and consume a long drink.

"I knew you would," he says, and takes a swig of his own chilled water.

The labor becomes intense for me. The heat index feels as if it is 225 degrees. Fortunately, I have the Marine to watch and keep focused: every move he makes; the nails he strikes into the oak boards by his powerful motion; the way he uses the back of his right arm to wipe sweat away from his brow; summertime perspiration dripping off his pointed nipples; sawdust clinging to the sweaty hair around his dented navel; flushed cheeks because it is far too hot.

Again, we stop for another break and replenish our bodies with water. In doing so, Rutger pulls his cell phone out of the front pocket of his shorts and sees that it is well past three o'clock in the afternoon. Immediately, he shares, "We need to eat."

"I'm game," I reply, happy to be his guest at Hotel Rutger, and hope that his body is on the menu, an all I can eat buffet, of course.

We have tuna sandwiches with light mayonnaise, strawberry lemonade, and slices of watermelon. The kitchen fan above his two-person table helps cool us down. Here, we sit across from each other and talk about: my writing and editor, the house he rents to a family in Annapolis, two war stories, and our likeness for guns. We talk about handguns in full: Derringers, the Desert Eagle, and the Mauser C96. Following our chat, he suggests we finish the closet in the foyer, although I want to object, but don't. Instead, I nod my head in agreement, and respond, "You have an incredible work ethic, Rutger."

"Trust me, I can be more incredible."

Yes, he can, I think, and agree with him, happy to call him my newfound friend, and imaginary summertime boyfriend.

We take our dirty dishes to the kitchen sink and place them in sudsy water: stainless steel forks, everyday china, two glasses that were used for chilled water. In doing so, we accidentally bump into each other: shoulders brush together with ease, hips touch, and chests partially meet. During this unexpected closeness, the Marine says, "My bad."

"It wasn't bad at all," I reply. "Don't worry about it."

He becomes silent at the sink, motionless, in deep thought. What is he thinking? What exactly rotates between his temples? Why is he still and silent ... and in deep thought?

I discover the answers to these prominent and boggling questions in a matter of seconds. Beside him at the sink, ready to hand-wash the dirty dishes, he turns to his left and faces me. The Marine's strong paws find my hips and press into my skin. We face each other, connecting eyes with steady stares. Our breaths mix with intended bliss. We stand like this for the next three ... seven ... eleven seconds. The Marine leans his face against my face and our lips connect for the very first time and discover ultimate bliss.

I swirl within his kitchen and palms. My heartbeat climbs into heart attack range. Sweat pours out of my body, and not because the day is desert-hot. The kiss is smooth and sweltering and enchanting and masculine and heated and spine-clenching and ...

Suddenly, Rutger pulls away and steps back from the sink and my body. The look he shares with me is shameful: slanted eyebrows, hollowed eyes, O-shaped mouth decorated with our combined spittle.

He shakes his head, clears his throat, and whispers, "This can't happen. I've made a mistake."

I'm numb where I stand, smelling lemons from the dish water, and the dense sweat from his body. Confusion locks me into position and a state of catatonic delirium sets into my system. What does he mean he made a mistake? Why can't this happen between us? Why does a single kiss throw off our day together? What exactly is happening between us, and why?

Rutger points to the kitchen door and rattles off with a scratchy voice that is thick with concern, "You have to leave, Islip … Go. You can't come back here. I'm sorry."

7. DISTANCE

I bolt out of the Marine's life with tears dripping out of my eyes and decorating my cheeks. I whimper in the woods between our houses like a lost boy, damaged and filled with much hurt. For as sweet and euphoric Rutger's kiss was, his relentless proclamation afterwards was biting. I realize for the very first time that … I have accidentally fallen for the man, unconditionally and inevitably. This is why my hurt stings with such brutal force. This is why I feel breathless in the miniscule plot of timber between our abodes. This is why I almost fall to the woodsy earth and bury my head between my knees in shock, pain, and what little humility I have left.

# # # # #

A week passes without the Marine's company. Two weeks. The first week of September arrives, but it still feels like a heated August beside the lake. I hear Rutger next door with his hammers and drills and saws, but he no longer welcomes me into his life. Our worlds divide by his single kiss within the realm of his kitchen. No longer are we connected.

I miss his company and presence. All I can do is think about that single kiss, my body aligned to his hulking body, our faces touching, and his massive hands on my hips. The thought recurs every single minute of each day. Again and again, I feel hot and lust-filled, just as I had felt while his lips pressed against my own lips. Again and again, a jolt of bliss skies up and down my spine because of our closeness. Again and again …

I write to keep my mind, heart, and soul off the Marine. Words spill out of me, filling my HP laptop. Articles build on my desk about breach loaded rifles, the AR-15, the 17 Hmr rifle, the M16, and others. My writing details the weapons in full, their history, and uses. I overwhelm Hilliard with my work, sending him a vast arrangement of articles. The man is taken aback by my progress and texts me a message that reads: "What's wrong with you?"

My response is rather simple and to the point: "I'm broken-hearted. Perhaps I need a vacation. I'm thinking about Key West again. You know I like it down there."

His response: "Take as much time as you need. You have loads of vacation days coming your way."

Following my communication with Hilliard, I hear a power saw buzzing next door. Curiosity drives me insane, and I find myself in the tiny plot of woods that walls Rutger from me. Here, I stand among a set of old oaks and observe him at work, sawing two-by-fours for another carpentry project. I study his every movement: arched back with its beautiful muscles, bulging biceps as he carries freshly cut wood into the house, ripped and sweaty abs from picking up tools off the dry earth.

"Beautiful," escapes my mouth; a mere whisper in the afternoon shade, still hidden among the trio of trees, unseen and being a voyeur … happiness discovered, but only temporarily.

Of course, I grow hard between my legs, sporting my own wood, excited to see his semi-naked body at work in the September sun, building again. Naughtily, I want to reach between my sculpted thighs and find the timber with my right palm, jerking it up and down while observing the man next door: consistent yanks and tugging with unyielding passion. I want to spray my sticky cock-juice inside the

246

woods, decorating the green ferns and moss-covered rocks at my stern feet, releasing man-ooze from my branch, and become spent while admiring the Marine at work. This doesn't transpire, though. Instead, I continue to be on my best behavior among the smallish forest, prevent my palm from manipulating the post in my khaki shorts, and continue to watch the Marine at his labor, sufficiently drooling.

I'm not surprised that he catches me spying on him. In fact, I half-hope he does, if the truth be told. As I adjust the firm goods between my thighs, clamping my cock in my right hand and providing it with a tug, my elbow is seen. Rutger just happens to be looking in my direction, becomes wide-eyed, and rather shocked to see that I have invaded his privacy and crossed a line regarding our neighborly status.

"Islip!" he yells at the top of his voice.

I'm not sure if his tone is filled with anger, enlightenment, or concern. Does he purposely call out my name to gain my attention, confirming that he sees me ... something?

"Islip!" he yells again. "Don't think I don't see you!"

Discreetly, I turn away, bolt back to my Tudor and feel embarrassed by my actions, ashamed, like an adolescent who was once in love with the neighbor's shirtless and well-built lawn boy so long ago.

I surmise in the kitchen with a glass of chilled water that the Marine is not gay. The kiss we have shared was nothing more than a freak incident between adult men, something that he is surely not going to act on. Rutger is straight as straight comes, I determine. The man is meant to be alone, harboring his post-war stress and his singlehood. I need to get over him and surface from my lust for our two bodies to mix together as one. The Marine is not capable of loving another man, let alone applying kisses and intimate licks to my skin. No longer do I believe we can meet against a wall, on the stairs leading up to my bedroom, or positioned on his bed, bound together by our chests, tongues, and upright shafts, fully.

# # # # #

September 6. It rains this evening, long into the night. The storm is brisk with a steady wind and downpour. I leave the Tudor's windows open, listening to the tempest's desirous rumble. Gold-white bolts of lightning zigzags the heavens, filling the night with an eerie and unsettling hue. I turn in early, cozy within my bed, positioned on the available sheet instead of under the sheet. Here, I sleep and dream, pulled into another world where I am coupled with the Marine. I believe we live in Kansas, surrounded by sunflower fields and semi-naked cowboys. The dream is a splash of vivid colors and the sounds of farm machinery and rodeo calls. I believe the faraway dream takes place for an hour … two hours … and long into the night, until I am pulled out of it with such brutal force: again, the Marine screams next door; this time at the top of his lungs; awaking from his own faraway place; somewhere in a war zone and trapped in the depths of a hellish Afghanistan.

Barefoot and wearing nothing more than a pair of lime-colored Unico briefs, I dash through the September storm. Hurriedly, I rush into the woods. Here, scared for the Marine, concerned about his safety, I careen through the upright timber, semi-protected from the rain by overhead foliage. Sprinkles still drop through the lush canopy and decorate my strong shoulders and pumped chest. Thunder alarms me, barking obnoxiously within the night. Flashes of daunting lightning crack from the ground into the heavens, around me. Here, I speed over the woodsy earth, having every intention of meeting the Marine again, assisting him after his Afghanistan nightmare that is polluted with the dangerous and sneaky Taliban.

8. BANG

I rush out of the woods, into the pouring rain, over his side yard, into his backyard, and traipse up the three steps to his rear door. Again, the kitchen light in his Cape Cod shines. And again, Rutger stands near the counter and kitchen sink, holding three pink pills in his left hand and a glass of water in his right hand. Unbeknownst to the Marine, I make my way into the kitchen, entering through its screen door. Immediately, I visually take in the hero as he stands in a pair of white

248

Rufskin briefs: molten chest in thin black fur, shaking right hand, mound of delicious cock hidden under cotton, and sweaty thighs.

Both of us stand still and observe each other. Both of us drip wet, but with different liquids. And, both of us breathe heavily and seem frightened, traumatized by this evening's event of his nightmare and screams in the night.

He finally moves, consuming the three pills in his left hand, medicine for his post-traumatic stress. Rutger downs the pills with two gulps of water and places the glass on the counter behind him, next to the sink. The Marine has tears in his eyes; a breakdown ready to occur. The nightmare of Afghanistan is still locked within his memory, which is stagnant between his temples.

I say, "I heard you screaming. I know you don't want me here ... but I had to see if you were alright."

He nods his head, understanding me. A line of tears fall out of his left eye, roll down and over his cheek, and eventually land on his chest, mixing with droplets of post-nightmare perspiration. The Marine's stare is still locked with my own. Now, he opens his arms to me, welcoming me into his world, for togetherness, and whispers in a scratchy tone, "I've fallen for you, Greg Islip ... I didn't mean to push you away."

He moves up to me with his outstretched arms and leashes me inside their bulkiness again. Our chests touch as our faces meet. Tongues greet each other as our mouths connect. Our underwear-covered packages kiss for the very first time, and grow hard, almost immediately. The kiss between us is inexorable and needed. Both of us tremble in each other's arms, locked together and mixed with bliss. Our breathing is intense, and our hunger for the other is unending; a dramatic and masculine combination between next door neighbors; a mesh between the damaged Marine and the magazine writer. The kiss is intense and fills the kitchen with fire and heat and erotic bliss, fully.

Rutger falls to his knees, dragging his extended tongue down and over my chest. The outstretched appendage meets my navel, the rim of my briefs, and falls to my cotton-cupped package between my wet thighs. His lips roll over my stiff, eight-inch uncut staff under its material. The Marine longingly moans and rubs his mouth against the length of my hidden tool, east and west motion that drives me into a state of sexual no return. Eventually, he pulls the Unico briefs down to my knees and allows my shaft to slap him in the face. His palms steady themselves against my hips as my pulsating rod slips between his lips. In a matter of seconds, he begins to blow me, bobbing his head to and fro on my protein-mast, sucking the life out of my cock. He seems to enjoy every bit of his motion, famished for my pole in the back of his throat, gagging on my meat with delight, and pleased that my balls slap against his chin again and again and again, for the next ten … eighteen … twenty-three minutes, while the storm becomes more frisky and wicked outside, having Edson within its dangerous grip.

My palms are clamped on the Marine's shoulders. Fingernails dig into his skin as I balance myself above him. A whirlwind of ecstasy by his mouth is discovered. I pump his throat with my hard mass, pull out, and pump the narrow canal again. My breath is lost, discovered again, and lost a second time. Helplessly, in a position of pure enchantment, I murmur his name a number of times, jack my pole into his system, and claim, "If you don't stop, Rutger, I'm going to shoot."

He listens and pulls his mouth off and away from my stick. As he rises from his knees, he wipes his lips with the back of his left hand. Following this event, he pulls down his own underwear to his ankles, steps out of the cotton, shows off his V-area of onyx-colored pubic curls, and the ten-inch post between his hairy thighs, which already drips with two bubbles of pre-ooze.

My fully naked body is pressed over his two-person kitchen table and my legs are kicked apart as thunder rips and roars overhead. The Marine's cut cock is protected with a roll of plastic, lubed up, and … he presses two of its firm inches into my rear, which cause a gasp of immediate pain to exit my mouth as I clamp palms on either side of the table. Another two inches break my middle apart, and four more inches seem to feel as if an M16 is being plugged into my bottom. The last two inches of his pole firmly snugs themselves into my rump, and I yelp with enjoyed pain/lust/fulfillment. Rutger now stands motionless behind me, allows all of his ten inches to linger inside my core, completely stationary and affixed to my man-crevice.

"Pump me," I chortle in front of him. "Do it, Rutger."

A banging ensues with elation-filled results. Hump after continuous hump is carried out to my bottom. Inch after inch of his pole slides into my opening, exits, and slides into me again. Bliss is discovered as sweat forms on my toned chest and sticks me to the table's wooden surface. I moan on the plane of wood, locked in position, and feel as if nothing can break us apart. Eight … eleven … fifteen minutes of his robust banging is endured. Hot perspiration flies off his furred chest and stings my back. The military man becomes hyper behind me, locked into my ass, pulverizing its tunnel-tight hole with all his weight.

Rutger's palms grip my hips as he steadies himself behind me. The man moans with heated undulation as he builds his orgasm. Cock-bump after cock-bump is felt at my middle. Chaotic but enjoyed thumps occur, which causes the shaft between my legs to bounce on its own with excitement. To my hungry surprise, the untouched post centered at my thighs explodes without even being touched/caressed/fondled/yanked. A rush of writer-sap sprays out of its uncut head and splashes against the kitchen's tile floor. String after string of the goo flies out of my joint, which causes me to feel intoxicated by the Marine's hefty ass-thrusts, his man-elation encountered.

"I had to have you," he calls down and over the splay of my rippled back. "I wanted you the first day I saw you," the Marine admits while he finishes finding his orgasm. Grunts escape his mouth as his final blows to my bottom are carried out. Caught up in his own act of pleasure, he releases his tool from my ass, removes the plastic that covers his beef, tosses the condom to the tile floor, and begins to jack his rod in an up and down frenzy, sure to get himself off.

What transpires is nothing less than Rutger's rapture. I watch him in motion over my right shoulder as he pivots his right fist in a quick and steady north-south motion, ready to explode. Moans of satisfaction escape his beautiful mouth. More hip-motion ensues, pumping into his right hand and … white spirals of gunk immediately blast out of his gun and puddle on my back. Ooze decorates my shoulder blades and spine. The spunk is sticky and hot like acid, but very much enjoyed – exactly what I desire.

We hug and kiss following our entanglement within his kitchen. Our chests heave for oxygen. Post-sexed and exhausted, he melts me again with his romantic kissing, circling the inside of my mouth with his tongue. Together we become locked as lovers, the handsome Marine and author. And together we compress our chests, having our nipples and stomachs touch, the way God intended for this romance between us to be carried out.

Lightning and thunder boom outside. The storm is at its fullest rage. The kitchen light flickers off/on/off/on and finally off. Rutger chuckles next to me in the fresh darkness, and whispers, "I have you, don't panic. I have no intentions of letting you go this time."

"You've always had me," I reply, comfortable against his skin and locked in his arms, broadly smile, together with the man I have helplessly fallen in love with, completely.

# # # # #

Naked, spent from our two-person gig during the thunderstorm, the Marine escorts me away from his kitchen table, into the depths of his Cape Cod, and welcomes me to spend the night with him. With my right hand locked within his left hand, I follow him upstairs, into his bedroom, and climb into the bed with him. Here, snuggled against his furry chest, I close my eyes, next to his skin, lust, and love. Sure of our long-term connection, I drift into warm sleep and realize that I have found someone I care greatly about and for, the man of my dreams, a Marine who is lost within me, swept up in everything I have to offer him, one who will never have a nightmare of being in Afghanistan again, safe with me … unharmed.

For Douglas Behling – He knows why.

THE EDITOR

ERIC SUMMERS resides in West Palm Beach, Fla., and more Marines have landed in his bed than on Iwo Jima.

BUTCH MEN PLAY HARDER!

BUTCH DIXON

ng any underwear. "Excuse me," I said, having a hard time looking

led by that bulge in his crotch, "but don't I know you?" "Maybe," h

of t   bout a m

n Ray   God, you

ser?   in?" he as

"Lik   s stronges

body   e on Gree

, he   I ever sa

o to t   ny ideas?

king   e same

coul   ery long t

l raci   ne swell.

with   e in store

go   behind s

see   in public

" he   vent to the

acy.   grabbed

d. I

traci   t, so firm

it, ha

h my   bing dick

ng, I   n cock, be

sound of unzipping filled the small space. I don't know who's hand

t before I knew it, I had his rod in my hand, and mine was in his. "

o do?" he asked, his tone challenging. I knew exactly, and sank to n

www.ingramcontent.com/pod-product-compliance
Lightning Source LLC
Chambersburg PA
CBHW052026020726
47501CB00004B/1268